A WITCHY TOUCH

Memory Guild Book 6

WARD PARKER

Mad Mangrove Media

ISBN: 978-1-957158-06-8

CONTENTS

CHAPTER 1

HUGO THE MEDIOCRE

Hugo the Magnificent downed his second glass of sherry as he watched Sophie levitate in my inn's dining room. The magic tutor with the pompous name should have been proud of my daughter's progress, but he looked nervous, as if she were already out of his league.

I was nervous, too, glancing behind me at the doorway to make sure no guests were around to see this, though it was late in the evening. Cory smiled at Sophie with pride as she hovered a foot off the floor, her long, straight black hair splayed out behind her horizontally as if it floated on the surface of water. I'd never seen her levitate before.

"Did you teach her how to do this?" I asked Hugo.

He shook his head no.

"Extra credit," Sophie said. "I was practicing a telekinesis spell, and I accidentally used it on myself. Kind of cool, right?"

"Very," Cory said.

I had hired Hugo in the past, after we learned Sophie had inherited the magic gene, to give her basic magic lessons. Her grandmother was teaching her potions and amulets, which were pretty much the extent of Mom's abilities. But we needed someone who could bring out Sophie's true potential by training the natural powers within her. She appeared to have much more power than Mom.

And I, of course, had none. The only non-witch of the family. The magic gene in the Chesswick line of witches occasionally skipped a generation. Lucky me.

Even Cory had magic in him. He hadn't known about it his entire life until a wizard recognized it, and drew it out, only to exploit Cory for his own benefit. We had discussed Cory taking lessons, too, but he decided he didn't want them.

"I've had enough of magic," he had told me. "I want to be normal again, to spend my days sweating over repairs to the inn. Taking up photography again. Fishing."

I couldn't blame him after the trauma he had gone through being the wizard's prisoner. But Cervantes, the black cat assigned to be Cory's familiar, had other intentions for his human witch. The cat would just have to be patient. But try telling him that.

Cervantes was on the floor beside the table where Cory and I sat. The cat watched with his yellow-green eyes as Sophie descended and landed softly within the magic circle she had drawn on the wood floor with chalk. His tail twitched with excitement.

He meowed in his trademark way that sounded like, "No."

"Cervantes, I give you permission to work with Sophie," Cory said, "since I've been a disappointment to you so far."

"Nooo," the cat said. I couldn't blame him.

"Very good," Hugo said to Sophie. "Now, why don't you try moving that wretched pink flamingo statuette? Like into the garbage can."

Sophie's lips moved as she recited a spell. She pointed to the flamingo that stood in the corner of the room, then raised her arm.

The flamingo rose from the floor.

Sophie moved her extended arm slowly to her right, and the flamingo floated across the floor as if tethered to her arm. She lifted her arm higher, then lowered it, placing the flamingo atop a nearby table.

"What a monstrosity that piece is," Hugo muttered. This guy, with the dyed-black hair in a bright yellow silk shirt and crimson scarf, had no right to judge my taste in decor.

"Good job, honey," I said to Sophie.

She beamed with pride. "It's almost easy."

She pointed to the flamingo again and made it levitate above the table. Hugo was right—the statuette was awfully tacky. Made of some rigid resin material, it was about two and a half feet tall and shockingly pink. I'd found it at Mom's antique store (who else but Mom would have it?), and I brought it here because of its tackiness. I wanted some Florida kitsch to lighten the seriousness of this historic room.

Sophie's lips moved with another spell. Then, my eyes must have deceived me.

The molded bird extended its wings and flapped them.

Even Hugo gasped in surprise.

The bird flew in circles near the ceiling. It looked as if its wings propelled it, but there was no way that was true, given its weight and material. It was Sophie's spell that gave the impression the bird was flying, and it was very convincing.

But the bird seemed to have a mind of its own. It sped up, and its flight became more erratic.

"Obey me," Sophie said.

The flamingo rose too high, got clipped by the spinning ceiling fan, and careened off toward the window.

"No!" I shouted, sounding like an angry Cervantes.

The bird smashed through the large-paned window and flew into the courtyard.

"Another repair to add to my list," Cory muttered.

"I don't know how that happened," Sophie said. "Sorry."

"You have a lot of power, but obviously need a lot of training," Hugo said.

The flamingo burst back into the room, its magically animated wings knocking the remaining shards of glass from the window. It headed directly toward Hugo like a kamikaze pilot.

Hugo shrieked. He ducked at the very last moment before the bird collided with his forehead. Still, it swiped off his toupee before crashing into the fireplace where a cozy little fire was burning.

The resin-molded bird bounced off the stone and landed on the dining room floor. The toupee fell into the fire and ignited.

With another shriek, Hugo dashed to the fireplace and retrieved his toupee, patting it frantically on his leg to extinguish the flames. He quickly replaced it on his head, though it smoldered slightly.

Sophie and Cory were polite enough not to react, but I accidentally let out a giggle.

"I'm sorry about that, Hugo," Sophie said.

"Okay. But before you get your ego all puffed up, let's do a little test, shall we?" Hugo said with barely concealed rage. "Leave the magic circle and try moving that pink horror again."

She stepped from the circle and repeated the spell. But this time, the flamingo only wobbled atop the table. It didn't levitate.

Sophie kept trying until her milky white complexion turned red.

"I can't do it," she said. "It's so frustrating."

"You see?" Hugo asked pompously, his jet-black toupee now singed and peppered with gray ashes. "Most witches wouldn't be able to do it without a magic circle, either. We want you to be better than them."

"How?" Sophie asked.

"When you're in the circle, you're gathering energy from the five elements and combining it with your own core energy," Hugo said. "But now that we've learned you're a water witch, you should focus on that one element."

"While I'm inside the circle?"

"Yes, at first. But we want you to learn to practice magic without the limitations of using a circle. The most powerful elemental witches don't need circles. They can tap into power in other ways."

Cory grunted. I glanced at him and saw the trauma in his eyes. Cory was an earth witch with the unique ability to harvest the immense power of underground ley lines. And he had suffered because of it.

"You need to learn to tap into power directly from the source," Hugo said. "And there's no source of water energy more powerful than the ocean."

"Does that mean I have to be at the beach in order to practice magic?" Sophie asked.

"No, because you're also going to learn how to charge your batteries, so to speak, and store the energy from the ocean inside you. So, you can bring it anywhere."

"That sounds awesome."

"For the time being, you *will* need to go to the beach to gather energy. Are you up for going tonight?"

"Yes! Of course."

Cervantes darted to her and rubbed vigorously against her leg.

"He wants to go, too," Sophie said.

"Is he leash-trained? He'll just run off and you'll lose him."

"This cat is too smart to run off."

"Well, he can't ride in my car," Hugo said. "My partner's allergic to cats and will go to pieces the moment he opens the door if your cat was in there."

"Don't worry, I'll take him in my car," Sophie said. "Cervantes shouldn't miss this. Familiars need to engage in magic regularly."

Hugo grumbled dismissively to himself. "I'll meet you at the municipal beach," he said as he eased his bulk out of his chair.

He walked out of the room with the aid of a walking stick. It was a tall one, more of a staff.

Cory flinched at the sight of the staff. Our eyes met. My telepathy picked up feelings of fear and trauma.

The staff reminded Cory of Texas Tom's wizard staff and all the terrible memories of Cory's servitude. I gave Sophie a kiss goodbye and a reassuring arm squeeze as she left for the beach.

"Don't be too late," I called out after Sophie. "I need your help with breakfast tomorrow."

I, the non-magical one, elected to stay home in case a guest needed me. There was nothing I could contribute to the magic session. I asked Cory if he wanted to go, too.

"I don't want to get in the way or affect her magic," he said. "I've taken a different path with my magic—one that probably won't go any further. She needs to find her own way."

His attention wandered as he bent to examine the flaking paint on the wainscoting. He'd been slipping easily back into innkeeper mode since he returned to me.

"Do you think it was a good idea to let Sophie go alone to

the beach at night with a man we don't know well?" I asked, slipping back into my over-protective mother mode.

Cory chuckled. "First of all, she's twenty-four. She doesn't need Mommy or Daddy chaperoning her. Second, I had the impression Hugo isn't interested in women."

"You're right," I said. Sophie had been through precarious situations before, from a foray into the drug world to being held briefly as a prisoner of vampires. She was a strong young woman. "So, you're saying it would be silly for me to wait up for her?"

"I won't mock you for staying up," Cory said with a smile. "I doubt they'll be late."

After he left to go to our cottage, I picked up the flamingo and returned it to its corner by the bookcase. I had a newfound respect for it now.

SOPHIE WAS LATE IN RETURNING HOME. THE FIRE HAD GONE out, and I was dozing, almost doing a face plant into the novel I was reading. The alarm system chimed when she came in the main door of the inn.

She was upset, her eyes wild, her cheeks wet with tears. Her milky white skin was flushed, making the dreadful tattoo on the bottom of her neck stand out.

"What happened?" I asked, jumping up from my chair.

"Total disaster. Cervantes ran off."

"Oh, no! I never expected him to do that."

"Me neither. He was totally mellow while we were doing the water-energy exercises. Suddenly, I heard him in my mind say that something was wrong, and he darted off like he was chasing something. He disappeared behind the coquina rock. I ran after

7

him but couldn't see him anywhere. There was enough moon-light that I should have seen him."

"Did he go into a crevasse in the rock?"

"Hopefully not. I used Hugo's flashlight, but still couldn't find him. I called him over and over, and he never replied. And then things got even worse."

"What do you mean?"

"Hugo. He came on to me."

"No!"

"Yeah, he put an arm around me to comfort me. But then the comforting got kind of creepy. I tried to slip from under his arm. But he squeezed me tighter. I was worried he was going to grope me, so I had to push him away. What a jerk!"

"I didn't think Hugo was interested in, well, women."

"He sure was tonight."

"Doesn't he have a male partner?" I asked rather stupidly.

"So what? Doesn't mean he wouldn't cheat on him or that he wouldn't come onto a woman."

"Do you want to report him to the police?"

"No. He didn't go far enough for that. But I don't want him as a tutor anymore, that's for sure."

"I'm sorry, sweetie."

"As soon as the sun rises, I'm going back to the beach to look for Cervantes," Sophie said, her voice breathy with exhaustion.

"I'll go with you."

"Let me lie down for a bit, then get me when it's time to go."

She went upstairs to 305, which had been converted to her living quarters. I retreated to the cottage for some sleep. But Cory must have sensed the hullabaloo, because the bedroom light switched on the moment I opened the cottage door.

"Is everything okay?" he asked, exiting the bedroom in boxers and a T-shirt.

"Not exactly." I recounted Sophie's story.

Cory wasn't the barbaric type who would exact revenge to protect Sophie's honor, but he was ticked off when he heard about Hugo. And he was equally distressed about Cervantes.

"Forget about Hugo," I said. "We'll never see him again. Let's focus on getting Cervantes back."

"I want to press charges against Hugo."

"Sophie said he didn't cross the line into sexual assault."

"If she was uncomfortable, he crossed a line," Cory said, angrier than I'd seen him in years. "That flamboyant, pretentious clown needs to learn a lesson."

"Okay, but let's get our fur baby back first."

Cory returned to the bedroom and came out again wearing shorts and sandals, his wallet and phone in hand.

"I'm going to the beach and look for Cervantes."

"Let me go with you."

"No, please stay here and get some rest. Before long, it will be time to make breakfast."

I handed him a flashlight from the junk drawer.

"We treat Cervantes like a human because he has the paranormal in him and is crazy smart," Cory said. "But he's still a cat. His hunting instincts trump everything. Shelters are overflowing with smart cats who got lost after chasing after some critter."

"Wait, take these, too," I said, handing Cory a package of cat treats. "The sound of the bag being opened always summons him faster than magic can."

"Yeah, he's a cat, all right."

We kissed before he strode out the door.

And now I was supposed to get some rest? How could I possibly relax after all this?

Running an inn and dealing with all the occult happenings in my life is exhausting. Somehow, I managed to fall asleep a few minutes after lying down.

I AWOKE TO MY ALARM. IT WAS JUST BEFORE DAWN AND TIME to make a hot breakfast for our guests. Cory wasn't around, but I assumed he was tinkering with something in the inn. Hopefully, he wasn't still at the beach.

After showering and dressing, I plodded into the inn, switched on the lights in the kitchen and began making coffee. The smaller of the two refrigerators was slightly askew. Roderick must have recently returned from stalking victims for their blood and had retired to his nest in the crawlspace inside the wall, the doorway of which was hidden behind the fridge.

It was a typical morning.

Until the buzzer rang at the main door. It was early enough that the night locks were still engaged on all the exterior doors.

I was slightly alarmed to see Detective Samson waiting at the door. It was common for him to stop by if he believed my psychometry could assist him with a case. The alarming part was this time he was accompanied by a uniformed police officer, a Latina, who'd been here before.

Both cops had grim expressions.

"Don't tell me another of my guests is dead," I said when I opened the door.

"Believe it or not, that's not why we're here," the Latina said. Her name plate said Fernandez. She'd made fun of me in the recent past about my growing number of deceased guests.

"No, not one of your guests," Samson said. "Was Hugo Starbright, AKA Hugo the Magnificent, here last night?"

"Why? And how would you know that?"

"I take it the answer is yes."

"He was giving Sophie mag—um, he was tutoring her." I couldn't mention magic in front of Fernandez or anyone not in one of the supernatural guilds.

"When did he leave?" Samson asked.

"Nine-thirty or so."

"Do you know why he went to the beach?"

"He was teaching Sophie something," I said, instantly regretting mentioning her. "Why are you asking? What happened?"

"Did he go straight from here to the beach?"

"Michael, will you tell me why you're here? Did something happen to Hugo?"

The two cops exchanged glances, and Samson nodded.

"A fisherman found Mr. Starbright deceased on the beach this morning," Samson said gravely. "It appears to be a homicide."

"Good Lord," I said. "How was he killed?"

"With his staff."

"In a surprising way," Fernandez said.

CHAPTER 2

NOT THE USUAL SUSPECTS

"Can we speak to Sophie?" Samson asked.

"She's still sleeping," I replied, a bit too defensively.

"We'll wait here."

Samson, he of the flirtatious grin, was uncharacteristically cold today. He sat in the foyer sitting area, normally a convivial place where I hosted my wine socials. Fernandez remained standing. Cops learn to endure long periods on their feet, holding vigil at crime scenes or because they rarely get offered a seat.

I texted Sophie, hoping she was already up, but she didn't reply. Climbing the stairs to the third floor, I knocked on her door. After a few raps, she groggily answered.

"Can you come downstairs, please?" I said into the doorjamb at a volume she could hear, but not the guests on this floor. "The police would like to ask you some questions."

"Who did you say?"

I guess I had dropped the volume on "police" too much. "The *police*."

The door popped open. Sophie's face was taut with concern.

"Come here, and sit down," I said as I led her back to her bed and waited until she was seated. "Hugo was murdered at the beach last night."

She stifled a sob. "Oh, no. Who would do that? Wait, they don't think I did it, do they?"

"Of course not," I said, hoping I was right. "It's because you were one of the last people to see him."

The last person, of course, being his murderer.

While Sophie pulled on sweatpants and a hoodie, she asked, "Should I leave out the part about Hugo coming onto me?"

I really, really wanted to tell her yes. Why give the police any reason to suspect her of the murder? But having worked with Samson for a long time, I knew lies, even by omission, were a bad idea when speaking to law enforcement. If they found out you were less than truthful, it could make you look guilty.

"No, tell them what happened," I said. "But it's okay if you downplay it a bit."

"This is so horrible. Why did it have to happen?"

"Did you like Hugo?"

"Yeah," she said, almost whispering. "I actually did."

AFTER RECENTLY LEARNING FROM A SPIRITUALIST GUEST THAT my elevator was haunted, I insisted on using the stairs. I'm not afraid of ghosts, but when suspended by steel cables dozens of feet above the ground in a rattling 120-year-old cage, it's not a good time to encounter the supernatural.

I have no issues with other people using the elevator. It is regularly inspected and in good mechanical shape. Other than the spiritualist, no guest has ever commented that the elevator was spooky. Besides, accessibility regulations require I have a working elevator. You're just not going to see me using it.

By the time we got downstairs, Cory was speaking to Samson. Why did Cory have to get involved?

"I told you already, I saw his car, but I didn't see Hugo," Cory said in a confrontational tone to the detective. The way they stood only feet apart was also aggressive. Why couldn't these guys leave their testosterone behind?

"You were looking for your cat?" Samson asked.

"Yes."

"Why was your cat at the beach? Who brings their cat to the beach?"

"I did," Sophie said.

Everyone looked at her.

"He's a very smart cat. I didn't think he'd run off."

"Do you believe the victim did something to your cat?" Fernandez asked.

Sophie shook her head no.

According to police procedure, Samson had to bring a woman cop along with him when interviewing women. The problem was, Samson was the only active-duty cop in San Marcos who knew the city was full of witches, vampires, and shifters like himself. Why Sophie and Hugo were at the beach was going to be asked—if they hadn't asked Cory already—and we couldn't mention magic lessons in front of Fernandez.

Samson was savvy about this, and I think he finally caught on that the cat in question was Cervantes, whom he knew was a witch's familiar.

"Why were you at the beach with the victim?" Fernandez asked.

"He's my tutor. Was my tutor," Sophie said sadly. "He was

teaching me about marine biology and the creatures that are active at night."

"Are you still in college?"

"Um, no. But I want to apply to graduate school for marine biology and didn't study it much as an undergrad."

Fernandez nodded, seemingly satisfied.

"What time did you leave the beach to go home?" Samson asked.

"Like eleven-thirty or twelve."

"Did you see the victim when you left? Was he alive?"

"Sure. He was fine. He was just standing on a rock staring at the ocean."

"Why did you leave without finding your cat?" Fernandez asked.

"Well, I guess I gave up looking." Sophie glanced at me. "And, um. Hugo was trying a little too hard to comfort me."

"What do you mean?"

"He hugged me. It made me uncomfortable."

Both Fernandez and Samson had their radars on now. Maybe I should have told Sophie to leave this part out after all.

"Did he touch you inappropriately?" Fernandez asked with fake tenderness.

"No. He acted like he had good intentions, but I just felt weird having a fat old guy hug me on the beach at night."

"Wouldn't we all?" I quipped.

I got icy stares from everyone.

"So, I left," Sophie said. "I planned to come back later to look for Cervantes."

"I couldn't wait until later," Cory said. "That's why I went to the beach. I love that cat."

"Did you know about the inappropriate hugging?" Samson asked.

I sent my own icy stare in his direction.

"Um. . ."

"Please be honest."

"Yeah, I knew about it. But I wasn't going to confront the guy. I'm not some hothead who flies off the handle for a minor thing like that." As if to reinforce what he just said, Cory put more distance between himself and Samson. "I went there to look for my cat and figured Hugo would be long gone by then. I was surprised to see his car there, but I saw no sign of him."

"His body was found only fifty yards from the parking lot's dune crossover," Samson said.

"I told you I didn't see it. There are lots of coquina rock formations around and I didn't see anybody. I was looking for the cat. I had a feeling he went south, so I did, too. Was the body found to the south?"

Samson seemed disappointed and shook his head no.

"Have you spoken with Hugo's partner yet?" I asked. "Aren't partners supposed to be the prime suspects?"

"I'm going over there next," Samson said. "We're here to speak to the people we know were on the same beach, not because you're suspects."

He emphasized the last part testily. But it was obvious that Sophie and Cory were suspects, at least to some extent.

And I truly hoped there wasn't any complication from a rivalry between Samson and Cory over me.

"We'll be on our way now," Samson said. "Thank you for your time." He handed business cards to Sophie and Cory, who both hesitated too long before accepting them. "Please call with any new information."

After they left, Cory said to me, "I thought that guy was your friend."

And only a friend. "I thought he was. Now, I'm not so sure."

IN THE EARLY AFTERNOON, SAMSON CALLED ME. FORTUNATELY, I was alone in the inn's kitchen removing an air plant from the counter near the sink. There was no logical explanation for an air plant being inside the inn.

"Boy, that sure was awkward," Samson said.

"You're telling me? You came to my inn and basically accused my daughter and husband of murder."

"Oh, come on, Darla. They were both at the scene where the murder occurred. We had to ask them questions, and that's all we did. I can understand why you're feeling defensive, but Fernandez and I are officers of the law, and we were just doing our jobs."

I forced myself to calm down. Somewhat.

"Yeah, you've got a point."

"Let me ask you some questions I couldn't ask in front of Fernandez. What were Sophie and Hugo Starbright really doing at the beach?"

"It turns out Sophie is an elemental witch, specifically a water witch. Hugo was allegedly showing her how to gather energy from the ocean."

"Allegedly?"

"I haven't had the chance to hear from Sophie how the lesson went. All I heard was about Cervantes running off and Hugo hugging her."

"Tell me honestly, do you believe Starbright tried to do more than hug her?"

"I don't think so. Sophie would have told me if he had. I didn't even think he was interested in women."

"You've told me Sophie went through a rough patch with

substance abuse. Has she ever committed violence?"

The anger was seeping back in. "Of course not!"

"Sorry. I had to ask. What about Cory?"

"No! He's not that kind of man. He tries to be a good father to Sophie, but my first husband is her actual dad. It's not as if Cory would need to kill a man to protect her honor."

"I've seen plenty of stepfathers do so."

"You haven't told me the specifics of how Hugo died. Was he clobbered in the head by his staff?"

"No, he was impaled. Speared through his torso. Personally, I suspect magic was involved, because it seems unlikely the tip of the staff was sharp enough to do the job. But I suppose the medical examiner could argue a strong enough person could have done it through brute force."

"I'm pretty sure Cory and Sophie don't know any spells that could murder someone," I said, "especially not in this way."

"It was a crude, brutal murder. But if it was done through magic, it was brilliant in a way."

"What do you mean?"

"Magic that can be disguised as non-magical. A great way for the magician to cover his or her tracks."

The idea fascinated me. I found my defensiveness replaced by curiosity. Being curious was the first step for me getting involved up to my eyeballs in a murder case.

"Did you interview Hugo's partner?" I asked.

"I gave him the news. And he was convincingly distraught."

"Did you get an inkling of him having a motive to kill Hugo?"

"Not yet. Give him a moment with his grief."

"Any evidence at the crime scene?"

"No. If there was, the tide took it away. The killer probably hoped the tide would take the victim away, too, but the body was caught in the coquina rocks."

"What about the staff? Did you find any prints?"

Samson chuckled. "Only the victim's. You sound like you're my supervisor. I thought you were my psychic consultant."

"I was getting to that. When can I read the staff for memories?"

"Whenever you can. The forensic team is finished with it."

"I'm on my way," I said, hanging up.

Despite my budding fascination with investigating murders, I was still only a humble innkeeper who had to return to her inn by 2:30 p.m. to prepare for Teatime. Priorities.

I FOUND SAMSON AT HIS DESK, TWO-FINGER TYPING ON HIS ancient computer. The staff at the police department was so used to me showing up, I could almost come and go as I pleased, as if I were the copier repair person.

"I've been swamped lately," Samson said, looking at me with strained eyes. "I'm spending a lot of time with the D.A. preparing for Tom Sykes' trial."

Texas Tom had been in the county jail for months while I waited anxiously for him to be convicted and sent to state prison. It made me nervous having an evil wizard so close to home. In fact, I heard he almost bonded out after his arrest, even with a super-high bail, until the feds investigating all his frauds and pyramid schemes froze his bank accounts.

"I sometimes wish you had shot him," I said.

"He's harmless behind bars. There's no indication he's tried to conjure any magic. You know, he probably can't do any serious magic without someone else to steal energy from, like he did with Cory."

"I wish I could believe you."

"Come on," Samson said, "let's go examine Hugo Starbright's stick."

"Staff."

"Whatever."

We went up to the evidence room. Tommy, the clerk, had his usual fashion accessory—crumbs from his recent lunch stuck in his beard.

"Tommy," Samson said, "I have some friendly advice. Don't get your sandwiches on the crusty baguettes anymore."

The poor guy turned red and hastily swatted at his beard, removing only half the crumbs.

Samson filled out the paperwork, then Tommy disappeared into the labyrinth of metal shelving units. He returned with Hugo's staff and a plastic container like you'd use to store your leftover meatloaf. Samson carried them to the small cubicle where I did my readings in private.

"I requested the property found on his person, as well," Samson said to me.

"Good idea."

"Well, I'll leave you alone to do your thing. Call me afterwards."

After his footsteps receded, I took deep breaths and cleared my mind. Hugo's staff was pretentious, just like its owner. Black lacquered, with brass paint on its tip, it looked like something a herald would rap on the floor to announce the king was entering the chamber. I was certain it had no magical use, unlike Tom's staff. The bottom of the staff appeared damaged, though it was the brass-painted end that had done the damage to Hugo.

I was careful not to touch the staff anywhere near the blood-stains at the top.

Laying it across the small table, I hovered my hands just above it. There wasn't much psychic energy here. No powerful memories tried to pull me in. I touched the staff with my index finger in a few places, only to find weak, inconsequential memories.

It appeared Hugo merely used the staff as a prop when he gave magic lessons. I guess it was an easy way for a dubious witch or wizard—or whatever he thought he was—to look more important.

I scolded myself for thinking ill of the recently deceased. But I resented paying him more than he was worth and then having my family put under a cloud of suspicion, thanks to him.

Stop it. *Focus*, Darla.

I searched for the most recent memories on the staff. Most were clustered three quarters of the way up, where he would normally hold it when standing. Here's a very fresh one. I grasped the staff and I—

—*feel so sorry for Sophie losing her kitty. Poor, poor Sophie. She must be so sad he ran away. I was only hugging her to make her feel better, but she took it the wrong way. She's leaving now, and I'm left here alone to take in the sound of the majestic ocean. I shall climb upon that rock. . . What? Maybe I'm not alone. I—*

—snap out of the reverie when he lets go of the staff. Not very informative.

Well, one thing I learned was he was rip-roaring drunk. He hid it well from me that night. He must have had a good buzz on before he arrived at the inn and drank my sherry.

That explains the unwanted hugging. I just wish he held the staff longer so I could see who or what he spotted on the beach with him. Searching for a more recent memory, I came up empty. The one I read may have been the last he ever had.

But why weren't there any memories from the attacker on the staff? For the same reason there were no fingerprints: the attacker must have worn gloves, thick enough to block psychic energy from adhering to the staff.

My eyes wandered to the plastic container. I pried off the lid. Inside was Hugo's wallet and a key chain with a car fob and house keys. The yellow label on the box lid that listed the contents said his cellphone was still in the custody of Forensics. I figured they were trying to unlock it.

The keys were a mess of very brief thoughts and sensory inputs. No one does much thinking in the brief moment it takes to unlock a door.

The leather wallet held memories, but they were also rather brief. I know, you think being in a guy's back pocket all day should cause it to collect a great deal of psychic energy. I hate to disappoint you, but buttocks aren't involved with any cerebral activity, at least for most people. Even when you "pull a thought out of your butt," your poor buttocks are left out of the transaction.

No, your fingers, lips, tongue, and feet leave the best memories when they do the touching. And the last time he touched his wallet, he was thinking about paying for a motel room and having some fun with a new partner.

I couldn't tell who the partner was. There was only a fleeting thought of the name Dorothy, and the quick image of a sad-faced woman in her early forties with dyed-blonde hair. I couldn't achieve a reverie with any memories on the wallet because they were too brief.

So, Hugo was having an affair with a woman. And if the partner he lived with knew about it, that was an excellent motive for murder.

I quickly poked my finger inside the wallet, touching the edges of his credit cards and license, but didn't sense any coherent memories. When I replaced the wallet in the container, a metal key slid out and bounced off the plastic.

The key was small and slim; the kind used in small padlocks or lockboxes. What caught my eye was its ornate, antique design. It was an old F-shaped key, and the eye at the foot of the F was cast with intricate scrollwork from an exotic long-ago time and place.

I couldn't resist. I held my finger just above the key. It was filled to bursting with psychic energy, though I couldn't make sense of it. The energy reminded me of the sort in the magic pearl given to me by the Fae.

I touched the key and was jolted by powerful thoughts in a lilting, sing-song language I didn't recognize. Images flitted in and out of my mind: a unicorn, a dagger, faeries flying on gossamer wings, silver goblets, an altar with a golden idol that resembled a bull, a harp, a Medieval-style battle in a distant field, a large ceramic jar or urn with curved handles, decorated with images of stars and planets.

Male and female voices sang a strange but beautiful song.

Suddenly, the key grew hot to the point I had to drop it.

This key was important, I knew. San Marcos had a bit of a Fae problem, and I needed to learn anything I could about the creatures.

More importantly, a faerie had told me I had a great destiny to fulfill and would either be a friend or foe of their species. How was I supposed to find out more?

I needed to keep this key. There was no mention of it on the inventory list. Stealing from the evidence room was surely a terrible thing to do, but I had done it once before and gotten away with it. Nothing would stop me from doing it now.

A quick glance told me Tommy had his back to me at his computer terminal, a bag of potato chips torn open beside him.

I slipped the key into my purse and buckled up for the ride ahead.

But first, back to the real world.

"Michael," I said when he answered his phone. "I'm pretty sure Hugo was having an affair. You'd better take a closer look at his partner."

"I had been planning to give him a couple of days for grieving before the heavy questions, but not anymore."

"Let me go with you when you speak to him. Hopefully, I can read some of his thoughts. Better yet, visit him at home, so if my telepathy doesn't work, I can use my psychometry."

"Okay. We'll go now. Meet me out back in the parking lot."

CHAPTER 3

STEROID-ADDLED

Hugo and his partner made an unlikely couple. They lived in a new subdivision of townhomes, which didn't fit Hugo's image as a witch. I would have expected an older home filled with cats and eccentric charm. While Hugo drove an antique imported sports car, his partner drove a brand-new American muscle car. It was parked in the driveway next to a visitor's car.

The garage had been converted into a gym. Hugo's partner's name was Vance Puggle, and he was a personal trainer. While Hugo had been middle-aged and overweight, this guy was a chiseled bodybuilder in his thirties with a shaved head and an air of repressed rage.

I didn't know what kind of clients I expected him to have, but the one at the moment was a little old lady who was amazingly buff.

"Hey, I'm paying for this session," she said to Samson and me as we walked up the drive. "You can't just interrupt us."

The white-haired lady was bench-pressing a barbell weighted

with several plates while Vance stood at her head, spotting her. When Samson flashed her his badge, I expected her to stop.

"Six. . . Seven. Three more!" Vance barked.

She growled with the effort, like an angry lion.

"Nine. . . Ten!"

"Two more," she grunted.

"Give it a rest now."

"Shut up, you steroid-addled freak!" she roared. "Nothing's stopping me!"

Samson cleared his throat but was ignored.

Meanwhile, I was busy scanning for thought waves. The old lady was thinking nothing but animal-level ferocity. Vance didn't seem to think much at all. Something told me he rarely did.

"Done!" she screamed.

Vance seized the barbell and helped her put it down on the rack above the bench. The lady sat up and wiped her face with a towel.

"Why are the cops here?" she asked. "Does this have anything to do with your partner dying?"

"Yes," Samson said. "I'm sorry to bother you again in your time of grief, Mr. Puggle."

"Alice refused to cancel her session, so I'm working through my grief instead," Vance said.

"Oh, come on, grief is for wussies," Alice said. "At my age, my friends are dying right and left. You have to learn to play through the pain."

"That's what I'm doing. But Alice, we only have time left for squat thrusts."

"That's okay. I won't stand in the way of justice. I'll get out of here now and let these two-bit *Law and Order* extras do their thing."

She threw on a warm-up suit and backed her luxury car out of the driveway.

"Quite a character," Samson said.

"She called me steroid-addled? She should look in the mirror."

Samson rolled through the standard questions about the victim: was he in debt? Was he involved in any disputes? Did he use drugs? Has anyone threatened him?

Vance answered no to all the questions, while I tried to capture thoughts from him about why we were here. I picked up plenty of wariness, but nothing specific. He didn't think we suspected him.

Until Samson dropped the bomb.

"Do you have any reason to suspect Hugo was having an affair?"

Rage washed over Vance.

How would they know about the cheating? The words popped into my head, clear as day. Followed by him trying to decide if he should lie or not.

"There was someone," Vance said in a tight voice. "A woman. Hugo said it was over and meant nothing to him."

Was it my imagination, or were Vance's enormous pecs and biceps rippling with anger? If anyone could impale a man with a blunt staff, this guy had the strength to do it.

"Do you know who the woman is?" Samson asked.

"Her name is Dorothy. I think he tutored her in magic. That's all I know."

He was telling the truth. The image of an appointment book appeared in his mind where he could find the woman's full name if he truly wanted to.

"Did Hugo keep an appointment book for his clients?" I asked.

He looked at me with surprise. "Yeah."

"Can we borrow it?" Samson asked.

"Yeah."

"Where were you last night?"

Now Samson was turning up the heat.

"Here. Working out. Went to bed around eleven. I expected Hugo would have been home by then."

I sensed he was telling the truth. Which was confirmed when I got a memory of him working out on the wall bars.

"Do you have proof you were here all night?"

"Um, no. But I guess you can check my cellphone's location. Don't you guys do that, anyway?"

"Of course we do," Samson said. "That's why perps leave their phones at home when they go out to do their dirty deeds."

I wandered into the garage behind Vance, hoping he wouldn't notice. There was no way I could let myself into the home and touch his possessions, but I wanted to try the wall bars. Hopefully, a client hasn't used them since he did.

I casually reached up and grasped the right-side bar, as if I was resting. I had to work quickly because—

—*Why isn't he home yet? Is he with that woman again? He told me it was over. Was he lying? I hate this, feeling like an insecure lover waiting at home while he runs around town like a tomcat. What does he see in her? Is she beautiful and hot? And why would he want her? He always said I was the guy of his dreams; the hottest one he'd ever been with. Was he lying? Man, it makes me so mad. I should confront him. No, that would make me look jealous. But I have to do something. Got to stop this. Time for a protein shake and—*

— "Can I help you?"

I let go of the bar. Because, back in the current world, Vance was staring at me with suspicion.

"Just resting," I said.

"You don't look very comfortable. You're too short and that bar's too high."

I smiled sheepishly and slowly retreated from the garage.

"I'll get the appointment book for you, Detective," Vance said as he went inside.

After the door closed, Samson asked, "Anything?"

"He's upset and jealous about the affair, but I couldn't find a specific memory about harming Hugo. This guy is still a prime suspect in my eyes."

"Don't be too quick to draw conclusions. I need to speak with this Dorothy, too."

"*We* need to speak with her."

"Maybe you should just go to the police academy and become a detective already."

"We've already been over this. I'm a consultant. An unpaid consultant. Maybe it's time to change the unpaid part."

"Don't get your hopes up."

We shut up when Vance stepped back into the garage. He handed a leather-bound journal to Samson.

"Hugo refused to use a calendar app for his magic tutoring." Vance said. "He was always so old-school."

He teared up, and I felt compassion for the big lug. You didn't expect to see such emotion from a guy with biceps wider than telephone poles.

"Excuse me," he said.

"Thank you for your time, Mr. Puggle," Samson said. "I'll be in touch soon."

WE STOPPED AT A COFFEE SHOP IN A SHOPPING CENTER TO

take a break and examine the appointment journal. The book was as flamboyant as Hugo.

The leather cover had an embossed pentagram on its cover. I had no idea you could buy a journal like this, but we have the internet to thank for that. Inside, the pages were thick, creamy and unruled. Hugo had written each entry with pen and ink using calligraphy. He treated this appointment book like a grimoire of magic spells.

The appointments were more like diary entries than calendar moments. Each page was headed by a client's name, the lessons planned, and progress made after each lesson. The book was about half filled, and it looked like he saw only two or three clients per week.

About a third of the way through the book, Dorothy Gilley's name appeared with a lesson scheduled for a year ago. The topic was "Finding Your Inner Magic." Beneath it was scrawled a note, with the same pen but not using calligraphy. It read: "Unhappy wife with no kids. Wants to believe there's something special about her. Potential for several lessons on core energies before we even get to spells and potions."

Dollar signs were scribbled after the note.

Yeah, Hugo found himself a goldmine. She wanted to believe she had magic in her, and Hugo was happy to string her along during the long process of becoming a witch.

I flipped the pages of the journal while Samson read it from the stool beside me, sipping his iced coffee. I was pleased to note the former sexual tension between us had evaporated. Ever since Cory returned, we had abandoned the flirtation that had begun when I thought I was an abandoned wife, inches away from dissolving my marriage.

Our new status as friends and professional colleagues suited me just fine, thank you. I felt blessed we could grow like this without hard feelings. But, then again, I hadn't had to deal with the two men in the same room at the same time until this morning. I hoped I wouldn't have to again.

As we progressed through the journal, magic lessons for Dorothy Gilley went from once a week to twice. And then to thrice weekly. Hugo was doing an excellent job of parting her with her money. Maybe he was even teaching her some magic.

Then her appointments abruptly ended, though the pages for his other clients continued.

"Does this mean she fired him after the affair? Or was this when their relationship went from making magic to making whoopee?"

"Who knows?" Samson said with a sigh. "We need to speak with her. Is there any contact information in here?"

There was no such data disturbing the beautiful calligraphy and poetic language about magic. Having a hunch, I opened the very last pages of the book, past a swathe of blank pages, and found a long list of names, numbers, and addresses printed in plain text with a ballpoint pen.

"Bingo."

Casually and confidently, so Samson wouldn't question why, I took a picture of Dorothy's contact information. Just in case I needed it.

Samson called Dorothy's phone number. He shook his head when she didn't answer.

"Mrs. Gilley, this is Detective Michael Samson of the San Marcos Police Department. Could you please call me at your earliest convenience?"

He rattled off his number and ended the call.

"Let's go visit her house," he said.

"You're not going to wait for her to call back?"

"What makes you believe she will? As a consultant, I thought you'd know more about investigative techniques."

I ignored that and followed him to his car.

The Gilleys lived far out in the countryside. During the drive, I used my phone to search the internet for more information about her. In public records, I found the name of her husband: Dick Gilley, manager of a hedge fund. I also saw they had a gigantic mortgage on their gigantic home.

"I suppose Dorothy's husband would be a suspect, too, if he found out about Dorothy's affair."

"Absolutely. We need to turn the rocks over methodically and see what's hiding beneath them."

More searching told me she was a retired public-school principal. I shared a summary of all the information with Samson.

"I'm impressed you're so good at getting info in non-psychic ways," he said.

"Enough of this, okay?"

He smiled and remained silent until we arrived at the address. An open gate greeted us, with a dirt road leading through a dense pine forest.

"Seeing as the gate is open, we'll go on in," Samson said, turning the car into the driveway.

It was a long driveway, enclosed by trees and with no view yet of the house. These folks sure liked their privacy. I couldn't imagine how many acres their property was.

Finally, the driveway curved to the left, and the house came into view. I had expected to find a country manor house, Tudor-style or Neoclassical. Instead, it was an ultra-modern behemoth. The architecture didn't fit into the rustic setting at all. The building was sprawling, with a detached garage. As we wound up the driveway, I got a glimpse of a swimming pool and cabanas behind the edifice.

Samson parked in front of the house, and we got out. We walked up a brick path lined by juniper bushes to the imposing front door.

"All we can do is hope someone's home," Samson said, ringing the doorbell.

Loud chimes echoed inside. But no one answered the door. He rang again.

"Okay," he said, inserting his business card in the door crack. "Dorothy will now know she's on our radar."

THERE WAS LITTLE OPPORTUNITY TO CHAT WITH SAMSON ON our return drive to town since he received a lengthy phone call. He said little, mostly grunts, interspersed with one-word questions. Maybe he didn't want me to hear anything.

"Thank you," he finally said. "And let me know as soon as your procedure is complete."

I didn't want to appear nosy about the call, but I was. I stared at him like a dog wanting a treat, which didn't hide my nosiness.

"You know when you made those quips about being a consultant?" he asked, his eyes remaining on the road. "Well, you're not the only one I use now."

"You have another psychic?"

"No, a witch. Of course, no one in the department knows she's a witch. With all the supernatural stuff going on in this town, I need someone to help me identify if magic was involved in homicides and serious crimes."

"Makes sense, but you said magic can't be used as evidence in court."

"No, but knowing the true cause of death keeps me from

charging the wrong person. And if we can't nail the perpetrator for using magic, sometimes we can find other ways to bring him or her to justice."

"Hugo's murder. Would that be a case where you'd use this witch consultant?"

"Exactly. That's why I brought the topic up. My witch checked out the crime scene, the staff, and the body in the morgue. She said magic was definitely involved."

"I'm not surprised."

"Well, I hate to be the one to tell you this, but I have to consider Cory and Sophie as persons-of-interest."

"What?" My pulse throbbed in my ears. "You already questioned them. They made it clear they had no motive and didn't do it."

"Darla, we have two witches at a crime scene where magic was used. That's too much of a coincidence. I *have* to take a closer look at them."

"It was obviously a different witch who did this."

"I'm sure it was. I'm only doing my due diligence."

"You're attacking my family. Please drop me off at my car before I say something so nasty to you that I get arrested."

CHAPTER 4

INTERVIEW WITH THE WITCH

"Mom, do you remember Gerta, the beach troll?" Sophie asked. "You know, the one Cousin Missy cured?"

"Of course, I remember her. She and her kids are the only beach trolls I know. The only trolls of any sort I know."

"We're visiting her today as soon as I clean up after breakfast."

"We are?"

"I want to ask her for help in finding Cervantes. Maybe he showed up at another beach troll's den to beg for food."

"I hope beach trolls don't eat cats," I said.

"Mom, they eat fish, shellfish, and seabirds. I think seaweed, too. But not cats."

It sounded like a long shot to me, but I drove us to where Gerta lived, in a state park with several miles of beachfront, not far from the spot where Hugo disappeared. I relied on Sophie to guide me to the den, hidden beneath a wooden boardwalk that crossed the sand dunes.

We climbed off the wooden walkway onto a dune, weaved

through the sea oats, and descended into the shadows beneath the structure. Facing toward the beach, at the back face of the dune, Sophie called in a sing-song voice,

"Gerta, we are your friends, Sophie and Darla. We humbly request your permission to visit you."

We waited. I'm no witch, but I felt a change in the atmosphere as magical energies began working.

The face of the dune shimmered. Soon, where only shadows had existed, the shape of a doorway with a rounded top appeared. It gradually came into focus to reveal a heavy wooden door with iron bolts.

"Upon your door, I'm knocking thrice. Answer it, please; I shall be nice."

The door opened outward. In the den's antechamber stood the hulking form of Gerta, her two children behind her, and an oil lamp hanging from a timbered rafter above them.

"Welcome, humans," Gerta said, beaming. She had a deep, rumbling voice with a vaguely European accent.

Trolls look like you think they would: humanoid, but taller and huskier. They have bulbous noses, bulging brows, and knobby skin. Their ears are pointed and rather hairy. I'm sure they think humans are the ugly ones.

Her kids, a boy and a girl, waved shyly at us. Each of them was larger than we adult humans.

"Gerta, thank you for seeing us," Sophie said. "I won't take much of your time. We've come to ask if you've seen a black cat named Cervantes. He has yellow-green eyes and a white collar. He's a witch's familiar, has magic in him, and can speak with witches and supernatural creatures. You would know right away he's not a normal cat. He escaped from us at the beach two days ago. I wonder if he has taken shelter with a troll."

"I have not seen him, no," Gerta said. "Nor has anyone

mentioned finding him. Yet I shall ask the other trolls so we can return him to you. It is not a safe time for supernatural creatures."

"What do you mean?" I asked.

"The Fae have been active of late. Hostile, they have been. They stole a child from one troll family. Another, they attacked. I'm afraid of the times to come."

Faeries had recently stolen a human child from witch parents but returned her. They threatened to take other children from non-witches. I was surprised they behaved belligerently toward the trolls, too.

"Are more faeries moving to the area?" I asked.

"Perhaps. Though I speak of the Fae community that has always been here, living in the forests and under the earth. They have existed here longer than we trolls and you humans. But only now have they become a threat. Something has awakened them and filled them with anger and hatred. They claim this land is rightfully theirs and they intend to rule it and suppress all the other creatures."

Great. It was difficult enough having supernatural creatures and humans coexist peacefully in the same world, with humans being none the wiser. Yet, it had worked, and the various communities of creatures could live as they wished and flourish. But now, it seemed the delicate balance would fall apart.

"Would the Fae harm a cat?" Sophie asked.

"I know not," Gerta said. "I hope not. The trolls of this area will look everywhere along the beach for your cat."

We thanked Gerta profusely,

"I'll check back with you tomorrow," Sophie said.

We left the troll den and climbed up the sand, then onto the dune crossover, crossing back into the human world. One that was oblivious to the storm clouds forming.

Before this, I had been reluctant to allow Sophie to be dragged into my strange relationship with the Fae. I had told her about the faerie's visit to my cottage and his announcement that I would be either a great ally or an enemy of the Fae. (I left out the part about my being destined for greatness, since what daughter would believe that of her mom?)

Our visit to Gerta reminded me of the young woman Sophie had befriended when they worked together at the restaurant. Imelda had the supernatural in her, as well, through the blood of the Aluxes. These creatures, from the Mayan region of Mexico, are like elves or faeries.

As we drove home, I asked Sophie if she had spoken to Imelda recently.

"I saw her at a party a couple of weeks ago," she said.

"Ask her if she or her family are aware of what's going on with the Fae and if they're getting dragged into it."

She looked at me with concern. "I hope they're not involved. I'm texting her now."

We drove over the Bridge of Memories and passed through Old Town, headed for the inn. Sophie's phone beeped.

"She says her family is aware of the unrest," she said. "They're trying to stay out of it. Her people consider themselves different from the Fae and have no desire to be involved. Unless they're forced to."

"Okay. Ask her to let you know of any new developments."

Sophie tapped away.

Frankly, I didn't want to get involved, either. Hopefully, the prophecy that I would be a friend or ally would not come true. As long as the humans and supernatural folk I cared about were not harmed, I was content to allow the world of mythical creatures to do its own thing.

My breath caught in my throat as I pulled up to the inn and saw Samson and Fernandez waiting on the sidewalk outside.

It looked like I had problems much closer to home than the Fae to deal with.

"Do you think they have good news about Hugo or Cervantes?" Sophie asked before we got out of the car.

"Unfortunately, no."

The grim expressions on the two cops' faces made that clear.

"Can I help you?" I asked as I walked toward the inn's door. "I'm afraid we're all full. No vacancies."

"Darla, we need to speak with Sophie."

"Why?"

"That, er, consultant I told you about," he turned away from Fernandez and dropped his voice. "She identified the magic used against Hugo as from a water witch. That's what Sophie is. We need to speak with her in greater depth."

"You can't arrest her based on that," I said in a loud, angry stage whisper.

"I'm not arresting her. I'm asking her to come with us to the station for an interview."

"Does she have to?"

"Technically, no. But it could make her situation worse if she doesn't."

"How could it be worse?"

"Non-cooperation often means guilt."

"I'll go with them, Mom," Sophie said. I hadn't realized she was within earshot of the discussion.

"We need a lawyer," I said.

"You don't have to bring a lawyer," Samson said. "It will only drag this out."

"Oh, easy for you to say. Of course, you don't want us to have a lawyer."

"The interview will be recorded to protect all parties. If she's innocent, she doesn't need a lawyer."

"I'm completely innocent," Sophie said. "Let's go get this over with."

I didn't know any criminal lawyers. Only a divorce lawyer and real estate lawyer. And what good would a lawyer do if this was about magic? I suppose I could ask the Magic Guild if any of their members were lawyers.

"Mom. Let's just do this, okay?"

I sighed.

"I'll drive her to the station," I told Samson. "We'll follow you."

ON THE WAY, I TRIED TO COACH HER.

"Detective Samson thinks Hugo was killed with a magic spell and that you might have cast it."

She laughed. "Well, I don't have the strength to spear him with his staff. So, it would have to be magic. The thing is, I don't know any spells that could do that."

"That's a good defense. The police are at a real disadvantage here. The prosecutors can't bring up the topic of magic in court. In fact, Officer Fernandez doesn't even know it exists. No one on the force except Samson does, unless they keep their knowledge secret. He can't charge you with murder unless he comes up with a method of death that can hold up in court."

"This is crazy," Sophie said.

"Yeah, but prosecutors have been known to use fabricated evidence before."

"Would Detective Samson let that happen? I thought he was your friend?"

"I thought so, too. Remember, the interview will be on video. So, Samson can't ask you direct questions about using magic. And if he dances a little too close to the topic, bring it up in your answers. That will make him back off."

Samson and Fernandez met us in the lobby of the police station. Normally, when I come here, it's to collaborate with Samson, and I feel I'm on his side. Today, that feeling was gone. I was no different from the other family members of criminals and suspects. Today, I wasn't on Samson's team.

The place felt unwelcoming and scary.

"Please wait down here," Samson said.

"I'm staying with her."

"You can't." He looked at me sternly.

"I'm acting as her attorney."

He shook his head. "Sorry. That's not going to work."

The two cops and my daughter walked to the elevator. Thankfully, they didn't lay a hand on her. Technically, she was a private citizen here for an interview.

To me, it felt as if she were a criminal in their eyes.

SOPHIE WAS GONE FOR OVER TWO HOURS. WHEN SHE FINALLY got off the elevator, she was alone. Samson didn't have the courtesy to escort her back to me.

She wasn't upset, but didn't seem relieved, either.

"How did it go?"

"It was kind of a waste of time in my eyes," Sophie said. "You were right—he couldn't ask about magic, so he asked a bunch of silly roundabout questions."

"What did you say?"

"I told him I had nothing against Hugo. I actually liked the guy. He made me uncomfortable when he hugged me, but I never felt in danger, so I feel horrible that he died. I also said I didn't have the strength or means to kill him."

I drove us home, furious at Samson. It seemed such a desperate reach to blame Sophie just because she's a water witch.

So why was he doing it?

CHAPTER 5

DARLA'S TREE-TRIMMING
SERVICE

N o more consulting. No more collaborating. No more congeniality. Samson and I were finished, I fumed, as I drove into the countryside on the way to the Gilley estate. Samson was the enemy now. I would have to find out on my own who killed Hugo, because Samson was too narrow-minded to do it. Sophie's name needed to be cleared. And if true justice was going to be done, an innkeeper-slash-psychometrist would have to do it.

Okay, maybe that last part sounded a little too egotistical. I had no power to bring about justice. But I sure as heck would not allow Sophie to be railroaded. At the very least, I needed to find some evidence that would lead the investigation away from her and toward the true culprit.

Unfortunately, I had no idea how I was going to do it. All I could think of was to speak with Dorothy Gilley and see if she looked guilty of the murder or knew who might be. And my only tools were my telepathy and psychometry. And my bad attitude.

The attitude worsened as I drove up the Gilleys' driveway and considered the gargantuan size of the family's property. Granted, land was cheaper way out here in the sticks. Even so, this place and the overly large house were over the top. I'd have to check out their property tax record online. No, strike that. It would only make me envious.

When the house came into view, one door of the four-car garage was open. A blue BMW was parked inside, as well as another vehicle I couldn't see fully. I parked in front and trudged up the front walk, trying to formulate a cover story.

I'm here to sell magazine subscriptions to support my kid's soccer team. Nope, I'm a bit too old to have a kid that age.

I'm here to convert you to my religion. Nope. I'd get the door slammed in my face.

I'm here to convince you to vote for . . . Oh, there's no election this year.

Do you need your trees trimmed? Hmm, that might work. They had lots of trees and I could say I had a tree-trimming company.

I rang the bell.

But why is my vehicle a beat-up Japanese import and not a pickup truck with a company logo on it?

The door opened. And the most amazing man stood there.

"Can I help you?" he asked with a slight accent, maybe French, maybe Italian, or something else.

I hesitated, then realized my jaw was hanging open.

"Hi," I said.

He was tall with thick black hair parted on the side. His face was aristocratic and European, with prominent cheekbones, square chin, and a delicate nose. Shimmering green eyes regarded me quizzically.

"Hi," he said with a polite but wary smile. "Can I help you?" he repeated.

"Is Dorothy here?"

"No, she's out now. Can I take a message for her?"

I had forgotten completely about tree trimming or whatever it was I allegedly did. I almost forgot why I was here. This guy was so captivating, and I admit I had expected Dorothy to answer the door, figuring her husband was off managing his hedge fund and raking in millions.

"Are you her husband?" I asked, regretting how stupid I sounded.

"Yes, I'm Dick. And who are you?" He was clearly losing patience with me.

"I'm Darla, and a friend of mine was murdered, and your wife was a friend of his, and I thought somehow that she might know something that might help me somehow figure out who murdered my friend, because I have to do this, since the police aren't doing their job and are fixated with my daughter as a suspect, so it's come down to me to look into this."

His eyes widened as I babbled uncontrollably until I ran out of breath. I guess it was nerves. Not much of an excuse, Darla.

"Wow," he said. "I'm sorry to hear your friend was murdered. You say Dorothy knew him?"

"Yeah. My friend was . . ." I couldn't say he was a witch. "He was a magician. He taught her how to do magic tricks."

"Really? That doesn't sound like her. What was his name?"

"Hugo Starbright. Also known as Hugo the Magnificent. He lived in San Marcos."

He shook his head. "Sorry, I've never heard of him. Give me your number and I'll ask Dorothy about him. She'll call you if she knows anything helpful."

45

I realized in my manic state I'd completely forgotten to use my paranormal abilities. Before I arrived here, I had imagined sipping tea with Dorothy in her living room with ample opportunities to touch household items in search of memories. Instead, I'm standing on the front porch like a rep for a tree trimming company without a truck.

Reaching into my purse for my inn's business card, I stopped. I needed a delay. Instead of my card, I grabbed a slip of paper and a pen. At the last second, I released the pen and left it in my purse.

"I'm sorry," I said. "Do you have a pen?"

My mind reached out, groping for his thoughts. He was a very guarded man, but I picked up feelings of suspicion. Then:

Magic tricks? Ha! That's what she thinks he taught her? They were tricks, all right, just not magical.

He sighed with impatience. "One moment."

He walked to a nearby side table in an immense foyer with a two-story ceiling and returned with a pen. I took it, hoping it had memories on it.

A woman's memory. Signing for a delivery from a florist. Angry thoughts.

Yeah, right, Hugo. Like flowers will make me forgive you for dumping me.

Not much, but I was lucky to get this, let alone anything, from a pen.

I wrote my number on the paper and handed it to Dick Gilley. He shoved it in his trouser pocket without a glance, as if he'd forgotten about it already.

"Thank you for your time hearing me out," I said.

"No problem," he said, closing the door in my face.

Feelings of resentment floated out like smoke escaping the house.

Wow. Both Gilleys had motives for killing Hugo. Motives more believable than any Sophie could have had.

As if to match Gilley's resentment, actual smoke rose in the distance as I drove back to town. Winding through the landscape of fields and dense patches of forest, I couldn't see the source of the smoke, but assumed it was a wildfire somewhere. It was the dry season, after all.

But as I got closer to San Marcos, fire department vehicles appeared ahead of me and poured onto County Road 117, the intersection of which I was approaching. By this time, the smell of smoke had penetrated my car, and it was not pure wood smoke. It had the acrid stench of manufactured materials, meaning a building was on fire.

County Road 117 led to the county jail. I prayed no one was hurt. I slowed as I approached the intersection. More emergency vehicles with flashing lights turned off onto 117, but these were law enforcement. If it was the jail that was burning, keeping the prisoners safe but still in custody would be tricky.

The thought crept into my head: Texas Tom was in the jail right now.

Ice filled the pit of my stomach.

Without even thinking, I took a sharp left at the intersection and headed toward the jail. I wanted to know what was going on.

After only a couple of miles, the road was blocked ahead of me by sheriff's deputies. I was close enough to see that the fire did, in fact, appear to be coming from the jail or adjacent buildings, but too far to make it out for sure.

A deputy approached my window, and I lowered it.

"Ma'am, I suggest you turn around and go back to the state road," he said. "This route is going to be blocked for a while."

"Is it the jail that's on fire?" I asked.

"Yes. They're getting it under control."

"Is everyone okay?"

"I believe so."

Right after he said that, flashing lights appeared in my rearview mirror. The deputy directed three ambulances to go around me.

So, not everyone was okay.

I was just backing up onto the shoulder to turn around when bright lights caught my eyes.

Fireballs arced into the sky. I've seen fireballs like those before. They had been fired at Cory and me by Texas Tom.

Two more ambulances came up, and I had to remain backed up on the shoulder to stay out of their way.

After they passed, something caught my eye again: a man sprinting from the woods.

It was Texas Tom.

He headed for the deputy's car that was used to block the road. The deputy saw him and sprinted toward his car to cut him off.

Then Tom noticed my car poised on the shoulder. He darted left, avoided the deputy, and rushed toward me.

Oh no.

My hands were shaking with panic. I tried to put the car in gear, but he was already upon it. He grabbed the passenger door, but it was locked. As I finally shifted the car into Drive, Tom rolled over the hood and thrust his hand into my open window, unlocking my door. He reached across me and pulled up the parking brake just as I punched the accelerator.

My tires spun in the dirt of the shoulder, the car inching forward.

Only now did Tom look at my face.

"Oh, it's you! What good luck! We're going to take a little ride together and get reacquainted."

He opened the door. I unclipped my seatbelt and scrambled out of my seat, over the parking brake, and into the passenger seat. Before I tried to open the passenger door, Tom had jumped into the driver's seat, closed the door, and pressed the master lock on the driver's armrest.

"Not so fast, Darla. Time to put a spell on you."

I got the window down most of the way before he found the child window lock. Crawling out the window, my body grew limp as a spell of some sort took hold of me. I was hanging painfully on the quarter of the window that was still above the door.

The sight of the deputy running toward me was the only thing that kept me from despair. I tried one last flop, like a fish on a boat.

The car jumped forward.

I tumbled to the dirt.

The deputy fired a round at my car that made my ears ring.

And I watched my cheap but beloved car drive away down County Road 117, back the way I had come.

"I'm not speaking to you. You're a traitor," I said to Samson.

"I'm a cop, and I do things methodically. If Sophie is innocent, you have nothing to fear except the inconvenience of me being methodical."

Samson drove me to San Marcos after I was interviewed by

deputies and prison officials. I had holes in my jeans, a scraped knee, and no purse or wallet.

"Methodical and completely lacking common sense," I said.

Samson shook his head and kept his eyes on the road.

"Sophie told you she doesn't have the skill to perform a spell that could kill a man. I can attest to that."

"You mean you wanted her to do it, and she couldn't?"

"You know what I mean."

"Well, thanks to the information you gave me about the Gilleys, maybe the investigation should take a different turn."

"Oh, you think?"

"You don't wear sarcasm well."

"I learned to be sarcastic before I learned to talk. It comes in handy when I speak with a detective who is so narrow-minded that he accuses a beginner witch of using magic to murder someone, just because she happened to be at the scene earlier."

"It's the standard way to investigate. You begin by looking at the people—"

"And ignoring the people with much stronger motives. Like the pupil he was having an affair with, whom he apparently cut loose. Or his partner, who knew about the affair. And now, after speaking with her husband, I know he's aware of the affair, too."

"You spoke to Mr. Gilley? Look, Darla, we can't have you interfering—"

"Listen, we have three people who could have killed Hugo. One of whom knows magic, because Hugo was teaching it to her. And maybe the other two do, as well. But we don't even know for sure magic was used to kill Hugo, only that spells were cast on the beach that night."

"Hold on, hold on. You were with me when I tried to interview Mrs. Gilley. I *am* investigating these other subjects. Like I told you, I'm very methodical."

"Enough about your methods. Tell me what exactly happened at the jail? Everyone I asked refused to say."

"I think they're refusing to comprehend it. From what I heard, it sounds like fires broke out in the jail in several areas simultaneously, including in places prisoners had no access. While the guards and firefighters fought the fires, they evacuated several prisoner pods under heavy guard. Tom's was one of them."

"So far, there's plausible deniability magic was involved," I said.

"Exactly. But then he had to find a way to escape when the prisoners were all shackled together."

"How did he manage that?"

"Obviously, it was low-profile magic. The guards tell me that one moment he was there, and the next he was out of the shackles and sprinting for the tree line."

"Why didn't they just shoot him?" I asked.

"Oh, they tried. That's when the fireballs began. Escaping the shackles could have been explained as a mistake by the guards who restrained him. But shooting fireballs back at them while he ran away? No one has an explanation for how he did that."

"I didn't think he'd be able to pull off that kind of magic. I thought he had to harvest energy from other witches."

"I guess he found one or more in the jail," Samson said. "There are all sorts of folks in the county jail at any given time. A much more diverse population than the convicted felons in the state pen or federal prisons. Who knows how many witches are in the jail?"

"Yeah." I stared glumly at the road. "The last thing I need right now is to have to worry about Tom kidnapping Cory again or getting revenge on my family."

"Don't hesitate to call the police, even if it's about a magic attack from him. Any information at all can help the marshals find him." He glanced at me. "And don't hesitate to call me."

"Call the enemy?"

"Come on, you know that's not the case."

"It is at the moment."

CHAPTER 6

THIS SMELLS LIKE A
HAUNTING

W hen I returned to the inn, I was pleased to find Sophie
and Cory preparing for Teatime in my absence.
Neither were great in the kitchen, but at least they had prepared
the simple stuff, like the finger sandwiches. Cory bought tarts at
a local bakery. And Sophie had the beginnings of the batter for
the scones in progress. I jumped in and took over. The scones
would come out of the oven just a little late, which shouldn't be a
problem.

Once things were under control, I told them about my
eventful day. I glossed over my clues about the Gilleys because
more investigation was needed. The main focus of my talk was
about Tom.

"I can't believe it," Cory said, clearly shaken.

"Let's hope they recapture him soon, but we need to take
defensive measures," I said. "Cory, stay armed at all times. I
know you don't like carrying a weapon, but you must be extra
careful."

He nodded.

"Let's test the inn's alarm system and all the locks."

"I'm on it," Cory said.

"Sophie, I don't believe Tom knows much about you, but you could be a target as well as Cory. Don't go anywhere by yourself until this is over."

"And to think being a murder suspect seemed like the worst thing in the world," she said with a bitter smile.

"We should place a warding spell on the inn, specifically configured for Tom," Cory said. "That's beyond my skill set, though."

"Me too," Sophie said.

Diana, the Memory Guild's astral witch, probably didn't practice that kind of magic either.

"I'll ask Arch Mage Bob to do it," I said. "He needs to know about Tom"

I texted him but didn't hear back yet. Surfers are among the few kinds of people who don't always have their phones in hand.

After Teatime, I patrolled the inn, checking to make sure all the unoccupied rooms had their windows locked. As usual, I had a lot of unoccupied rooms.

To save time and energy as I went from floor to floor, I took the elevator. And today, of all days, I finally had an encounter with the ghost.

The darn elevator shook and rattled like it was on its last legs. I was already nervous about the experience, when something made me turn my head to find a man riding the car with me. A man who hadn't been there when I got in. I jumped in surprise.

"Hello," I whispered, not sure what one was supposed to say to a ghost in this situation.

The ghost was a man in his forties, with shaggy brown hair, a mustache, corduroy pants, and a cardigan sweater. He turned to me with sad eyes and opened his mouth to speak.

Then promptly disappeared.

That was freaky. He didn't seem malevolent, but I couldn't imagine ever getting used to encountering a ghost. Even Sage, from the Memory Guild, still made me feel a little uneasy.

After I finished my paranoid window checking, I resolved to learn more about this ghost. If anyone would know, it would be my cantankerous resident gargoyle, Archibald. Unfortunately, this required waking him up. And I didn't have Cervantes to help me.

No guests were around downstairs, so I headed straight for the parlor and stood before the giant English Medieval fireplace and its mantel supported by four stone gargoyles.

"Archibald. I need to speak with you, please."

He never answered right away.

"Archibald, I need to access your unique knowledge of the inn. Only you have the experience and wisdom that can help me."

Sometimes, flattery worked. Today, it didn't.

"Archibald, please. I don't have all day."

Of course, my time constraints were meaningless for a creature of stone who has existed at least eight centuries.

After calling his name several more times, and even knocking on his head, I took it up a notch.

"Hey Archie, wake up!"

The stone face of the gargoyle shimmered as it animated into life. His expression was even more devilish than normal.

"What do you bloody well want? I told you I absolutely despise that name."

"I know. Sorry."

"Get on with it, then. Tell me what you want. This better be worth my while."

"I need your help to identify a ghost in the hotel," I said in the sweetest voice I could muster.

He sighed. "There are literally dozens of them."

"There are?" I had only encountered three. Aside from the elevator ghost, there was the bride in 303 and the Elvis impersonator in 202.

"Indeed. I thought you would have met most of them by now. Perhaps they find you as off-putting as I do when you call me Archie."

"This ghost haunts the elevator." I described his appearance.

"That sounds like Darren."

"Who was he?"

"The former owner."

"Oh my. He didn't die here at the inn, did he?"

"He most certainly did. How or exactly where, we do not know."

"Wait a minute," I said. "If you don't know where he died, how do you know he died here? I don't believe ghosts have to haunt the exact place where they died."

"Oh, we're convinced he died here. He simply disappeared one night. No sign of him. The authorities searched everywhere. Years later, shortly after you came along, a horrible odor was detected in the inn."

"If there was a decomposing body, the police would have found it back when Darren disappeared. And I haven't smelled anything," I said.

"The odor was detected by Roderick, not by any humans. And I have to say, as a vampire, his senses are not as sensitive as one would expect. Now, allow me to explain. After Darren disappeared, his heirs eventually closed the hotel, and it remained empty for over three years until you purchased it. Roderick is nevertheless convinced the smell is Darren's fault."

"I knew the inn was empty for three years. But I didn't know the owner died here. My realtor should have told me."

"This is a place of lodging. It's inevitable that people would die here over time."

For a moment, I became defensive, as if Archibald was pointing out my high rate of guests getting knocked off. Until I realized he was talking about the three centuries of the inn's existence.

"Roderick can't locate the corpse?"

"He is a vampire, not a ghoul. He hunts living creatures, not dead ones. The existence of a foul odor was as specific as he could describe."

"The body decomposed years ago. Why is there a foul smell now?"

"Roderick and I believe the odor is a manifestation of the haunting. It's a cry for help from beyond the veil for someone to find his remains."

"I wonder why he's haunting the elevator. He couldn't have died in there, or in the shaft, because someone would have found him," I said.

"Precisely."

"Could he be signaling us to look upstairs?"

Archibald shrugged with his little impish arms.

A switch clicked in my brain. "Room three-oh-three. The previous guests complained about a foul smell in the bathroom. I had a plumber make sure the toilet wasn't clogged. He couldn't explain where the smell was coming from."

"Roderick never mentioned that particular room. However, you should investigate there further."

Before I could ask another question, Archibald had returned to stony slumber.

So, there I was. My daughter was suspected of murder. Our cat was missing. A psychotic wizard, who kept my husband hostage for a year and holds a grudge against me, has escaped from prison. And I had to deal with a haunting by the owner who preceded me. I could ignore his apparition, as long as he didn't freak out any guests in the elevator. But a foul smell *had* to be dealt with.

You can't have guests complaining about stinky bathrooms. It really looks bad in the online reviews.

I rode the elevator to the third floor, hoping Darren would appear again. Could I convince him to help me solve this? Unlikely, but I was willing to try. Of course, he didn't show up. Ghosts weren't known for their dependability, Sage being the rare exception.

Could two ghosts be haunting the same room? You'd think they would be territorial. Wouldn't Helga, the original ghost of 303, kick Darren out?

I let myself into Room 303, covering my hand with a shirt-sleeve to avoid the long-ago memory of Helga's murderous husband. Sunlight streamed through the gauzy curtains, putting a warm shine on the Victorian-era furnishings. The room was welcoming and attractive, with no hint of what had happened here in 1889.

But sure enough, a smell came from the bathroom. It wasn't exactly the odor of raw sewage, nor did it scream of a rotting corpse. It was simply noxious. Sort of like a stew made of boiled cabbage, gym socks, bad breath, and a porta-potty during Oktoberfest.

The bathroom in 303 was sparkling clean, including the toilet. The sink and bath faucets emitted no odors. Was the smell coming from a dead rat inside the walls? It was the only non-supernatural explanation I could think of, but I wouldn't think dead rats smelled this bad. Cory would have to use his handyman skills to check it out, anyway.

I returned to the bedroom and sat in an armchair.

"Helga, are you here?" I asked the empty room. Like Archibald, ghosts don't come running the moment you call them.

As I've noted before, having the paranormal in my blood makes me popular with supernatural creatures. Ghosts seek me out. Perhaps they believe I'm more sympathetic, or at least more likely to pay attention. I'd had contact with Helga before and hoped she'd heed my call.

Something moved in the corner of my eye. I looked in that direction but saw nothing. Still, I sensed a presence in the room.

"Helga, is there another ghost haunting your room?"

A dresser drawer opened slightly, and I jumped.

"Close the drawer if your answer is yes."

I waited. The drawer remained open. This wasn't helpful.

"Is there a corpse hidden in the walls?" I asked.

No answer at all. I felt suddenly alone, as if my spectral visitor had departed.

Oh well. I needed Sage to inspect the inn. Only a ghost could tell me another ghost's secrets.

Before I left the room, I poked my head in the bathroom.

The smell was gone. I shook my head and went downstairs, riding the elevator alone, without Darren.

Cory was waiting when the elevator doors opened. He held a plunger and a bag of tools.

"Two-oh-two called down with a complaint," he said in response to my questioning look. "They said a terrible smell is coming from the bathroom."

"Oh boy. This is getting weird."

I explained about Darren and 303.

"Two-oh-two is haunted, too," he said. "Is there a pattern here?"

"Maybe Darren's ghost is marking his territory to drive the other ghosts out. Or, the choice of rooms could be a coincidence. The question is, why is it happening now? Darren died three years before I bought the inn, and I've been running the place for over a year. Why is he raising a stink now?"

"I wish I knew. Anyway, I have to respond to two-oh-two. Who knows, it could simply be a clogged toilet after all."

Cory later reported the toilet wasn't clogged. All my alternate theories were being eliminated in place of one: this was ghost gas.

With all that was going on, I honestly didn't have time to deal with spectral stinks. But as an innkeeper, I couldn't afford to ignore it.

GLORIA, THE MEMORY GUILD'S PSYCHIC AND MEDIUM, arrived visibly alone, but I knew that Sage's spirit was with her. Sage would be my supernatural version of a cadaver dog. And she might also serve as my negotiator with the spirit who was taking the living hostage with his odors.

"Do you want to cleanse the inn of Darren's spirit completely?" Gloria asked. The petite, silver-haired woman was all business tonight.

"Not really. I have plenty of room for ghosts. I just want him to stop the stink bombs. And, if possible, stop appearing in the elevator. That's a scary place to encounter a ghost. He's welcome to show up elsewhere."

"Not in the shower when a guest is using it," Cory said. "That's kind of freaky, too."

"True. Sage, you can begin your search for him in the elevator."

"If Sage can't make contact, we'll try a seance," Gloria said, "though direct ghost-to-ghost, or I should say peer-to-peer, communication is the best, in my opinion. Now, you say you don't know how Darren died?"

"No. But I assume he died on the property," I said. "Archibald believes his body is still here, but I have my doubts."

"How gruesome."

"Yeah. And damaging to property values."

We chit-chatted in the living room for another twenty minutes until random snatches of Beatles songs began playing on the slightly out-of-tune piano. A transparent apparition of Sage appeared on the bench, bent over the keyboard.

"Sage confirms the ghost is Darren's," Gloria said. "He admits he is responsible for the odors. He doesn't create them deliberately—they're an embodiment of the feelings of decay and uncleanliness that torment him without a proper burial for his remains."

"Where are his remains?" Cory asked.

"That's the problem. He doesn't know. His death was so surprising, he doesn't remember it at all. It's a big part of why he's haunting the inn."

"Wonderful," I said. The stink problem went from a plumbing issue to a supernatural puzzle I couldn't solve. If Darren doesn't remember where he died, how could we figure it out without demolishing the entire structure? "But he's certain he died at the inn?"

"Yes. The last thing he remembers clearly is riding the elevator to the third floor."

"I would say the rickety old thing gave him a heart attack, but then his body would have been found," Cory said.

"Can't Sage sniff out his remains?" I asked.

"Only if his spirit was connected to them. Otherwise, they're nothing but bones."

"The inn has been reopened for a year. Why has this stink problem begun now?"

"That's the way ghosts behave," Gloria said. "With a logic known only to them."

CHAPTER 7

FOUL SPELLS

"I almost had a freaking heart attack when I heard Tom escaped," Arch Mage Bob said, standing on the street corner outside my inn.

"I hope he's left the area and is on his way to South America or someplace far away to hide," I said.

"No, he's probably still nearby," Cory said, frowning. "Tom's ego is too big for him to walk away without getting revenge on everyone he thinks wronged him. Specifically, the three of us."

"Wonderful," I said. "Like I really need another thing to worry about."

"He's probably still indebted to the Fae," Bob said. "Let's hope they keep him busy enough that he leaves us alone. Okay, let me cast this warding spell."

Bob was experienced and powerful, not needing any amulets, talismans, or magic circles to cast his spells. I did, however, suspect the seashells on a leather thong he wore around his neck contained magical energy.

He chanted words I didn't understand in a powerful rhythm.

The language sounded Native American, though I recognized some Latin words here and there. With alternating hands, he motioned in straight lines up and down, side to side. He shuffled down the sidewalk along the exterior of the inn, down the Cadiz Street frontage and up Hidalgo Avenue. Next, he went into the alley on the east side, and, since a neighbor abutted my property to the north, he went through my courtyard.

Finally, he had covered the entire perimeter of the inn and the cottage, too. He completed the spell with a loud clap of his hands.

"How strong is the protection?" I asked.

"I challenge you, dude, to find a witch who can cast a stronger warding spell. Remember, the spell blocks psychic incursions and magic attacks. Not physical creatures. You and your guests can come and go. But Tom could stroll in, too."

"That's why we have a gun," I said.

Cory glanced at me with dismay.

"I gotta tell you, I picked up traces of someone else's magic," Bob said. "I think Tom has already sent out some feelers."

"I had a dream last night about him," Cory said. "Of him standing over the bed, staring at me."

"Why didn't you tell me?" I asked.

"I didn't want to alarm you. It was just a dream."

"It was Tom probing you," Bob said. "Probably to test the strength of your magic. Have you been practicing at all since you escaped from him?"

"No. I just can't right now."

"I think you should. For your own protection."

"Too bad Hugo's not here to give me lessons."

"With all respect to a departed fellow witch, Hugo wasn't famous for making his students into powerful witches," Bob said.

"Was I being fleeced by hiring him to tutor Sophie?" I asked.

"He was okay teaching the basics. Sophie needs to find a better tutor if she wants to advance. Wait, why are you guys looking at me like that?"

"Sophie is a water witch like you," I said.

"I don't give magic lessons."

"You used to give surfing lessons. I heard you're a brilliant teacher."

"Dude, I don't have time anymore. My surf shop and the Magic Guild rule my life."

"Think about it," I said. "How much do we owe you for the warding spell?"

"It's on me," Bob said. "We all need to stick together to get rid of Texas Tom once and for all."

I DON'T LIKE TO LIE. NO ONE DOES, EXCEPT HABITUAL LIARS, and they're too dishonest to admit they enjoy it. There was no way, however, that I could get Vance to meet with me without my saying I was interested in becoming his personal-training client. I had to convince him I wasn't a cop and had come with Samson that day only because I was a friend of Hugo's.

"You seemed very interested in my equipment," he said, drinking a protein shake at a juice bar in the Old Town neighborhood near my inn.

"Yeah, you've got a great setup for a home gym."

"It's a professional-level gym."

"That's what I meant." I slurped my mango smoothie, trying to pick up his thoughts.

He was all business. His eyes roved over my body, assessing my fitness and strength.

"I've never had a personal trainer," I said. "I feel almost too old."

I can tell, he thought.

"Nonsense," he said. "You saw Georgia at my house. She's seventy-seven."

He went on to list his hourly rates and different training programs. I had to pretend I cared. I mean, I would have cared if I didn't have a job that demanded my attention day and night. So, I nodded and took notes, looking for an opening to change the subject.

"This is kind of ironic, isn't it?"

"What?" he asked. I don't think he knew what ironic meant.

"My daughter was a client of Hugo's for magical training, and now I want to become a client of yours for fitness training."

"I didn't know Hugo was tutoring your daughter. I thought you said you were Hugo's friend."

"I was. That's how I got to know him. He was a lovely man."

Vance's jaw muscles flexed. With a jaw like his, he would have a bite that put pit bulls to shame. "Yes. He was."

Thoughts of sorrow rolled from him and washed over me like waves. I pondered my plan of attack. Asking him directly about Dorothy could reveal my true intentions, so I had to be careful. I would have to take an indirect route.

"What did you think about Hugo's magic?" I asked.

He was surprised. "What about it?"

"Did you believe in it?"

He tugged at the shoulders of his shirt, as if his deltoids were too big for the fabric.

"At first, I thought it was just some illusionist act, like in Vegas. And it was—he used to perform on stage back in the day. After we met, though, he showed me some things that weren't tricks at all. They were real magic. He could make things levitate, like someone's plate of food at a diner. He messed around with some drunk guy one night, kept moving his plate and utensils. Man, I laughed my butt off."

His eyes grew dreamy. "That's when I began to fall for him."

"Did he teach you any magic?"

"Not like that. But yeah, some stuff."

Like how to kill someone?

"What kind of stuff?" I asked.

"A spell to help me focus better on my exam for my personal trainer's license. Spells to enhance my stamina. Some potions for muscle growth. It was all simple stuff. He said I didn't have magic in my genes but could do more if I learned to gather my internal energies, or something like that. But I couldn't do it. All I knew how to do was to focus on my strength and willpower."

I doubted he knew enough magic to murder his partner with it. He might know enough to subdue him there on the beach, enough magic that Samson's witch consultant detected it. Vance was strong enough to kill Hugo with his staff through sheer muscle power alone.

"My daughter has magic in her genes, and Hugo was working with her on gathering her internal energies. She's not quite there yet. It's difficult."

Vance nodded.

"Were any of his clients powerful witches?"

"A couple, I think. He didn't tell me much. It's like when you're a doctor you can't talk about your patients' health with other people."

"He had one client he mentioned to us," I said carefully. "A woman who was pretty advanced. Does the name Dorothy sound familiar?"

His brow creased, and jaw clenched.

"Nope."

"He canceled on my daughter twice to accommodate Dorothy's schedule. I didn't appreciate that." This was completely fabricated, but my lie was in pursuit of justice. Right?

"I guess the woman was a well-paying client."

"I guess. I wonder what she was like."

A quick mental movie of him approaching her in a super-market and giving her a warning. A sense he had been stalking her.

"I guess loyalty is rare these days," I said.

I think I went too far. Vance's face was red. His plastic cup cracked loudly, and protein shake oozed over his hand.

"Hugo was a loyal partner. Don't you ever say he wasn't."

I received a quick flash of images from Vance's memory. A shouting match with Hugo. Vance pushing him against a wall and punching a hole through the drywall near his head. The searing pain of betrayal.

"I'm so sorry, that's not what I meant at all," I said in a soothing voice. "I was just talking about money."

"And I'm loyal to my clients, no matter how many sessions they do in a week."

He wanted to bring the conversation back to where it had begun: me hiring him. But I had one last angle to cover.

Why did Hugo have a key that was loaded with memories of the Fae?

"Did Hugo know any faeries?"

His expression darkened even more. "That's a derogatory term."

"No, I mean the supernatural creatures from folklore," I fake-laughed nervously over my faux pas. "Also known as the Fae."

"What the heck are you talking about? Do you think I'm an

idiot? Just because I believe in magic doesn't mean I believe in unicorns and leprechauns and crap like that."

"There's a lot more to the world than our human eyes can see."

"You know, maybe this isn't such a good idea, you being my client. I work my clients hard and expect them to be focused on fitness, not fairy tales. If you want to get in shape, join a gym where you can watch TV on your treadmill." He abruptly stood, knocking his stool over. "Thanks for the shake."

He stomped out of the juice bar. Patrons looked at me questioningly. I just shrugged. Vance's client was proven correct in calling him steroid-addled.

I threw away my smoothie cup when I left. But I wrapped Vance's half-crushed protein-shake cup in a napkin and took it with me. I wanted to read it for memories.

THERE WAS AN EMPTY BENCH FACING THE CATHEDRAL IN THE city square. Based on Vance's reactions, and what I picked up with my telepathy, he was really upset by Hugo's affair with Dorothy. And with a guy like Vance, extreme anger could lead to violence.

I placed his cup on the bench and removed the napkin I had wrapped it in to shield it from my psychometry. I held my palm close to the plastic, the way you would measure the heat in a pan. It was burning with hostility, but not with substantial memories. No surprise: he had held it for only a short time and was too focused on our conversation to dwell upon much else.

My fingers touched the cup. I—

—didn't think she looked much like a cop, but does she really want to

69

hire me as her trainer? I don't buy it. She could use some resistance train-ing, that's for sure, the scrawny little thing. What does she really want?

What does ironic mean? Yup, I knew it. This is something to do with Hugo. Does she suspect I killed him?

. . . How does she know about Dorothy? This is a freaking fishing expedition. I bet she knows about the affair, and she wants to see if I knew about it. Man, I wish I didn't. I'll never get over it. . . Pulling my punch at the last second before I broke his face. Going right through the freaking drywall. The hole not repaired for weeks, like a black stain reminding me of what he did. I'll never forgive him, even after he got what he deserved. . .

She knows about the Fae, too? How?

And she fell for my stupid joke about the derogatory term. Man, I can't deal with this chick. She's a nutcase. I've got to get out of here before I—

— can't believe how intense his anger was.

I was hoping he'd leave a memory of committing the murder or paying someone to do it. He left nothing that told me for sure whether he was guilty. Still, he was surely angry enough to do it.

Then there was the topic of the Fae. He knew about them, most likely through Hugo. But how did Hugo learn about them, and, more important, how did he get their key?

Before I went down that rabbit hole, I had to get this investigation on the right track.

"To what do I owe this unexpected pleasure?" Samson asked with a smarmy tone when he answered his phone.

"I'm trying to prevent you from derailing your career, which you seem so intent on doing. I just met with Vance Puggle."

"Darla, you can't freelance with this investigation and inter-fere with witnesses. I might even call it witness tampering."

"I'm calling it doing your job. I used telepathy and psychom-etry on him and saw a lot of anger and a violent streak. He got into a physical altercation with Hugo and punched a hole in the wall next to his head. And he threatened Dorothy Gilley. He also knows a little magic."

"Enough magic to impale someone with a blunt stick of wood?"

"Maybe. He might know more than he let on. But even if he doesn't, he easily has enough brute strength to have killed Hugo that way with his bare hands. He could have done other magic on the beach that night, which your witch consultant—I'm using air quotes here—picked up on."

"Maybe you're right about the magic. Brute force is a much simpler, easier explanation."

"So, will you investigate Vance further? And leave Sophie alone?"

"I hear you, I'll take your tips into consideration, and I'll continue with my methodical—"

I hung up on him.

CHAPTER 8

A STUDENT SCORNED

Knowing Dorothy wouldn't answer a call from my unknown number, I texted her instead, using the number I found in Hugo's appointment book.

Hi, I'm Darla, a good friend of Hugo's. So sorry for your loss. He wanted me to give you a message if anything ever happened to him. Can we meet?

It was a brazen lie, but what else was I supposed to do? Tell her I wanted to talk to her to see if she killed her tutor and lover?

She answered me quickly, which surprised me.

Yes, but not in a public place and not at my home. Can I come to yours?

Of course, I typed, *331 Hidalgo Avenue in San Marcos.*

As soon as I sent it, I had a moment of doubt. Was it foolish to give my address to a potential killer? But I assured myself that this was a place of business, and you only had to go to our website to learn I lived here.

We agreed on 1:00 p.m., a good time because my guests were usually out and about that time of day.

I was standing at the main door when a blue BMW pulled up to the curb. I think it was the same one I saw in their garage.

Dorothy's appearance matched the image from Hugo's memory. Thin, dyed-blonde, signs of multiple cosmetic surgeries. A face marked by perpetual sadness. She lived in great wealth, but apparently her marriage was not happy, so she tried to find joy with Hugo, of all people.

She came to the door, and I let her in.

"I'm Darla. Nice to meet you."

"Dorothy."

We shook hands briefly.

"You live here?" she asked, taking in the ancient dark wood of the foyer.

"Yes. A lot of bed-and-breakfast owners live onsite. Can I get you coffee or a cool beverage?"

"No, thanks." She seemed like she wanted to make this brief.

"Let's have a seat in the living room," I said, mentally preparing for the fabricated message I was about to give her.

"That's okay. I can't stay long. What did Hugo want you to tell me?"

Here goes. "He wanted you to know how much he cared for you. It was not like him to fall for a student, and he realized it was unprofessional of him. But he couldn't help himself. He also wanted you to know that you have great potential for becoming a powerful magician and you shouldn't give up."

I didn't know if my malarkey would be believable, but she became choked up. I felt guilty for doing so much lying lately, but it's difficult to get people to reveal information. Besides, I believed this lie made Dorothy feel better.

"I changed my mind," she said. "Can I sit down?"

"Of course. Follow me."

In the living room, she sat on one end of a loveseat, and I sat across from her in a wingback chair.

"I'm so sorry for your loss," I said. "It's such a tragedy he was taken from us. He was teaching my daughter and was like a member of our family." It's okay to exaggerate when talking about the dead.

She dried her welling eyes with a tissue. "Thank you for sharing Hugo's message. It didn't sound much like him. I see why he couldn't say those words to me himself. But I wish he hadn't told anyone else about us."

"Yes, he told me." This wasn't a total fabrication, because his memories told me of the affair.

"Did he tell you why he dumped me?"

"No. Why?"

"I don't know, either," she said angrily. "He claimed our thing was interfering with my studies. But I believe he romanced me just to make his partner jealous, and then they reconciled. He only used me."

"I'm sorry. Do you have any idea who would want to kill him?"

It sounded to me like she would. I fixed her with my eyes and opened my mind, looking for the smallest reaction of guilt, hoping her thoughts would enter my head.

Her eyes met mine, as if she were trying to read *my* thoughts.

Does she think I did it? Her words appeared in my brain.

"I had the impression Hugo had many enemies," she said. "People who paid big money to learn magic and came away with nothing."

I decided to take a risk.

"I will tell you this because you believe in magic. There is some cause to believe Hugo was killed with magic."

No reaction. "How?"

"He was killed with his magician's staff. And it may have been wielded through magic rather than human hands."

Comprehension filled her face.

What was she thinking about? She was so guarded right now that even her own thoughts weren't flowing freely.

"Does that fact give you any ideas about who the murderer is?" I asked.

"Probably a disgruntled student."

"Like who?"

"I got the impression there were many. But if magic was used, this student must have learned more than most of his students."

"You don't give him your endorsement of his teaching?"

"He promised more than he could deliver."

"To you, too? How much did you learn?"

Oops. I sensed her closing herself off defensively.

"I didn't learn attack spells," she said in a flat voice. "Hugo taught me the power of concentration and how to focus my inner energies. How to enhance my self-esteem. And how to protect myself."

"You mean general self-defense, like martial arts?"

"Sort of. How to hold my own against an assailant on the street."

And protect myself against magic.

I wondered how I could get her to tell me more.

"Is there anyone threatening you?" I asked.

She gave me a fake smile. "I have no enemies that I know of."

"You're certain you can't think of anyone who would kill Hugo or harm you?"

An image filled my head of Vance, Hugo's partner. In a supermarket, his red, angry face was up close to hers, shouting at her. It was the encounter I had read from Vance's memory, but now from Dorothy's perspective.

It dissolved into a scene with a group of men in a room lit by candlelight. This image appeared for only a second or two. I thought I recognized her husband's face, but couldn't be certain. Both images were laced with Dorothy's fear.

"No, I can't," she said.

"Please let me know if there's any way I can help you. I'll keep anything you tell me in absolute confidence."

"I appreciate that. But don't worry about me. I have nothing to worry about."

She stood up. The worry radiated from her in waves.

"Thank you for sharing Hugo's message with me."

"My pleasure. Again, I'm sorry for your loss. If you want to talk more, please call or text me. Any time, day or night."

"You're very kind." She smiled and walked out of the room, and out of the inn, without looking back.

I wasn't any closer to figuring out who murdered Hugo. Dorothy had a motive, but there was someone else, or others, she feared. Her husband included.

Vance was still the most likely suspect in my book.

If only Samson would get his head out of his butt and take this investigation in the right direction.

"Mom!" Sophie rushed into the utility room with the enthusiasm she once had as a child. I was helping Bella, the housekeeper, fold sheets. "Cervantes was seen on the beach yesterday!"

"Where exactly?"

"Gerta said on the rocky stretch a mile south of the North-point Park beach."

I fixed her with a warning stare and glanced at Bella, so Sophie wouldn't let slip any reference to beach trolls.

"One of Gerta's friends saw him," she said. "He was hunting among the coquina rocks, crawling into holes and stuff."

"What was he chasing after? Bella, do you mind finishing up? We need to go to the beach immediately."

"No problem. I hope you find your cat."

Bella was young and easygoing. A recent history graduate of San Marcos College, she was saving money for grad school. She'd been recommended by Dr. Noordlun, whom she'd had several classes with, not knowing he was also the director of the Memory Guild.

I grabbed a bag of cat treats, and we drove to the beach. Parking at the public lot, we fanned out to the south along the wide stretch of sand. Soon, the dark brown lumps of limestone appeared, formed millennia ago by pulverized coquina shells.

The first rocks we encountered were half-buried in the sand. As we moved south, more rocks appeared until they covered the beach, and we had to walk upon them. There were long, flat shelves of rock, partly adorned by remnants of seaweed and dotted by small barnacles. Atop and between them, large craggy rocks were strewn about as if by a bored giant.

It would be easy for a small animal to hide here. There were gaps between the rocks and pockets of space beneath them. Many had holes bored into them by sea creatures. Some holes held water from the receding tide. Others went completely through the rocks and led to dark crannies beneath them.

Not only were these rocks a good place to hide, but they were also an easy place to break an ankle if you weren't careful.

We saw seashells, a crab, and plenty of shorebirds. But no Cervantes.

"Cervantes," Sophie called again and again.

I shook the bag of treats like a maraca. It felt a little silly.

If he was spotted here yesterday, what were the chances he was still around? And I worried about him finding food and fresh water over the time he'd been gone.

Most of all, I worried that he'd gotten a foot caught in the rocks and possibly drowned by a high tide. I tried to wipe that thought from my mind.

"Cervantes, please come out!" I sounded desperate.

We'd searched for him just like this on the night he disappeared with no success. Just because he'd been spotted by a beach troll the day before didn't mean we'd have better luck today.

The sun was low over the dunes. It was getting late. Fortunately, I'd had the foresight to bring a flashlight.

"Cervantes," Sophie called. I assumed she was also calling to him with her witch-familiar telepathic connection.

"Is Cervantes a black cat?" asked a high-pitched male voice that startled the heck out of me.

Even though it wasn't dark yet, I turned on my flashlight and panned it 360 degrees. There was no one else here but Sophie and me.

"Yes," Sophie said. "He was last seen on this beach yesterday."

"I saw him, too," said the man.

"Who are you?" I demanded.

"Lukas."

"I don't see you."

"He's a sea sprite, Mom," Sophie said.

A what? Another supernatural creature I hadn't known existed. We humans are truly ignorant of all the wondrous things around us.

"I apologize, but I'm not familiar with sea sprites."

A tiny hominid rose on buzzing wings and hovered a few feet away at face level.

He wasn't like the faerie I had recently encountered, who initially was a tiny, winged human-like creature about two feet tall, before he transformed into a handsome man. Which was before he transformed into a fearsome goblin.

No, this was a tiny human-like creature only a few inches tall wearing clothing that looked like fish skin. He didn't have his own wings; rather, he had harnessed several dragonflies to a small snail shell he rode inside, like a basket beneath a hot-air balloon.

Had someone slipped a hallucinogen into my coffee?

"Hi Lukas. I'm Sophie, and this is my mom, Darla."

"Pleased to meet you," he said, bowing inside his shell-basket.

"How do you know about sea sprites?" I asked Sophie.

"Being of the supernatural and paranormal world, we have the privilege of seeing and communicating with wonderful creatures like Lukas."

He bowed again, then tugged at one of the gossamer lines attached to the dragonflies to maintain their position in front of us.

"Where do you live?" I asked.

"Right here on the beach. I'm part of a small colony. We often take over ghost crab burrows and fix them up with fixtures made from shells and pieces of driftwood. There's a rather large family that took up in a gopher tortoise burrow on the other side of the dunes, an enormous space and rather ostentatious. I call it a McMansion."

Unbelievable. But I'd better get used to discoveries like these.

"That brings me to the topic of your cat," he continued. "He was hunting all over this beach for faeries. He said they had hostile intentions, and he wanted to interrogate one. Probably by batting him around and torturing him like cats are wont to do."

"Cervantes would never do that," Sophie said.

"Oh, yes he would," I said under my breath.

"As I was explaining, your cat was exploring a gopher tortoise burrow that we'd left alone because it actually housed a tortoise. And a rattlesnake. Well, it turns out those creatures had been evicted, and the Fae were using it as part of a tunnel complex. I regret to say they captured your cat."

Sophie looked at me with dismay.

"Why would they take Cervantes?" I asked.

"Because he's a witch's familiar and has powers they want to use," she said.

Harvesting magical energies from someone to use for their own magic was a practice the Fae had taught the wizard Texas Tom. He, in turn, had used it on Cory.

But I wondered if the Fae had another motive. Maybe it had something to do with me. If they believed I was destined to be a great ally or enemy, stealing my cat would surely turn me into the latter.

"Come, I'll show you the burrow," Lukas said.

He snapped his reins, and the dragonflies flew westward and over the dunes. We followed slowly, climbing up a hill of sand, picking our paths through the sea oats atop it.

Down below, Lukas hovered over a standard gopher tortoise

burrow, a hole about a foot and a half wide and eight inches high, with a mound of excavated sand in front of it.

Sophie and I knelt before the opening. The beam of my flashlight only went so far before the burrow angled downward.

My skin prickled. Yes, there were traces of magic in there.

"Cervantes?" I called, knowing I would be unanswered.

"What are we going to do?" Sophie asked.

"Take the battle to the Fae. I want our cat back."

CHAPTER 9

ROID RAGE

Darren struck again. Bella was turning over Room 301 and noticed a foul smell. I couldn't allow that to happen because the room was booked tomorrow. I prowled the bathroom, armed with a plunger, certain the smell wasn't coming from the plumbing. It wasn't that kind of odor, if you know what I mean.

Apparently, Darren varies his odors each time. Today, it was unwashed armpits with accents of rotting meat. It was worse than sewage. My eyes were watering.

I was obsessed by the possibility that Darren's body was trapped in a wall somewhere, even though the odor didn't come from a corpse that would be mummified by now. The spectral stench, this olfactory haunting, couldn't be pinpointed to a physical location.

Still, I felt like I had to search for the source. What else was I to do?

After hours of frustration, my phone buzzed. It was a text from Samson. He was downstairs, wondering where I was.

Maybe it was time to put the stink behind me. I avoided the elevator and took the stairs down.

"What is that smell?" Samson asked, nostrils flaring.

"Don't tell me you can smell it down here?"

"Yes. It's wonderful."

"What?"

"Cinnamon, and something else."

"Oh, the cinnamon rolls I baked for breakfast. I thought you were talking about the ghost stench."

"The what?"

"Never mind. You don't want to know."

"I stopped in because I'm heading to Vance Puggle's house to ask him more questions and possibly bring him to the station for an interview."

"Finally!"

"I wanted you to come along to read some of his stuff while I have him in the other room. Can't use your psychometry in court, but you might find something that I can investigate further."

"Sure. Did my information about him finally change your mind?"

"Cellphone location data. One tower placed him in the vicinity of the crime scene the same night. Let's see if he has a good explanation."

VANCE WAS WORKING OUT IN HIS GARAGE WHEN WE ARRIVED. Not that I expected to find him reading Shakespeare, but didn't this guy have any other interests in life? He was always working out, training someone else to work out, or drinking protein shakes to enhance the muscles he just worked out.

He was not happy to see us.

"Now what?" he growled.

"You have a moment to answer a few questions? Good. Let's begin then," Samson said, pulling out a small notepad. "On the night Mr. Starbright was killed, you said you were at home."

"I was."

Of course, he was working out.

"We subpoenaed your phone records, and lo-and-behold, you seem to have taken a drive to the beach. Convenient of you to leave that out."

"I should have mentioned it, but I knew you'd assume the wrong thing. When Hugo didn't come home, I went to see if he was still at the beach. He told me he was going to bring his student there."

"The records place you there early enough that Mr. Starbright would still be alive. Did you see him?"

"No. I thought he was going to be at Northpoint Park. He wasn't."

"You didn't check out Pelican Park, where he actually was?"

"No. He didn't say he'd be there."

"Vance, can I use your bathroom?" I asked.

He looked at me as if noticing me for the first time. "Yeah, whatever. It's past the dining room."

He didn't seem worried I'd find something incriminating, not knowing about my ability.

The door from the garage led to a laundry room. A hamper of smelly workout clothes sat atop the washer. The odor was nowhere near as noxious as Darren's ghost could produce.

I entered the kitchen. It was in great condition, since the townhome was new, and was decorated with retro kitchen accessories, with lots of root vegetables and herbs in jars. I assumed

Hugo was responsible for the look. The room was messy, though, with dishes piled up in the sink.

The place was filled with psychic energy on the many surfaces touched by the two men. Kitchens are among the most-touched rooms of a home.

Now, where to begin? How to sort through all the mundane memories accumulated here and find something incriminating?

First, to save time, I scanned the surfaces to find where to focus. I began at the most popular spot of a kitchen, the refrigerator. Of course, the handles held layer upon layer of memories from the two men. Most were short and inconsequential, and they were mixed together. Except, the most recent ones on the French door model were Vance's, of course.

They were dark, brooding, and self-pitying. Just what I expected. I held my hand closer to the handles, feeling the psychic energy radiating from it like heat. With my index finger, I touched—

— *the last of our savings. How did we spend so much? Hugo's life insurance better pay out soon or I'll end up maxing out the credit cards again. Hm, how old are these turkey burgers?* —

— I bet they're too old, Vance. Nothing earth-shattering there, but the life insurance could be an additional motive for killing his partner.

There were more memories on the handles I should check out. Most people are thinking about food while they hold the door open and gaze at their bounty, but if something is troubling you, it can invade your thoughts at any time.

My index finger followed the gradual curve of the right handle, since I had observed Vance to be right-handed. However, now I scanned the left handle and quickly found a concentration of intense energy. It had come from Hugo. With my full hand, I grasped—

— the possibility that he's not just threatening me, he really means it. This gym rat, whom I rescued from poverty and gave a good life to, would actually kill me? No, no, it has to be a threat. I already broke it off with Dorothy, so why is he still threatening me? Is it because of Manuel? That's only a flirtation. Nothing to see here, folks. (Chimes ringing) Held the darned door open too long. I—

— lost the memory when he closed the door and removed his hand.

That was interesting. Another clue pointing toward Vance that hinted at a more complex motive. If the affair with Dorothy was already over, why would Vance kill Hugo? Because of his honor? An overabundance of jealousy? This Manuel character? Or was there another reason, aside from the life insurance policy?

My hand swept the horizontal handle of the freezer below the fridge. No powerful memories stood out. I looked around the kitchen for my next target.

Ah, the coffee maker. No pod machine in this kitchen. These guys had an old-school drip machine. The pot's plastic handle would be a great place to—

A loud clatter of steel against steel came from the garage, followed by something large slamming against the other side of the laundry room wall. I rushed to see what was happening.

Samson was pinned against the garage wall, his head at the ceiling and his feet dangling a few feet above the floor. What was pinning him there?

Magic.

I looked over to see Vance charging toward him with a dumbbell in his hand.

"No!" I screamed.

A large inflatable yoga ball was on the floor near me. I kicked it at Vance. Yeah, it wouldn't stop a charging bull with heavy steel in his hand, but it distracted him. He stopped and crouched on the balls of his feet.

"Assaulting a police officer with a deadly weapon will put you in prison for the rest of your life," I said.

It appeared Vance had come to the same conclusion already. He ran through the open garage door to his muscle car and jumped in. The engine roared to life, and the car sped away.

"Can you hand me my radio?" Samson asked. "I dropped it by that bench over there."

I retrieved the compact, hand-held unit and reached up to give it to him. Still attached to the wall, he called in a request to apprehend Vance.

"Obviously, Vance knows more magic than he let on," I said. "And has anger-management problems. It's probably 'roid rage' from all the steroids he's taking."

"Obviously. Now help me get down from here."

"Give me your hand."

With my short stature, I had to reach a little higher than I care to admit. I grabbed him by the wrist and tugged.

He didn't move.

I grabbed him with both hands and pulled, putting all my weight into it. No dice.

"Can't you pull any harder?" Samson asked.

"In case you haven't noticed, I don't have a lot of weight on me. It doesn't matter, though. The magic is too strong."

"I can't stay up here all day," he said in a demanding whine.

"Be nice, or I'll take your picture and post it to the Police Department's social media."

"This is not a laughing matter."

"I know, I know. You don't get paid to just hang around all day."

"Darla, I'm warning you."

"We need a witch to undo the spell Vance used. My cousin, Missy, could do it, but she lives five hours away. Arch Mage Bob could do it."

"He's too high-profile. I don't want him involved."

"I believe Cory learned Bob's negation spell. He could probably do it with the help of the pearl the Fae gave me."

"Come on, I don't want your husband to help me out of this embarrassing situation."

"Sophie wouldn't know how to do it. Maybe my mother does. I can ask her."

"Okay, ask her," Samson said, looking doubtful.

I pulled out my phone and called.

"Hi, Mom. Since you're so good at manipulating Billy, I thought you could help move a different detective."

While I described the predicament, Samson winced.

"Yeah, stuck like a fly to flypaper."

"I can't undo powerful magic," Mom said, "but I have a potion that helps free you from a habit you're stuck with. Do you think that would work?"

"Doubtful, but it would be amusing to try it. Let me give you the address."

After I hung up, Samson said, "'It would be *amusing*'? I don't have time for you to get your jollies."

"To be honest, you don't have a choice right now. If you insist on being too macho to have a man help you."

He simply glowered at me.

Samson behaved like the wait was intolerable, but Mom needed time to create her potion or amulet, or whatever she planned to use. By the time she arrived, his face was beet red.

"Doesn't he look cute up there?" Mom said as she entered the garage carrying a tote bag. The clink of glass bottles came from within.

"He's not in a cute mood, that's for sure," I said, peeking into the bag. "Is that sage?"

"Yes. Burning it will cleanse the garage of evil and weaken the spell that binds Detective Sansom."

She held aloft a clump of tightly packed sage stems and leaves wrapped in newspaper.

"This is called smudging," Mom said, lighting the package on fire with a kitchen match.

Thick, pleasant-smelling smoke poured from her bundle. She paced around the garage-gym, smoke trailing behind her. Finally, she reached the wall where Samson was suspended and held the sage as close to him as she could reach.

He coughed. "Enough already."

"I still sense evil here," Mom said. "It's the spell that binds you to—"

The fire alarm went off.

"You better get me down before the fire department gets here," Samson said. "I know a bunch of those guys."

"Just one step after this," Mom said.

The fire sprinklers began shooting water everywhere.

"Oh, heavens," Mom said. "Let's get out of here."

She and I stepped out onto the driveway while Vance's gym was drenched. One sprinkler was right next to Samson's head. His soaking-wet clothes hung from him like he'd just crawled out of the swimming pool.

"You're going to regret this, Darla," he said through clenched teeth.

"The homeowner's insurance will cover it," I said.

"No, I mean you, personally. I will get revenge. I swear it."

After several minutes, the water turned off. Mom re-entered the garage and withdrew a small bottle from her tote bag. She removed the cork stopper.

"This is the potion that breaks habits as well as frees and unblocks you," she said, handing it to Samson. "Drink all of it, even if it tastes bad."

His arms were free below the elbow, allowing him to chug the potion.

And then choke to the point of gagging.

"That is horrible!"

"Yes, I know. Now, we wait for it to work."

"How long?" Samson asked.

"I don't know. I guess we'll find out. Just be patient."

A siren came from far away but grew louder.

Samson's stomach gurgled.

"Oh, no," he said.

Mom and I exchanged glances.

Samson's face had turned deathly white. No, it was greenish.

"Oh, no," Samson repeated.

"What's wrong?" I asked. "Being seen up there by firefighters is not the end of the world. I'm sure they see people in all sorts of unflattering ways."

"It's not just that. It's. . . Mrs. Chesswick, you said this stuff unblocks you?"

"Yes."

"Unblocks you, like intestinally?"

"That could be one of the benefits."

"It's not a benefit to me right now. Not at all."

"Oh, no," I said.

Samson moaned.

"We should give the man some privacy," Mom said.

"It looks like you'll be getting plenty of revenge on Vance and his gym for casting that spell on you," I said.

Samson appeared to be sweating, but it was difficult to tell, since he was already soaking wet.

The siren was much louder now. The firetruck must be just around the corner.

Samson whimpered, and said, "I don't know how I'm going to—"

With a sound like Velcro ripped apart, he separated from the wall and landed on his butt on the garage floor. Fortunately for him, training matts cushioned the fall.

"It worked!" I said. "Aren't you relieved?"

He didn't hear me as he raced inside. The slamming of the bathroom door echoed out into the garage.

"Yes, dear, he'll soon be quite relieved," Mom said.

CHAPTER 10

THE KEY TO IT ALL

Cory, Sophie, and I sat around my cottage's tiny dining table after dinner. When I lived alone, I ate most of my meals here, unless dinner consisted of scarfing down the leftover canapés from wine hour. Even now, when I had my family to eat with, we preferred to eat here rather than in the inn's dining room. This dining nook felt more like it belonged to us, while the much larger room in the inn belonged to my guests, and not just during breakfast and teatime. Sometimes, they went there to eat takeout meals. Often, they used the tables for card games.

"How can we locate the Fae?" I asked. "It's the only way we can get Cervantes back."

"The pearl from Tom's staff the faerie gave you is supposed to help summon magical creatures, such as the Fae," Cory said. "I don't know how to do it, though."

"And I'd rather not summon them here. I want to find them where they live. Ideally, without them knowing in advance."

"You think we can raid them and rescue Cervantes like we're

commandos?" Sophie said, dripping with sarcasm. More sarcasm than I'd heard since she was thirteen.

"Well, not when you put it that way."

"Texas Tom probably knows where to find them," Cory said. "I wouldn't be surprised if he's with them right now to evade capture."

"He's the last person I want to deal with," I said.

"Instead of being on the defensive, waiting for him to attack, we should take the initiative and track him down."

"If the police can't find him yet, how will we?"

"Magic will find a way."

"I should mention I have an object connected with the Fae," I said. "It has their memories on it, but I can't understand their language or make any sense of the visual images. Still, perhaps it can help in our search."

"You never mentioned this before," Cory said.

"I didn't know if it would be important. It's a key. I think it unlocks the lid of a large storage jar I saw in a memory. I think the jar is called an amphora."

"Wait, where did you get this key?"

"Um, it fell out of Hugo's wallet."

"Do you mean when you read his stuff at the police station? Did you steal the key?" Cory was getting worked up.

"Stealing is too strong a word. Borrowed."

"Are you crazy? You can get arrested for that."

"The police don't know it exists. They didn't inventory it with the other stuff in the wallet."

"Darla, you're taking such a risk."

"Listen, I've been taking many more risks than you know about. Not just when helping free you from that wizard, but also dealing with all the crazy stuff that has come up since I became a member of the supernatural club."

"Mom has a thing for trying to solve murders," Sophie said.

"You've changed a lot in a year," Cory said.

"You bet your booties I did. And you're going to have to let me call the shots here. The Fae have a fascination with me that could be an advantage or be my downfall. But either way, it's on my shoulders to resolve it."

"Fine," Cory said, raising his hands in surrender. "Just remember, you have a family that doesn't want to lose you."

I smiled. "Of course. I've fought hard to get you back and keep Sophie safe. I'm not going to throw it all away stupidly."

"And don't get yourself arrested, either," Sophie said.

"I'm not planning on it."

"What if the key would be a helpful clue for the police investigation?" Cory asked.

"They don't seem to be looking beyond Sophie now. Does this key belong to you?" I removed it from my purse and showed it to her.

"Definitely not."

"I doubt it belongs to Vance, who should be the primary suspect now."

"The key could send the police in the right direction," Cory said.

I was tiring of being second-guessed. "Or it could be completely irrelevant to Hugo's murder. Who knows? What I know for certain is it has psychic energy from a faerie on it. So, first I'm going to see if it helps me find where the local Fae hang out. Then, I'll find an excuse to examine the wallet again and tell the evidence clerk, 'hey look, a key fell out of the wallet.' Are you satisfied?"

Cory shrugged angrily. Sophie glowered. I stewed. We weren't exactly a portrait of the quintessential American family at the dinner table from a Norman Rockwell painting.

I WAS ALONE IN THE COTTAGE'S SECOND BEDROOM. IT WAS MY office, but was also intended to serve as a guest bedroom with a convertible couch. However, the room was so full of boxes, I wouldn't have the heart to make someone sleep in here. Since this master of marketing always had vacancies at the inn, I always put visiting friends or family in one of the empty guest rooms.

Tonight, I sat at my desk, its surface cleared of everything except the strange golden key that had fallen from Hugo's wallet. It was about one and a half inches long, delicate yet strong, possibly meant for the lid of the ceramic vessel I had seen in a faerie's memory.

Where had Hugo gotten it? The key had to have at least a fleeting memory of his on it. While I couldn't understand the language of the Fae, Hugo's thoughts could be helpful.

Holding my fingers close to the key without touching it, I took stock of what memories were here. The problem was, the Fae psychic energy was so strong, nearly overpowering, that it overwhelmed any human memories.

Yet human memories were here. I sensed them now, unlike the first time I had read the key. In fact, here was one, near the end of the key. I touched it—

—While he sleeps, I decide once and for all to steal it. I will use it as a bargaining tool when I divorce him. He values it tremendously. I slip it back into the velvet sack—

—The brief memory ended when the fingers lost contact with the key. They were not Hugo's fingers, but those of a woman. The voice of the thoughts was familiar. Was it Dorothy's?

There had to be more human memories on here. I flipped the key over and traced its shape with my finger, almost touching it. It was so difficult to get past the powerful Fae memories. Wait, there was something here—

—I don't understand why she's giving it to me. She worries he'll find it, but why doesn't she put it in a safe deposit box or something? She and I aren't going to last. Doesn't she see that? If this is as valuable as she says it is, why entrust it to the guy you're having a fling with? I slip it into my wallet, the safest place for the moment—

—I remove my finger from the key. Another memory that was too brief. But I recognized Hugo's voice and the visual image of Dorothy when she pushed the key into his palm.

Hugo knew it was valuable, but little else about it. I needed more.

I moved my finger over the bow, or head, of the key and I heard a male voice speaking in English. I plunged into another reverie—

— "It is only fitting that you keep a copy of it."

"This is fine craftsmanship."

"It is a gold overlay. The base metal is not found here on earth, and is much stronger even than titanium. If you admire the workmanship of the key, you should see the lid of the amphora it unlocks. The lid is a beauty of mahogany, mother-of-pearl, gold, and silver. I believe it is the original lid."

"And the jar has never been opened since the first time?"

"So, it is said, though I honestly couldn't say. Only Her Majesty would know. You must appreciate the honor of her wanting you to keep the spare key. That is how much she trusts you."

"I am indeed honored. But let me ask you, is she afraid she will lose her copy of the key, or that it will be stolen?"

"We live in uncertain times. One never knows when a war or other conflict will erupt, and our people will be forced to flee."

"Her Majesty feels this way?"

"She does."

"It is unsettling to hear such worries from even the Faerie Queene."

He drops the key back into the velvet—

—I snap out of the reverie. It takes a long moment to process the memory I just read.

This key is for a vessel owned by the Faerie Queene?

And the lackluster magician, who called himself Hugo the Magnificent with no trace of irony, possessed this key.

All I could say was, you've got to be kidding me.

Let me review. Hugo received the key from Dorothy. And she stole it from some male. It could be any number of men, but let's assume it was her husband. Why did the Fae entrust him with a spare key to this super-valuable jar belonging to the Faerie Queene? As far as I knew, the guy was a hedge fund manager. Were the Fae his clients?

Weird, to say the least. Then, a chilling possibility occurred to me.

I had been proceeding on the likelihood that Hugo had been murdered because of his affair with Dorothy. His partner, Vance, killed him out of jealousy. Dorothy killed him in retaliation for being spurned. Or her husband did it out of jealousy.

But what if Hugo was killed because he had the key?

The key that now sat atop my desk.

Uh-oh.

CHAPTER 11

THE FAE AREN'T OKAY

I visited a state park south of San Marcos, the same one Summer had taken me to recently, where I had discovered I could, in a fashion, perceive the communications between trees. She said I was reading the mycorrhiza fungi, the fungal system in the trees' roots that transmits information between the trees and helps them in other ways. Being able to do so must be another facet of my psychic abilities.

Of course, I couldn't understand what the trees were saying. Except, one word made its way into my mind:

Mother.

Why were the trees sending me that thought? How did I understand it? What did it mean?

I wandered along a trail through a thick forest, home to Southern live oaks, long-leaf pines, and cabbage palms. Ostensibly, I came here for peace and quiet, to clear my mind of the complex plots and motivations behind the mysteries of Hugo's murder and Cervantes' disappearance.

I told myself that was why I was here. Yet, I also hoped to

learn something from the trees. Anything would be fine. I wanted only to understand *why* I felt this connection with them and illuminate a part of myself I hadn't known existed.

Sure, I've always loved trees. Who doesn't, aside from real estate developers? The oak tree in the backyard of my childhood home had been a play site for as long as I could remember, from playing with dolls and toys in the sandy soil at its base, to flying up and down on the tire swing my dad had attached on a rope tied to a sturdy limb high above. And, even in my adolescent years, as I sat, leaning my back against the trunk, writing in my journals, and imagining magic in my distant future.

By magic, I had meant love, fame, and wealth—not literal magic. Instead, the years had brought me love, certainly not the other two. And it had taken me into a world of the paranormal and supernatural I never knew existed beyond the simple kitchen witchery of my mother.

Throughout my childhood, across those mornings and afternoons in my backyard, the oak had stood over me like a companion, a sentinel. Yes, even like a family member.

The trail was winding, and I had to take care not to trip over roots protruding from the vast underground network woven by the trees, linking them to each other.

It felt almost as if the trees, and the entire forest, were aware of my presence. I had the sense of being watched, but benevolently.

Speak to me, forest. Tell me what I need to know.

Instead, all I heard was the sighing of a breeze through the leaves and branches, and the distant calls of birds. The buzzing of insects. Sounds that have been unchanged since before human ears were on this planet to hear them.

As my mind emptied of my concerns, I became more perceptive to the organisms around me. I had a feeling that the forest was here to protect me, but it also expected me to protect it.

And the strangest thing was I felt older than my actual years. As if I had known this forest since the beginning of time.

I shook my head. My imagination was getting the best of me, just like when I was a kid below the oak in my backyard.

Up ahead, just off the trail to my right, was an especially large live oak. It bore the scars of removed limbs on the portion of the trunk facing the trail. Spanish moss was draped from its branches, and tiny ferns covered its trunk and larger limbs. The tree looked ancient.

On a whim, I sat beneath it, as if I were a kid in my backyard. But, this time, I placed my palms against the ground to use my ability of psychometry that had come to me only in midlife.

Almost instantly, I picked up the buzzing energy of thousands of data transfers among the roots from tree to tree, like the forest's internet. There was a tremendous amount of energy passing along this network below me.

And I couldn't understand any of it. But how could I expect to?

I was patient as the energy flowed from the ground, through my hands, and into the paranormal part of my brain. Pushing away my human thought process, I became a pure receptor of whatever it was I was absorbing from the roots.

It seemed like hours went by before recognizable images appeared in my mind.

A troop of faeries, dozens of them, passed along this trail recently. It was night, and they were in the form I had seen once before: human-like, but only a couple of feet tall, flying on insect-like wings. They darted between trees, staying off the trail, but following it. I sensed hostile intent.

And the forest was alarmed by the incursion. The faeries

were not from around here, and the trees were on alert, as if this was a swarm of damaging pests. I got the sense that other similar incursions of the Fae had happened here recently.

The trees felt threatened, though the faeries did not damage any of them in the vision I had. Still, there was a mood of malignancy from this incursion.

The Fae have existed on this planet much longer than humans. Their relationship with the forests was deeper and more complex than I could ever imagine. Surely, humans were the most destructive creatures the trees encountered, but there was no mistaking the sense of foreboding that flowed in my mind from the root system.

My connection faded as human thoughts returned to my brain and intruded on the conversation. I wondered what the Fae were up to.

The memory came to me of Gerta, the beach troll, telling me the Fae had grown tired of all the humans who had invaded their lands over the centuries. The Fae would no longer lurk in the shadows, but would take back what they considered theirs. Rule the land as they once had and stamp the humans out.

Long after the faerie had appeared in my cottage and shared the prophecy that I would be a friend or foe of the Fae, the answer was coming into focus.

I couldn't see myself being their ally, like evil Texas Tom. Plus, they took our cat, for crying out loud.

Would I be their enemy, then? Frankly, I would prefer to not be involved in any conflict that was brewing between humans and the Fae.

But did I even have a choice in the matter?

I AWOKE AT 3:00 A.M. FROM CORY TALKING IN HIS SLEEP. Since he'd returned to me, snoring was an occasional problem, one he'd never had before his disappearance to the In Between. What caused this change, I don't know, but siphoning massive amounts of energy from ley lines could surely mess up your sinuses, wouldn't you think?

Talking in his sleep, though, had never been an issue.

It didn't seem to be a bad dream. He mumbled in a conversational tone, and I didn't have the heart to shake him awake.

Suddenly, he sat up in bed.

"What is it?" I asked.

"Cervantes communicated with me," he said, smiling down at me. "He confirmed he's a prisoner of the Fae, but he's okay. It was weird. I was dreaming about him, and he spoke to me in my dream. It was so real. I gradually woke up and realized he truly was speaking to me telepathically."

I'm a telepath, but I've never had the honor of speaking with Cervantes. He only communicated with witches. I was forced to resort to the usual human-cat interactions of guessing whether he was being affectionate or hungry. Usually, it was the latter.

"Tell me what he said."

"He knew we'd be worried about him, and he told us not to be." Cory rubbed my arm. "Typical Cervantes, hiding his concerns. He had sensed the Fae's presence at the beach and was hunting for them. Several faeries ambushed and ensnared him deep in the gopher tortoise burrow. It leads to an extensive network of tunnels that stretch beneath the city."

"Did they harm him?"

"No, but they are treating him like a feral cat captured in someone's backyard. They keep him in a cage, which he's not happy about, and have been trying to extract energy from his magic."

"Stealing energy must be a Fae thing," I said. "You told me they taught Texas Tom how to do it."

"Yeah. Cervantes said they haven't had much luck with him, though. Maybe because he's a cat. The good news, he says, is they've taken a liking to him, sort of as their pet, not knowing he can understand their language. So, they've been letting him out of the cage more often and allowing him to mingle with them, but only in parts of the underground tunnels where he can't escape."

"I hope they lower their guard more and give him a chance to slip out."

"Me, too, of course. The concerning thing, though," Cory said, rubbing his eyes, "is the number of faeries is growing. Cervantes believes they are amassing an army. Their populations have been in decline throughout the Americas, but if they all come together, they could be a formidable danger to humans."

"I've heard they believe humans are invaders in lands the Fae consider their own," I said.

"That's what Cervantes said. The Fae believe humans are an inferior species and want to subjugate us. They'd prefer to find powerful people who will submit to them and then influence the rest of us to do the same. Tom is an example of that."

"I guess that includes me, too, when they told me I could either be a great ally or foe. I suppose by ally they mean a collaborationist. But I don't have a bunch of people I influence."

"Cervantes said if we humans don't submit to the Fae, it will lead to war."

"War? Really? They're supernatural creatures humans don't believe exist. If they were stupid enough to expose themselves to us, we would wipe them out with the military power we have."

"Our armies don't have magic," Cory said grimly. "And from

what Tom told me, the Fae's magic is beyond what any human witch or wizard is capable of."

"What should we do? We have to alert someone. The president? Central Command? Our congressman? My hairdresser?"

"We have to keep it in the supernatural world."

"Then I have to go to the Memory Guild," I said. "And you, to the Magic Guild. I don't believe that's enough, though."

"It will have to do for now."

I stopped in the bathroom, planning on returning to bed and getting a bit more sleep. As I was washing up, something caught my eye.

A vine had snaked its way beneath the sash of the small window. It dangled lazily off the sill. I didn't want to deal with it now.

"When you have time, please trim the vines beneath the bathroom window," I said to Cory as I crawled back into bed.

"There aren't any vines growing there."

"Well, there are now."

"That's strange. I found seedlings growing in an empty vase in the foyer yesterday. I don't understand how that could have happened."

"How interesting," I mumbled as I dozed off.

CHAPTER 12

LIVING MEMORY

I passed along my request through Archibald for an audience with the Memory Guild. Then, I returned my attention to the mundane work of running an inn. The fate of the world could be resting on a knife's edge; nevertheless, scones and scrambled eggs had to be prepared.

I lit the butane burners on the long table in the back of the breakfast room and set out the chafing dishes of eggs, home fries, and sausage. Next, came the tray of freshly baked muffins and bread. The crock pot of oatmeal and the pitchers of fresh orange juice topped it off.

My first guests to arrive were an elderly couple from Buffalo. I greeted them warmly.

"What's that smell on the second floor?" the husband asked grumpily. He wore his trousers up nearly to his ribcage and had more hair coming from his ears than was on his head. "It smells like rotting fish up there."

Darren strikes again.

"It's a phantom odor," I said. "Courtesy of a ghost."

"Are you sure there aren't any guests with a dead flounder in their room?"

"Quite sure. The odor should go away shortly. I'm sorry for any inconvenience."

I returned to the kitchen to get more butter when I suddenly found myself orbiting the earth. Talk about inconvenient. Getting summoned to a Memory Guild Meeting never came with any warning.

Fortunately, if we ran out of butter at the buffet, I would return to my inn only a second or two after I left, no matter how long the meeting ran. In fact, my body would remain in the kitchen the entire time while I astral traveled. I believe if someone tried to talk to me while my spirit was at the meeting, I would barely hesitate to answer. They would never know I had left my body to orbit the earth, attend a meeting, and then return to my body in a blink of an eye.

So, why was I orbiting the earth? No clue. My astral trips usually showed me something educational. I supposed the awesome view of our planet without the need for a space suit and oxygen was a lesson in itself.

Then, a mushroom cloud appeared over North America. Followed by two more.

Okay, this wasn't fun anymore. Was this a vision of a destined future, or a warning of a potential calamity to be avoided?

That was my question when I landed in the torch-lit chamber where we held our virtual meetings.

"The lesson intended," said Dr. Noordlun, "is that all civilizations have the seeds within for their own destruction. Whether the enemy is foreign or domestic, a strong, self-aware society can prevent those seeds from germinating."

"All right, then. Who wants to hear about our enemy?" I asked.

The nine other members of the Memory Guild looked at me, stone-faced.

"Are you going to talk about the Fae?" asked Diego, the vampire.

"Yep. Are you aware of what they're up to?"

"Those of us who are entirely supernatural," Diego nodded at Archibald and Sage, "have sensed the Fae's increased presence in and around San Marcos. There have always been some in this area, certainly before I arrived in the sixteenth century, but their numbers were small, and they kept to themselves. There's no ignoring how many are here now, while even more keep arriving."

"I'm pretty sure their intentions are hostile," I said. "They want to do more than steal human children to compensate for their low birthrate. Many of them now insist they're victims of humans who have invaded their lands. They want to take back all the territory they claim and treat us as inferior creatures."

"They sound quite a bit like humans, don't they?" Archibald asked.

"Indeed, they do," Dr. Noordlun said.

The group broke out into comments and questions about what the Memory Guild could do, until Dr. Noordlun spoke.

"I believe the supernatural guilds of the city need to come together and meet this challenge. We don't want normal humans involved, unless the guilds fail. If the humans ever grasp the concept of faeries being real, then the cat's out of the bag, as they say, and all supernatural creatures are in danger."

"But what exactly can we do?" I gestured to the others in the room. "We're a bunch of intellectuals. Are we supposed to take up arms and fight the Fae with force?"

"You answered your own question, Darla. We use our brains." Dr. Noordlun tapped the huge mane of white hair atop his head. "We learn more about the Fae, their strengths and weaknesses, then formulate a plan for how to counter them."

"Sounds great," I said. "But how do we do that?"

"Our greatest assets are the memories we preserve and protect. The chronicles of history we correct and record. The verified truths about humankind and the other creatures that have called San Marcos home throughout time. We probably know more about the Fae of this region than they do themselves."

"We do?"

He laughed. "The Memory Guild does. It's all in our archives."

It occurred to me I knew nothing about "our" archives. This chamber where our astral selves met was the only "property" I knew belonged to the Memory Guild. And it didn't even exist! It was only an illusion.

I worked with the other members in the field, gathering information and solving mysteries. But I had no idea where the information was kept. Dr. Noordlun's office at San Marcos College was the only physical location I associated with the guild, and it technically belonged to the college.

Dr. Noordlun smiled at me as if he'd read my thoughts.

"We don't have crates of stone tablets, or vaults filled with paper records, or shelves of books, or server farms filled with data. Museums, universities, public libraries, and governments around the world have those. For the Memory Guild, history is a living entity, as are the memories that come from it."

Everyone was smiling at me and my dumbfounded expression. I was still considered the new kid.

"Are you certain she is ready for this?" Archibald asked. Of course, he'd be the one giving me a hard time.

"It's long overdue," Dr. Noordlun said. "Diana, please send us to the Hall of Records."

Diana, the astral witch, murmured an incantation, and before I even had time to glance at her, we were all in a new location. It was a massive hall, built with stone like the previous chamber, illuminated by light pouring in through skylights high above us.

Surprisingly, it was a conventional library, despite what Dr. Noordlun had said. There were twelve rectangular bookcases spaced evenly throughout the space. Each was about forty feet long, twenty feet wide, and two stories tall, solidly filled with giant leather-bound books. There wasn't a single gap anywhere from a missing volume.

I approached the nearest bookcase cluster. The leather cover of each book was shiny and scored in roundish patterns. The books exuded a rich smell, but not quite like leather. There was no trace of dust or mildew in the scent.

The oddest thing was, none of the books were marked with titles or numbers. How in the world could you find the book you were looking for?

"I thought the archive was not books," I said.

"You're coming to a conclusion too soon," Dr. Noordlun said. "Take a closer look."

I stepped up to the bookcase, and then I saw it.

The entire wall of books nearest me was moving ever so slightly. Each spine, all at once, moved toward me, then away. The movement was regular, rhythmic.

It was almost as if the wall of books was breathing.

No, it *was* breathing.

"They're . . . alive?"

"Exactly," Dr. Noordlun said. "These are our living memories. Twelve immortal creatures called Tugara. Some say they are distant relatives of dragons, but they also have plant-like characteristics. They contain all the history and memories of the world, keeping the information alive and vibrant, always adapting as we learn new things, correct errors, and debunk lies."

"You say they're immortal?"

"Yes, but only if they are not harmed and killed. We must forever protect and nourish them."

"Do they need to eat?"

Dr. Noordlun laughed. "They have a process akin to photo-synthesis. But they also eat insects and fungus from time to time. Believe it or not, they appreciate good chocolate, too."

"Who doesn't?" Gloria said.

"How do you find information inside them?" I asked. "Is there some sort of index?"

"That responsibility falls to me," Dr. Noordlun said, "since I'm the scholar of the guild. Though the process is anything but scholarly. I must go into a trance and commune with the creatures in a telepathic fashion. Other members of the guild are learning how to do this, should something happen to me."

"I would like to learn," I said, the words escaping me before I could even think.

"The new girl will learn when she's ready," Archibald said.

"You won't be the one to decide when I am," I said to the snarky imp.

I stared at the twelve amazing creatures, giant slumbering bulks, filled with all the wisdom of the world. It was reassuring to know the knowledge was here, in safekeeping, instead of merely scattered across the globe in often inaccurate, fragile, and decaying documentation systems kept by unreliable humans.

It was also frightening to think of all these valuable assets in one hall.

"Are the Tugara safe here?" I asked.

"Safer here than any other place or dimension accessible to humans."

"Um, where, exactly, are we?"

"A plane of existence unique to our needs," Diana said.

"Is this like the In Between?"

"That's one way of looking at it. This is like our own little private island in time and space."

"Here, acts of nature can't harm our records," Dr. Noordlun said. "Vandals or invading armies shouldn't be able to come here. The only known enemy of the Tugara is the Father of Lies himself."

Ah, the nemesis of the Memory Guild. While Satan is referred to in the Bible as the Father of Lies, the Guild's arch foe is a more specific incarnation of Satan, who spreads untruths and distorts facts. He can manifest himself as a demon, a human, or any other creature. Or, he can simply be a madness spreading through humankind that infects minds with conspiracy theories and paranoia.

"Needless to say," Dr. Noordlun continued, "we must protect the Tugara from him at all costs. But let's not speak anymore of such a dreadful topic. We're here to do a little research on the Fae. What's remarkable about our archives is that they contain history and memories from before humans existed. When the Fae, and other creatures we call mythological, dominated the earth."

"How did that information get into the archives?" I asked.

"We put it here—our current team, and those who came before us. Psychometrists, mediums, ghosts, witches, vampires, wood-speakers, metal-speakers, stone-speakers, and other specialists dug up this data from the earth around us and put it here. Historians, like myself, interviewed the living descendants of faeries, elves, trolls, sprites, and the other creatures who lived before humans did. It was quite an effort that took generations."

"I should say," Archibald piped in.

"The archives mean so much to us," James, the metal-speaker, said. "And not just because of all the work we've put into them."

While James spoke, Dr. Noordlun walked among the Tugara.

"He's about to connect with the archives," Diana said.

"How, if we're here only virtually?" I asked.

"His spirit can do it. He doesn't need to make contact physically with them, although he can come here in person if needed. Didn't you notice the scent of the Tugara? That shows you how sensitive our spirits are and how much they can interact with the physical work."

"I can attest to that," Sage said. In our astral meetings, she always appeared perfectly solid, just like a living person.

Soon, I lost sight of Dr. Noordlun among the Tugara. But his voice came to me as loudly as if over a loudspeaker.

"The Fae arrived in the Americas from Europe, Africa, and Asia, like the first humans did, but they didn't walk here over the Bering Strait land bridge. They flew, in their winged forms, in a big swarm like locusts, across the Pacific in the eastward winds of the jet stream.

"They spread out across North, Central, and South America. This was long before the elves, trolls, and other supernatural creatures we're familiar with arrived. Instead, there were native supernatural creatures living here, with which the Fae warred. In some places, the Fae wiped them out. In others, like Florida, they coexisted.

"The first humans who arrived also coexisted with them. But as humans thrived, the Fae and other creatures hid from them for safety. By the time Europeans colonized the continents, the

Fae completely retreated from view, like the other supernatural creatures. The Fae survived in the deep forest and below ground. In Florida, they flourished in the Everglades.

"But more and more humans kept coming. Our numbers grew, our axes destroyed the forests, and we filled the swamplands with homes.

"More than a century ago, a mysterious illness swept through the Fae, killing some of them and making others infertile. Which, of course, caused their numbers to decline even more. They're still suffering from this illness today.

"The more belligerent faeries claim the disease came from humans. That was the initial impetus for them to become hostile to us. Kidnapping human children to raise as faeries began decades ago and now has spread to San Marcos, thanks to the wizard Texas Tom and other humans who have collaborated with the Fae.

"Now, there are faerie warlords who have amplified the rhetoric against humans, blaming us for every ill of their society. Encouraging their people to fight to retake their lands. To drive humans away, or to enslave them.

"There is talk, even, of wiping out humans. It is a dire situation we're facing.

"The Fae worship a pantheon of gods. One of them is named Aastacki. Based on the religious writings in our archives, Aastacki is an incarnation of the Father of Lies."

The members of the Memory Guild let out a collective gasp.

"The Fae warlords worship him in particular, to help them spread hatred, misinformation, and paranoia amongst the Fae, driving them in their impending war against the humans.

"The warlords are the ones who want to wipe out humans. And the Father of Lies, as you know, wants to wipe out our memory. As well as every one of us in the Memory Guild."

There was nothing but stunned silence that seemed to last forever. Until I ruined it.

"Where are all these Fae hiding? They stole our cat and I want to get him back."

The entire membership of the guild stared at me like I was nuts. Dr. Noordlun emerged from the Tugara with a similar expression.

"I'm not talking about going down into their tunnels myself to rescue my cat," I clarified. "It would be helpful to have a general idea of where he is, and maybe magic will help him escape."

"There are records of their traditional homes in this area, down in caves and pockets of the underground limestone formations. However, with all the additional Fae congregating here, they've expanded their tunnel system. We don't have information on it."

"No offense to the odious miscreant who regularly attacks my face," Archibald said, "but don't you think Cervantes is of less importance than the survival of your human race?"

"Oh, but he's a very special cat," I said.

Many heads shook in incomprehension.

CHAPTER 13

UNWELCOME GUESTS

I was back in my kitchen again, a plate of butter in my hand, only a second or two after my astral self had been whisked away to the Memory Guild. The feeling I had was severe disorientation, but I had to shrug it off and return to the dining room.

Everything here was normal. Two couples ate at their respective tables. The young family with two kids, who had checked in the previous night, were at the buffet table creating a mess I would have to clean up as soon as they sat down.

My morning was completely mundane, and boy, how I appreciated that fact. After hearing about the Fae invasion and the Father of Lies, even laundering sheets and towels would be delightfully dull in comparison.

Then my phone rang.

"Darla! Are you at your inn?" It was Arch Mage Bob. He never called. He never answered my calls. The only way to speak with him was to find him, usually at the beach or at his surf shop.

Hearing him on the phone put a knot in my stomach.

"The warding spell I put on the inn alerted me. It just fended off a bunch of magic attacks, one after the other. Someone's trying to get at you or your family, probably Texas Tom. And if he can't hit you with magic, he might show up in person."

I thanked him for the warning, then texted Cory.

He didn't answer.

I texted Sophie.

She didn't answer, either. Probably because she was still asleep, but I couldn't be sure. Cory was Tom's most likely target, but Sophie would be the most vulnerable one.

I sprinted for the stairs, taking two at a time to the third floor. (You should be impressed someone of my height could do that.)

Racing down the hall to 305, I pounded on the door.

"Sophie, are you okay?" I pounded harder. "Sophie, answer me!"

The door to 304 across the hall opened. A small owlish man peeked out. Mr. Wittington from Milwaukee.

"Is everything okay?" he asked.

"Everything's just fine." I was practically singing in soprano with my nerves so tight. "Breakfast is served downstairs."

He seemed dubious at the thought of leaving his room.

The lock clicked, and Sophie's door opened.

"What is it, Mom?" she said, her face creased from sleep. "I was going to be downstairs in time to clean up after breakfast."

"Just making sure."

I smiled at her and Mr. Wittington, like everything was normal in my mundane world.

Then came the gunshot from downstairs.

Everyone flinched. Mr. Wittington looked at me as if to say I should have known, and slammed his door, followed by a flurry of locks clicking.

"He went after Cory. Stay in your room until I'm sure Texas Tom is neutralized." I turned from Sophie and ran toward the stairs.

By the time I got downstairs, the guests in the breakfast room were gathered at the French doors, looking out at the courtyard. Avoiding them, I went down the hall to the other door to the courtyard, burst outside, and ran through the ajar door of my cottage.

It had to be the stupidest tactical error I could make, running right into trouble without knowing the situation. But I was lucky.

Cory sat in the dining alcove, my Glock pistol on the table in front of him. He looked really shaken up.

"Are you okay? Where is Tom?"

"He's gone."

"He's dead?"

"No. I didn't shoot him." Cory looked at me, half relieved and half embarrassed. "I hit the TV."

He sure did. The set wasn't super big, but it took up the length of a hutch. A hole was placed right in the center, with a spider's web of cracks radiating from it. Our LED was DOA.

"Hopefully, you nailed one of those annoying morning show hosts."

"Darla, he came here to take me away to be his energy slave again. He's taken refuge with the Fae, and they want his magical energy. We all know he can't harvest it from ley lines like I can, so he wanted me to go with him."

"Bob called and told me the warding spell blocked some magic attacks."

"Yeah, so Tom showed up in person to convince me to join him in serving the Fae. When I refused, he tried to capture me. He was casting a binding spell, but I had placed the pearl in my pocket after I sensed the magic attacks. I put together a rudimentary protection spell around myself and it seemed to work. Still, he wouldn't leave until I nearly shot him. He seems weaker, and I can tell he's low in magical energy. But he's going to come for me again, Darla. Tom doesn't give up this easily."

"So, he's here in present-day San Marcos, not back in 1891?"

"It seems so. He's staying with the Fae. He said I should join them, too, because they are going to rule us humans. There are thousands of them here, he said."

"But where? Last week, when there was a dental convention in town, you couldn't avoid bumping into a dentist. So, where are these thousands of faeries?"

"He said many are living underground, while others are in human form and live among us unrecognized."

"Don't you see the irony here?" I asked. "Not long ago, Tom was using skills he learned from the Fae to take over the Magic Guild and rule all the witches. Now, he's just a lackey of the Fae and is helping them try to rule us all."

"Tom is nothing but an opportunist."

"We now have a warrant for Vance Puggle's arrest for Hugo's murder," Samson told me over the phone. "The problem is locating him. I got a search warrant and led a team searching his home for evidence to strengthen our case for murder. We also looked for clues for where he would hide out."

"Find anything?"

"A life insurance policy for the victim, with Puggle as the beneficiary. Nothing else. And as far as clues to where he might have fled, we found nada. I knew it was a long shot. He ran away on an impulse, but I was hoping he'd have made plans for where he might go if he became a suspect. That's where you come in."

"You think he left memories of where he would go?"

"Yeah. And now you don't have to sneak around to read his stuff. You can take your time. Can you meet me at his house at noon?"

"Okay."

Truth is, I really didn't want to go. Now that Sophie wasn't a suspect, I wasn't as driven anymore to find Hugo's murderer. Don't get me wrong—I wanted poor Hugo's killer to be punished, but it wasn't my job. Samson could handle that. I had bigger worries. An escaped madman wizard trying to kidnap my husband. An ancient race of mythological creatures who want to conquer humans. Unpleasant odors popping up in my inn. You know, the stuff that makes finding a steroid-addled muscle-head seem unimportant.

Being a psychometrist was a gift and also a responsibility. Samson truly needed my help, so I suppose I could sacrifice a couple of hours to search for Vance's memories. The guy didn't have a whole lot going on upstairs, so it's not as if there would be a lot of coherent thoughts to read.

I told Cory where I was going, and he said to be careful. Careful of what? Vance's house was absolutely the last place he would be right now, while the police were looking for him.

Therefore, I was stunned when I drove up to his townhouse to see his red muscle car parked in the driveway and the garage door open. I was about to hightail it out of there when Samson's car pulled up behind mine. His jaw undoubtedly dropped onto his chest from shock.

His car quickly drove around mine and pulled into Vance's driveway, blocking his car from leaving. Samson remained in his car, talking on his radio. Then, he got out and walked up to my window.

"I called for backup. When they arrive, we'll go in and get Puggle. You can have the place to yourself after that. You won't need to look for memories of where he's hiding out, of course. But anything you find about Starbright's murder will help me find more evidence that can be used in court."

Barely a minute later, two patrol cars arrived. One of the officers went with Samson into the garage gym while the other stood in the driveway. I approached this one.

"Hi," I said. "I'm a consultant working with Detective Samson."

The cop, a young guy with short dark hair, nodded at me, then returned his gaze to the garage.

Apparently, the door leading inside was unlocked. Samson and the other uniformed officer walked right in, guns drawn. The cop with the dark hair moved to where the driveway met the garage. I followed him, trying to peer into the open doorway to the house.

Samson and the officer didn't have to go far. Even from where I stood, I could see the feet of a man lying on his back in the laundry room.

The third cop rushed to join the others, and during the flurry of radio calls and cops going back and forth from their cars, I slipped into the garage and headed toward Samson, who stood in the laundry room over the dead body.

The body belonged to, you guessed it, Vance.

There was no blood on the body or on the floor beneath it. I wondered how he'd died. The only things amiss were two burn marks on his head, one at each temple.

"Why is Vance here? Is he an idiot?" I asked Samson. He didn't seem annoyed that I had intruded on the crime scene.

"A very simple reason." He pointed to a suitcase on the floor nearby. "He probably realized the police weren't watching the house around the clock anymore, and he couldn't do without some personal items. They weren't worth dying for."

"How did he die?"

"Electrocution. He got zapped in the head. Your average stun gun or cattle prod couldn't have done it. I'm guessing it was magic."

"Texas Tom," I said, and explained his attack on my inn. "Cory said Tom's magic was weak, but it was almost strong enough to breach the warding spell Bob put on the property. And possibly strong enough to do this to Vance."

"Could be. What would Tom want from Vance?"

I couldn't think of a single thing. Until I remembered the key that had fallen from Hugo's wallet, the one that came from a faerie. Maybe Tom was doing the bidding of this faerie and was searching for the key when Vance happened to come home at the worst possible time.

"Tom has been working for the Fae. Maybe they wanted him to search for something."

I couldn't mention the key, or else I'd get in trouble for stealing evidence.

"I'm going to take a quick look at something," I said, hurrying into the house. For me, "look" meant touch.

"Wait! You can't touch anything until the crime scene techs go over the entire house."

"Don't worry, I'm putting latex gloves on." The gloves would prevent me from leaving or disturbing fingerprints, while being thin enough to allow the psychic energy through.

I had to be fast. Heading upstairs, I was surprised to find both the master and guest bedrooms were being used. It only took a quick glance at the decor and the flamboyant clothing lying around to realize Hugo used the master bedroom. The other one was decorated with bodybuilding posters. Vance was such a cliche.

Someone had ransacked Hugo's dresser and bedside table. Drawers were all pulled out, and clothing and personal items were scattered across the floor. On top of the dresser was a dark-wood jewelry box. The bracelets and ear studs Hugo liked to wear had been spilled upon the dresser.

I touched it with my gloved hand. Years of Hugo's memories were on here, but there was very recent energy. I moved my fingertips to—

—*find any secret compartments. Where would he hide a small key? It could be anywhere, and I've looked just about everywhere. They're so confident this Hugo dude had it. No, it's not in here. Wait, is someone in the house? I better—*

—Let go of the box lid and get out of the room before Samson has me arrested. Unfortunately, I couldn't identify whose memories I'd just read. It was a male—my guess was Texas Tom, but I didn't know him well enough to recognize his thought patterns. The individual was so focused on his search that he didn't think about himself. There were no identifying marks on his hand seen holding the box lid.

As I was coming down the stairs, Samson walked to the bottom of the staircase and frowned at me.

"I didn't disturb anything," I said. "I touched one surface, gently, and I was wearing these." I held up my gloved hands.

"Still, you shouldn't have."

I finished descending the stairs and pushed past him.

"Well, did you learn anything?" he asked.

"Oh, I wasn't supposed to do it, but you're happy to benefit from my findings?"

"I insist upon it."

"It was a man. I'm not sure who. He was searching for a key with the sense that he was following orders and didn't know what the key was for. Then, he heard someone entering the house."

Of course, I omitted the fact that I had the key. Even though I, too, didn't know what the vessel it unlocked was for.

"Well, all this sure is a kick in the butt," Samson said.

"Because now Vance can't be tried for Hugo's murder?"

"No. Because he might not have been the murderer."

"Come on, Michael. I found a bunch of incriminating memories. His phone records show he was near or at the scene. And he freaking attacked you and fled! How many innocent men attack the detective investigating them? Really, your whole 'methodical' schtick is getting on my nerves."

"It was miles away from an open-and-shut case. He had a motive and was at the scene. We can't bring to court the dark thoughts you found. So, what does that leave us? A case not much stronger than one against your daughter."

I almost blew my top before swallowing my anger. It burned in my stomach like a locally grown datil pepper.

"Sure, Detective. Hugging someone too long is as powerful a motive as cheating on a long-term relationship. Makes tons of sense."

"Crimes of passion rarely make any sense at all."

"The people who investigate them need to make sense."

"Anyway, I was going in a different direction before you hijacked my train of thought."

"*I* hijacked it?"

"If you would let me finish. It stands to reason the person searching Mr. Starbright's possessions is looking for a key, a person who doesn't have any compunction killing someone who gets in his way killed Mr. Starbright for the same reason.

Believing the victim had the key on his person. Obviously, he didn't, because the perp came here."

Actually, Hugo did have the key, but it easily could have been missed in a search, tucked away in his wallet like that, until I accidentally turned the wallet upside down. Now that Sophie wasn't being accused, my mind was open to this possibility.

"So, Texas Tom, or whoever killed Vance, also killed Hugo, all in pursuit of the key. Right?" I asked.

"Yeah. It's worth checking out."

Samson turned away to speak to a crime scene tech who had just arrived. I used the opportunity to sort out what I knew before I said something stupid. The key belonged to the Fae. For some reason, it was given to Dorothy's husband. She stole it from him as a bargaining piece of sorts. Then she gave it to Hugo. Now, let's say the Fae wanted their key back. If they found out Hugo had it, they'd come after him. With Tom serving as their human errand boy, he could be the one who went after Hugo.

Then, I remembered: Tom was in the county jail when Hugo was killed. Dang it.

I also remembered Tom was good at long-range magic attacks. He basically brainwashed the entire magic community of San Marcos when he was in another time period. Potentially, he could have killed Hugo from his jail cell.

Could he have retrieved the key from Hugo's body using long-distance magic? Seems like a stretch, although I knew very little about magic.

But wait—what if he used a gateway to transport himself from the jail to the beach and back again? That was a possibility. Though, I couldn't imagine why he would return to jail, unless the gateway gave him no choice.

When Samson had a moment, I explained my theory to him, leaving out the memories I read on the key itself.

"Interesting," he said. "I'll check with the jail to see if they have surveillance footage of his cell. I'd be interested if he disappeared, even if only for a few moments."

"Yes, the time you're physically absent after you pass through a gateway is usually less than how long it feels you're gone."

"It messes with my head to try to understand gateways and the In Between. I'd rather not experience it again."

"You might have to if you want to catch Texas Tom."

Samson sighed with exhaustion. "I wish I could investigate a normal crime. Why is magic always involved? Is it because you always seem to be involved?"

CHAPTER 14

FAERIES IN THE BACKYARD

I needed to know more about the faerie key and who would kill to get it back. It could be whomever Dorothy stole it from. Or it could be the Fae.

Either way, since I now possessed it, I could soon end up on the hit list.

The most obvious person to ask was Dorothy. But it was risky to reveal that I knew about the key. It could put me on the hit list really quickly.

Unfortunately, my curiosity was more powerful than my discretion.

I composed a text to her:

Sorry to bother you. Hugo's attorney sent a package to my daughter, his student. It contained a key.

No, no, no. I can't risk Sophie like that. I hit the delete key and revised my text:

Hugo's attorney sent a package to me, since I was his friend. It contained a key. Hugo claimed it was a gift from you, but he wanted me to have it, since he feared for his life. Can you tell me anything about it? Do you want it back?

I hoped she didn't see through my blatant lies. Or want the key back.

She didn't respond. So, I went about my mundane day, hoping my phone would buzz with her text.

"What in the infernal blazes is that smell?" Mr. Wittington, the elderly gentleman from Milwaukee, asked me in the third-floor hallway.

"What smell?"

"It reeks like I just jumped headfirst into a landfill."

"Oh, that. I'm sorry. It will go away in a minute or so. It's a phantom odor from a haunting. You know that ghosts can make noises or present visual apparitions. In this case, it's an odor apparition."

"And there's a plant growing in my sink."

"I'll take care of it. It's just another supernatural thing."

"Oh. Of course!" He smiled and continued down the hall.

I made up the part about the plant being supernatural because I didn't know how it got there. Curiously, my explanation didn't faze Mr. Wittington one iota. Looks like my inn's reputation of being haunted was spreading.

Still, I really needed to find Darren's remains. His odor apparitions were embarrassing. And, let's face it, a bad smell is a bad smell, even if the reason behind it was out of the ordinary.

My phone buzzed. I yanked it from my back pocket.

I don't know what key you're talking about, said Dorothy's text.

Rather than being coy, I took the aggressive route.

You do know. It's a small, intricate golden key. The kind used for jewelry boxes and the like. It looks valuable.

There must be a mistake.

I was having none of it. *I'll be happy to bring it to your house. Maybe once you or your husband see it, you'll remember.*

No response for several minutes. I wondered if I'd gone too far.

Then she finally replied:

May I stop by your inn?

Sure. I'll be here all day. Thank you.

DOROTHY ARRIVED RIGHT IN THE MIDDLE OF TEA SERVICE, hair perfectly coifed, wearing a purple dress. Bad timing on her part.

"Thanks for coming," I said. "Come, join us in the dining room and have some tea and scones." I tried to sound as nonchalant as I could.

She glanced across the foyer to the hall leading to the dining room and the tables of guests enjoying finger sandwiches and scones.

"I'd rather speak privately."

"Then come to the kitchen," I said, leading her in. I gestured to a stool beside the butcher-block island. "Have a seat, and I'll pour you a cup."

I thought she'd decline, but she allowed me to pour the hot water. She took a packet of herbal tea from the open box of selections I presented her. The box was mahogany and triggered the memory of the ornate lid of the jar to which the key presumably belonged.

"How big was the key you received?" she asked.

I held my finger and thumb apart. "About an inch and a half. Do you want to see it?"

I was bluffing, hoping against hope that she wouldn't want the key.

She shuddered. "No, thanks."

"There's something special about it, isn't there? I never saw a key quite like it."

"Yes." She paused, as if gathering strength. "I don't know why Hugo left the key to you. I didn't realize you were that close to him."

"He knows I have a keen interest in antiques. My mother owns an antiques shop."

"I didn't explain enough to Hugo how important the key is. It shouldn't be circulating among people."

"Why?" I asked.

"I'll be honest with you. I took it from my husband out of spite. And I thought I could use it for leverage if we divorce. I shouldn't have done it. But I can't take back what I did. He now knows it's missing, and if he discovers I took it, well, things could go badly. That's why I gave it to Hugo for safekeeping. I couldn't return it to my husband because then he'd know I took it. I don't want him to realize I even know about the key."

"What's so special about it?"

"I only know it was given to my husband by very important people. He was safeguarding it. I knew if I took it, he would be at my mercy."

"Sounds dangerous," I said.

"It is. I regret doing it. But there's no going back now."

"Who are the very important people who gave it to your husband?"

"I don't know."

I thought she was lying. Maybe she didn't want to tell me about the Fae.

"What lengths would your husband go to in order to get the key back?"

She stared at me for a while, eyes blinking.

"You mean, would he kill Hugo?"

"Yeah."

She seemed to come to a resolve. "He might."

"That would mean he'd have to know you gave it to Hugo. That you were seeing him."

"Yes, it would. Dick never confronted me about cheating on him, but he might have known."

I poured more hot water into her cup. It was time for me to make the rounds in the dining room, but I didn't want to put this interview on hold. I decided to go on the offensive.

"Do you know anything about the Fae?" I asked.

Her face turned white. "No. What's that?"

"Faeries. Like from folklore."

"Why would you ask me about that?"

"Because I'm a kook." I gave a big grin. "The funny thing is, the older I get, more and more things that used to be only folklore turn out to be true."

Her face still looked stricken. She knows about the Fae, I thought. Since she took their key, she must not be on their side, though. Maybe I could convince her to join my side.

"I don't care if you think I'm crazy," I said. "I believe in the Fae. Well, it's not only a belief. I know with certainty they exist. And they're a threat to us humans right now. I think the key once belonged to the Fae. And I think you know that. Anything you can tell me about them would help immensely. Besides, they stole my cat."

She was frightened. She stood up as if to leave, but hesitated.

"I'll keep whatever you tell me in confidence," I said. "Don't worry about your safety."

"Okay," she said, releasing a pent-up breath. "I've heard of them. You know, some people see ghosts. I've seen a few faeries."

I've seen both, I thought.

"But I have nothing to do with them," she added. "I doubt they're a threat."

"They are. And, like I said, they have my cat. Do you know where I can find them?"

"No."

"Where was it you saw the faeries?"

She hesitated again. This was like pulling teeth. Finally, she said, "In the forest that surrounds our house. There are hundreds of acres of woods. Somewhere in there, far from the house, I saw them while hiking."

She pulled her purse over her shoulder as she mentally shut herself off from me.

"That's all I know," she said.

"Thank you for your help. But I forgot to ask, what does the key unlock?"

"The key? Some box, I assume."

"Where is the box?"

"How would I know? Thank you for the tea."

She turned and walked from the kitchen and out of the inn.

MY TALK WITH DOROTHY MOVED THE BALL A LITTLE FARTHER down the field, but there was so much I didn't know. We now needed to learn more about Dick Gilley, because getting his key back was an obvious motive for killing Hugo and Vance. There were hints suggesting he associated with the Fae. Which could support the theory that Texas Tom was the magic hitman ordered to do the jobs.

The key still bothered me. The tiny piece of metal may have been the reason two men died. It might become dangerous for me to have it.

The remaining question, though, was why? What was so special about the jar it unlocked?

The Memory Guild could help me answer these questions. Namely, James, the metal-speaker. If I was lucky, he could tell me more than I learned from reading the memories left on the key.

After I cleaned up from Teatime, I assigned Cory and Sophie to host the nightly Wine Hour. I retrieved the key from its hiding place in my bedroom and hid it in my pocket. Then I hopped on my motor scooter, the only ride I had since my car was stolen by Tom, and headed to a street that ran parallel to Royal Avenue, the pedestrian-only tourist mecca of San Marcos.

I parked the scooter in view of the bay and cut through an alley to the entrance of the historical reenactment village. James worked as a blacksmith in this recreation of San Marcos in the early colonial days of the sixteenth and seventeenth centuries.

Beneath electric lighting that mimicked torches, James stood at his forge, pulling a metal rod from the fire, and hammering it upon an anvil. A small crowd of tourists watched the large, bearded man. His ample pecs showed beneath a leather apron.

I had to wait while he shaped the rod into a curly decorative thing with no purpose I could ascertain. Next, he answered questions from the audience. Finally, I approached him.

"Darla! What brings you here? Let me guess, you need me to read something."

"Yes, James. I'm ashamed it's so obvious I'm using you for your paranormal abilities."

"When I have so much more to offer," he said with a wink. "What do you have for me?"

I showed him the key. He held it in his beefy hand.

"Wow, this is beautiful. What's the story behind it?"

I explained what I knew so far.

"Uh-oh," he said, "one tiny key that could open some big trouble. Right away, I can tell it's extremely ancient. Let's go to the shed where we won't get bothered by anyone."

Behind the smithy was a shed, built in the historical style, where tools were stored, and James took breaks. We sat upon two anachronistic plastic chairs.

With the key in his palm, James pressed both hands together and closed his eyes. We were both silent seemingly forever, with the words and laughter of tourists drifting into the shed along with the music of a distant fiddle.

James' breathing grew loud and steady, and a low nasal humming escaped him. I'd never heard him hum before while metal-speaking. I saw, in the artificial torchlight, beads of sweat appear on his brow.

His breathing became irregular, his shoulders twitched erratically.

I grew concerned. Was he all right? I said nothing, though, not wanting to break the spell.

His eyes fluttered open, revealing only the whites.

"James? Are you okay?"

He moaned and twitched. He appeared to struggle to pull his hands apart. I didn't know what to do.

With a pop of air pressure, his hands separated. The key fell to the wooden floor, and I swiped it up instantly, returning it to my pocket. At last, James relaxed and opened his eyes.

"Wow," he said. "I've never encountered metal like this before. There's gold covering a metal I can't identify. I don't believe it's even found on the earth, or, if so, only deep in the planet's core. And it's incalculably old."

"I was concerned about you. You looked like you were experiencing trauma."

He smiled weakly. "I don't remember what was happening to me, only what I was reading. There's nothing magic or evil about the key itself, but it has been associated with immense forces of magic and power. I don't even know where to begin."

"Take your time."

"Most recently, it's been handled by humans, but before that, there was a lot of Fae energy in it. And before that—I don't know what to call it. All I can say is the key was in the presence of immortals."

"Immortals?"

"I don't know. Like angels, or gods, or something."

"What would angels or gods need a key for?"

"Beats me. I'm only telling you what I experienced."

"Did you learn anything about what it locks?"

"Only slight impressions from the metal of the lock it touched, made millennia ago from the same metal I can't identify. The key hasn't been used in centuries."

"I know I should let it go, but a key is no good without something to open," I said. "This key is so intriguing it haunts me. I've picked up memories that have shown me a large ceramic jar or amphora with a wooden lid that has the lock. I feel I must find this jar, though I don't know why."

"It's just human nature."

"We're talking about creatures other than humans now."

"Yeah. Maybe you don't want to open the jar after all."

I thanked James for his help, as inconclusive as it was. The subject of immortal entities freaked me out, I have to say. Since I joined the Memory Guild, we've tangled with demonic entities, but certainly not gods or angels. Or major demons.

That was something I truly wanted to avoid.

CHAPTER 15

THROTTLED

My motor scooter, once it was freed of the bumpy cobblestones of Old Town, picked up speed on the smooth asphalt of the Victorian-era neighborhood just to the north. I was headed to Mom's on a mission of magic. With little hope of succeeding.

I had asked Sophie and Cory to meet me there so the three witches could work on a spell to help me locate the mysterious jar. All we had to work with was the key that unlocked the lid. And the combined magic of one hobbyist and two novices. It was the best option I had. I couldn't ask my cousin, Missy, to travel all the way up the state to work on a farfetched mission. Nor could I ask Arch Mage Bob for yet another favor.

This was to be a family affair. The Chesswick family of witches. Cory, of course, is not of the Chesswick line of women, but I'm giving him an honorary membership.

My growing curiosity about the jar was turning into an obsession, and it could prove to be an unhealthy, dangerous one. Yet, by the very nature of obsessions, I had no choice but to obey it.

How I justified it was that finding the jar would help us locate the Fae. They had the jar with them where they lived or stashed away somewhere. Either way, it would help us zero in on them.

When I arrived, Sophie's car was parked at the curb in front of Mom's house. Behind it was the four-door Ford I recognized as Detective Billy Reyna's, a normal sight at Mom's most mornings. It was part of their flirting ritual, in which Mom served him freshly baked scones and freshly brewed coffee, while the magic love-inducing ingredients in the scones went to work on the aging detective.

Today, there was freshly brewed trouble, as well.

I parked my scooter in the driveway that ran along the side of the house leading to the detached garage, which was too full of junk to hold a car. Before I stepped through the back door to the kitchen, Sophie warned me off.

She and Cory were sitting in the backyard gazebo (which was also filled with junk).

"I wouldn't go in there just now," Sophie said. "Mom and Billy are arguing."

"About what?"

"Their relationship. What else? Things have been weird ever since they were entranced by Texas Tom's spell."

The evil wizard's spell had briefly turned the entire magic community of San Marcos into brain-dead lust zombies, so he could manipulate them. It also accelerated Mom and Billy's flirting and moved the action from the kitchen to the bedroom. Which could lead to a life of bliss together. Or multiple rounds of two hard heads knocking into each other.

I faced the door again and looked through the windowpanes. Billy was in his usual seat at the table with his coffee and a plate of scones. Mom leaned against the counter, facing him, a scowl upon her face.

Both threw loud words at each other. I couldn't hear the conversation, but the words "freedom" and "controlling" were clearly audible.

I didn't have the patience to sit in the gazebo and wait for the storm to pass. There was too much stuff I needed to do today. Therefore, I forced the issue and opened the door to the kitchen.

"Good morning!" I said in my cheeriest voice.

The two lovers ignored me.

"I'm not 'controlling' you," Billy said to Mom. "I thought a relationship meant spending all your time together."

"I've been independent too long to become your slave."

"Slave? Your hyperbole is not helping. Does hanging out with me this weekend mean you're my slave?"

"It means you want me attached to you like a submissive wife. I know how you old-school men are."

"I'm younger than you, Sadie."

"Why must you bring that up? I'll outlive you, anyway. You're so high-strung your heart is going to explode any day now."

"What are you talking about? I'm in great shape." He patted his pot belly. "Most guys my age retire from the police force, but I'm never going to retire. They call me an institution."

"A mental institution."

"Now, now, kids," I said. "Let's behave."

They finally noticed I was there.

"Oh, good morning, dear," Mom said. "Is it time for our workshop already?"

Billy slid his chair back. "I'll get out of your way. I have to make the rounds of my informants. See you this weekend, Sadie.

Good seeing you, sweetheart," he said to me, squeezing my shoulder.

He truly was old-school. In an annoying way.

After the door closed behind him, I asked Mom, "What's all this about being Billy's slave? You've been feeding him scones laced with love potions for years. Didn't you want a relationship with him?"

"I wanted a boy toy. Not some insecure guy mooning over me who won't let me out of his sight."

"That doesn't sound like Billy at all."

"It will, as soon as he becomes fully enraptured by me."

I sighed and poured myself a cup of coffee in a stained and chipped yellow mug, the same one I used when I last lived here as a teenager. It's the little things that keep us grounded in this crazy world.

Sophie and Cory meekly entered the kitchen.

"Come on, grab yourself some coffee and scones so we can get to work," Mom said. "No, not those scones, Cory. Try these."

She yanked away the platter of remaining magic-infused scones and slid a new batch from a baking sheet onto a different platter.

When all four of us were seated around the table, I gave a brief introduction to their assignment. Cory knew most of what I'd been up to. Sophie and Mom got the abridged version, the one less likely to freak them out over the perilous situation I'd gotten myself into.

"This will be the foundation of the spell." I pulled the key from my pocket. "Do not, under any circumstances, lose this key or allow anyone to steal it."

Everyone nodded. I placed the key in the center of the old table.

"Beneath the gold coating, the key is made of an unidentified metal that might not even be from the earth."

"You mean it came from an asteroid or meteor?" Sophie asked.

"Maybe. Or from another planet." How that would be possible, I couldn't explain.

"Using the key," I said, "you're going to come up with a spell that helps us locate the lock it belongs to. Okay, start conjuring."

The three witches of my family looked at each other blankly, then back at me.

"How?" Cory asked.

"Why are you asking me? I'm not a witch. You guys have the magic genes, so figure it out."

"Witches don't just wave a magic wand," Mom said. "Spells are complicated. We need a grimoire with instructions."

This was a bad idea. Why was I so naïve to think they could simply whip up a spell, like making a meal with whatever ingredients you have in the pantry?

"Wait, before you give up, let's think about this," Sophie said. "We each know a smattering of magic. Let's see if we can put our smatterings together. Grammers, you know how to make a potion that signals if magic is in the air. You used it to confirm that Texas Tom was sending magic attacks."

Mom nodded.

"Maybe we can adapt it to locate objects that contain magic. Hugo, may he rest in peace, taught me how to amplify spells by drawing up the energies within myself and from the ocean. Of the few basic spells he showed me, I have one that helps me find my phone. That could help. What about you, Cory?"

He rubbed his face. "I can draw tons of energy from ley lines, but that brings back a lot of bad memories, and I don't think we need that much power for this spell. Let me see, I can do a basic protection spell, but that won't apply here. Um, oh yeah, I have a spell that helps me see for long distances. That could come in handy if we adapt it."

"Good," Sophie said. "Next, we need to put our spells together to create a bigger spell that will find the lock."

"Cory, do you think the pearl will help?" I asked. "Not only does it have power of its own, but it's also associated with the Fae."

"Good idea!"

I pushed back my chair. "You guys stay here and keep working. I'll run home and get the pearl. Be right back."

Outside, I started my scooter, turned it around, and rolled down the driveway into the street. Transporting a priceless object like the pearl made me a little uneasy, but I truly believed it would help my family of witches build a spell to locate the jar and the Fae.

As I drove toward Old Town, I realized I wasn't clear about exactly what we would do if we achieved our objective. Finding the Fae could help us free Cervantes. That was the most important thing for me personally. I reminded myself it was much more important than satisfying my curiosity about the jar.

As to the larger issue of stopping the Fae from starting a war against humans, there wasn't much we could do ourselves. That would require all the guilds of San Marcos and Northern Florida banding together. They would need to know where the Fae were hiding and amassing their forces.

See, finding the Fae was more than a personal crusade. The fate of my fellow humans hung in the balance.

I was waiting at a red light when my beloved motor scooter attacked me.

There's no other way to describe it. As I sat there, balancing the scooter on my left foot, the engine began revving to a frightening pitch. Not being mechanically minded, I didn't know what to do. I played with the throttle, thinking it was stuck, but nothing worked. The engine roared and whined like I was a motorcycle racer.

When the light turned green, I was afraid to put the scooter in gear. The machine would probably lurch ahead so suddenly I would lose control and fall off. So, I turned off the engine.

Tried to turn it off, that is. The engine wouldn't shut down.

Meanwhile, a car had come behind me and honked its horn. Jerk. Being in neutral, I walked the scooter to the curb to allow the car to pass. All along, I kept turning the key, trying to turn off the engine. I helplessly looked down at it, wondering if there was a wire I could pull or something else to shut it off.

Then, the scooter put itself into gear. With a lurch that snapped my head back, it shot forward, popped a wheelie, and like a bucking bronco rearing on its hind legs, threw me onto the sidewalk. The scooter's front wheel touched down. Somehow, it remained upright and drove away.

That's when I realized I was the victim of a magic attack. My scooter had become possessed. It drove away from me on my intended route as if a demon were riding it. But I knew magic was the cause.

The scooter turned around flawlessly, without wobbling or tipping over.

And came at full speed right at me.

Though I didn't intend to, I stood there and watched it streak toward me like a charging bull. At the last second, I regained control of my frozen legs and stepped to the side, allowing the scooter to just miss me as if I were a matador.

Well, I wasn't brave like a matador, that's for sure. I screamed and ran down the sidewalk and into a parking lot.

The scooter was right behind me.

The parking lot was nearly full, since this was tourist season, and I ran between and around cars, making myself as difficult a target as possible. Even so, my beloved scooter stayed only a few yards behind me. It bounced off car doors, scraped bumpers, and knocked off side-mirrors while still keeping up with me.

I was tiring quickly. If I tripped and fell, I was a goner.

Someone whistled, and I looked over to see a college student filming me with his camera. Great. The video of a middle-aged woman being chased through a parking lot by a riderless motor scooter would surely go viral. My reputation as a kook would be enhanced locally.

Would the video include footage of me being caught and killed by my own vehicle? Probably.

"Would you freaking help me out here?" I shouted at the videographer. He waved at me and kept on filming.

I calculated how much gas was left in the tank and if my human energy would outlast the gas. It didn't look good for me.

In the end, the only thing that saved me was an old lady in a big boat of an American car from an earlier era. She flung open the door of her just-parked car right after I ran past it. The door dinged the car next to her and stayed open a long time as she struggled to get out.

The scooter, roaring not far behind me, smashed into the inside of her door. It flipped into the air, did a somersault, and went through the windshield of a blue BMW parked across from the old lady.

The old lady didn't even notice it as she clawed her way out of the low front seat.

The scooter's engine revved, the rear wheel continued to spin, but the scooter, tangled in shattered glass in the front seat, wasn't going anywhere.

I stopped, bent over, gasping for air. My life was saved.

Who was responsible for this? It had to be Texas Tom. Perhaps he found out that I have the key. Glancing around, I didn't see anyone watching, aside from the videographer, the old lady, and a woman who had heard the crash and came running. I think she was the owner of the BMW.

"My car! What did you do to my car! Were you driving drunk?"

The woman who owned the BMW was Dorothy Gilley.

"It was an engine malfunction. Sorry."

"Darla, what on earth are you doing here?"

"Just trying to survive."

It occurred to me I was going to receive a big fat traffic ticket for this. And that I no longer had any means of transportation, with my car stolen by Tom, and my motor scooter having gone to the dark side.

I gave the videographer, who was still shooting me, a one-finger salute.

CHAPTER 16

RECIPE FOR MAGIC

Dorothy called the police. Both of us and the old lady needed accident reports for the insurance claims. While we waited, I texted Cory to tell him about the accident. I told him I could walk home from here, but obviously couldn't bring them the pearl. He replied that Sophie and he would pick me up.

His text was full of typos. Not using a smartphone for a year in earth time, twice that duration in In-Between time, had caused his phone skills to deteriorate. We had to buy him a new phone after he escaped from Texas Tom. We were going to buy him a car, too, since he was sharing Sophie's. Now, she had the only running vehicle in the household.

"Of all the cars in the parking lot, why did you have to crash into mine?" Dorothy whined.

"I didn't choose yours. My motor scooter did. It was out of control and the engine wouldn't turn off. The scooter hit this lady's door and flipped into your windshield."

I couldn't tell her the scooter was possessed by magic. Dorothy surely thought I was crazy already. Telling her that would send a valuable source of information running from me for good.

Dorothy sighed and pouted. I have to admit, at first, I was happy that the car my scooter had leaped into was a luxury car, not a vehicle that belonged to a working-class person. However, now I felt pretty rotten about it.

After the police officer left, I offered to buy Dorothy a coffee.

"No, thanks. I need to be on my way as soon as the rental car gets here."

"Please," I said. "I want to make amends."

"You don't need to. I know it wasn't your fault."

She wants to pump me for information again, her thoughts said in my head. *Dick will be suspicious if I'm not home soon.*

"Another time, maybe?" She glanced at her watch.

"Sure," I said. "Have a nice day."

I trudged to the street and waited for my ride. Dorothy was truly afraid of her husband, I thought. Their marriage sounded toxic. She probably regrets stealing his key, and I hoped her safety wasn't at risk.

THE DEALERSHIP THAT SOLD ME THE SCOOTER RETRIEVED IT from the accident scene and brought it to their own repair shop. The rep I spoke to over the phone assured me that my scooter's malfunction should never have happened. He didn't go so far as to blame me, but he left the possibility lingering in the air that I was somehow at fault.

I was boiling mad, but controlled myself, because all I wanted was my scooter to be fixed. I wished I could defend myself by telling him the malfunction was surely caused by magic, but I didn't. It would probably mess up my insurance claim.

That evening, Cory, Sophie, and I had a simple meal of baked chicken thighs with a salad. And wine. Yes, even though I had finished a leftover bottle at the end of the wine reception, I opened another for dinner. Call it self-medicating, if you will. I called it a de-frazzle process after almost being killed by my magic-possessed motor scooter.

When the meal ended, Sophie left, and I got ready to go to bed early. Mom showed up uninvited at the cottage.

"After you left my house, we made good progress on creating a spell," she said. "The more I think about it, the more I believe the pearl will make it work. The way Cory described the pearl's ability to summon the Fae, it's just what we need."

"Alleged ability to summon them," Cory said. "According to Tom, and he's a big liar."

"It can't hurt to try, can it? I brought all the ingredients for the potion I plan to make." She held up a stuffed tote bag.

"Mom, how 'bout we try tomorrow? I want to go to bed soon."

"Darla, are you drunk?"

"Tipsy," I said. "In case you haven't noticed, I'm above the minimum drinking age. Way above."

"You don't have to stay up with us. You're not a witch, after all."

"Thanks for reminding me I'm the only non-witch of the family."

"Oh, get over yourself," Mom said, pushing her way into the cottage. "Where's Sophie?"

"She's in her room."

"Get her down here. This will be fun."

It wasn't fun for me. I lay on the couch while the three witches sat around the tiny dining table. The pearl rested on an oven mitt in the center of the table, an icon of perfection amid the confusion. Mom went into the kitchen to boil water and ruin my spice grinder by using it on foul-smelling plants and who knows what else.

After she brewed her potion, and stank up the entire place Darren-style, she poured the nasty brew into a mason jar. This, she set on the oven mitt beside the pearl. Cory produced the golden key and placed it on the oven mitt, as well. He'd had it in his wallet, not realizing the irony of keeping it there.

The three leaned in and put their hands atop each other on the lid of the mason jar. Sophie claimed she was transferring to it energy she had harvested at the beach. Cory mumbled an incantation he said was for a spell for long-distance vision.

To be quite honest, the whole thing looked really corny. My family members reminded me of young children having a tea party. Don't accuse me of being jealous—if you saw this scene, you'd think the same thing.

But an unexpected thing happened: the pearl began to glow brightly.

"Is it working?" Sophie whispered with excitement.

"The pearl glowed like this when Arch Mage Bob used it with his magic," Cory said.

"By Jove, I think we've done it!" Mom exclaimed.

"Done what?" I asked from the cheap seats. "You made the pearl glow. How are you going to find out where the Fae are?"

The three witches looked at each other in puzzlement.

"Can we connect the pearl to the map app on my phone?" Sophie asked.

No one answered, rightly so. Until a thought popped into my head.

"You know, there might be something to what Sophie just said."

The three looked at me with the same puzzled expression.

"I mean, what the heck? Sophie, cast the spell that finds your phone. That will connect the phone to magic. Then, open the map app and hold the phone up to the pearl and the potion," I said. "Let's see if anything happens."

Sophie mumbled an invocation and opened her map app.

"Put it in satellite view," Cory said.

Sophie held the phone just above the objects on the oven mitt. Nothing happened. She did so until she complained her arm was tired. She set down the phone with one end on the pearl and the other angled upward to lean against the mason jar.

"Okay, I concede it was a ridiculous suggestion," I said.

The phone buzzed, not from a notification, but with a long, sustained vibration. Everyone crowded around to look at the screen, myself included. It showed a satellite photo of the countryside: a few green fields and a vast forest.

"Pardon me," I said, reaching to the screen.

Careful not to knock the phone off its perch, I used my fingers to zoom out on the image until we could see the lines of two state and county roads bisecting. Now I knew the general location west of San Marcos. I zoomed back in, closer this time, and realized what we were looking at.

The forest surrounding the Gilley estate.

Dorothy claimed she had seen faeries in these woods. Now, I believed her.

"I know where this is," I said. "It's near the home of the woman Hugo had an affair with."

A unified, three-way gasp came from the witches.

"That's a pretty big piece of forest," Cory said.

"Yeah. If it's true that the Fae are living below ground, we'd have to find an entrance to their tunnels. We can't zoom in that tight with the app. We'll have to locate it on the ground."

"Perhaps, if we bring the pearl and the potion with us, they'll help with our search," Mom said.

I looked at her with concern. "Us? I don't know if it's a good idea for all four of us to be traipsing around in those woods. It's probably dangerous."

"You think I'm too old?" Mom asked testily.

"I didn't say that."

"Well, I say you're correct in this circumstance. I'll stay in the car."

"We'll go out there in the morning," I said, "after we finish breakfast service."

No matter how much I tried to live a life of action and adventure, there's no avoiding my mundane responsibilities as an innkeeper. James Bond I was not.

"So, if we find a tunnel entrance, what do we do then?" Cory asked, always the practical one.

I was tempted to say, "improvise," but that would be reckless when my family members were involved. Also, it was important to set realistic expectations. We weren't going to explore a network of tunnels looking for Cervantes and an ancient jar. Especially not with faeries running around.

We wouldn't go into the tunnels at all. Cory and Sophie would, however, try to reach Cervantes telepathically and see if he could escape.

CORY'S SNORING WOKE ME UP. I STIFLED THE URGE TO smother him with a pillow and rolled over, slowly drifting off again.

Short dreams followed, each one strange and unsettling. I was giving birth, but it wasn't like when I had Sophie. I was lying on my back on an animal skin beneath the stars, a campfire flickering at the edge of my vision. A midwife held my hand while her other hand rubbed my stomach with a foul-smelling ointment that was warm on my skin.

She chanted in a strange language I'd never heard before. She peered down at me, her face only inches from mine, and spoke. Now, I could understand what she said.

"The world is grateful to you, Mother of Life."

Mother of Life?

My contractions increased in timing and severity, while sparks from the fire swirled in the sky. No, it was the stars themselves that were swirling.

The pain was intense, and I was drenched in sweat. What happened to my epidural? I wondered.

"Where's the doctor? I need another shot."

The midwife didn't answer me. Instead, she placed a branch of aromatic leaves upon my heaving stomach.

I think I fainted briefly. When I came to, the midwife was helping the baby from me. I moaned in pain. The midwife smiled with delight and held the baby up for me to see.

It was slick with amniotic fluid. But it wasn't my baby. It couldn't be.

It was a tiny calf.

I screamed in horror.

And went straight into the next dream. I was deep in a vast forest of towering trees. Although it was daytime, the forest was dark from the tree shade. I wore a soft tunic of silk and strode upon sandals through the trees, listening to the happy cacophony of voices coming from beneath the soil.

The trees were talking to each other. And I was their mother

—not just the mother of the trees, but of all the creatures in the forest and the countryside. I walked among the trees and bushes feeling their love for me, returning it with all my heart. My purpose was to protect and nourish them, while their purpose was to grow and reproduce, bringing oxygen for other creatures to breathe, as well as produce fruit and nuts for the forest creatures to eat.

The birds were mine. The insects were mine. The creek that ran nearby was inhabited by my children, too.

With my love, I felt an enormous responsibility for the welfare of my children. I also felt power. I didn't know exactly what the power was, but it made me feel invincible and able to shape the world in beneficial ways.

I felt as if I could tear the evils of the world asunder. In fact, I heard the walls of an evil city tumbling down—

No. That sound was Cory snoring.

I lay awake, thinking about my dream, still vivid in my memory. It wasn't like me to have grandiose dreams like that. Maybe it was something I ate the night before.

My dreams are usually forgotten the moment I set my feet on the floor. But this one remained with me, pestering me to figure out what it meant. Unfortunately, I didn't have time to research dream symbolism.

I had the weirdness of my real life to interpret. For instance, why was a seedling growing out of the grout in the corner of my shower?

Yeah, really. I keep an immaculate inn, but with my heavy workload, I occasionally neglect my own bathroom. So, yes, I've had to remove mildew from the shower now and then.

But a three-inch-tall seedling? How did this get here and how did I not notice it until now?

What was the deal with all the plants invading our home? We

didn't exactly live in a jungle, after all. Maybe there really was something supernatural going on.

I didn't know what kind of plant this was. Strangely, I had no urge to yank it out like a weed and toss it in the trash. Carefully, I pried out its tiny roots, carried it outside, and replanted it in a courtyard flowerbed.

"You'll like it much better out here," I said to the seedling.

Funny, but I sensed it agreed.

CHAPTER 17

SEE THE FOREST

"This seems kind of random," Cory said. "We're just walking around in circles."

"It's not random," I said. "We're walking in *concentric* circles."

"Not exactly circles," Sophie said.

She was right. The forest was so dense, we had to zigzag a lot to avoid thick clumps of palmettos, fallen logs, and places where the undergrowth was simply too dense to push through. Cory carried the pearl, Sophie held Mom's magic-sensing potion, and I had the key.

In theory, if we approached a tunnel entrance or a place where the Fae were active, the spell tying the three objects together would alert us. In theory. I know it was a slapdash way of doing magic, but absent a highly experienced witch or wizard, this was the best we could do.

Some families spend quality time together hiking in the woods. Mine carried around improvised magic in search of hostile faeries who would imprison or kill us if we were caught. True quality time.

"Watch out for snakes," Cory said.

"Great, like this wasn't messed up enough," Sophie said.

"I'm watching out for faeries," I said. "In their natural form, they're around two feet tall and have wings like an insect. They could hide easily in the underbrush. They can also take human form. I saw one who turned into a goblin. There's no missing a goblin—you'll know if you see one."

"This is insane," Sophie said. "We should go back to the car now."

"Don't you want to find Cervantes? My theory is the closer we are to him physically, the easier it will be for you guys to contact him telepathically. We'll try to lead him to us, then take him home."

In theory.

We weren't relying totally on magic. I had my map app open, helping us navigate our concentric circles through the forest. Unfortunately, it could zoom in only so far.

Cory stopped suddenly. "Look up there."

He pointed to the twisted branches of a southern live oak tree. A red ribbon fluttered from an upper branch.

"That has to be a marker of some sort from the Fae," he said. "A human surveyor would have placed it more at eye level."

"Does it mean a tunnel entrance is nearby?" I asked.

Of course, no one had the answer. We searched around the circumference of the tree. There was no sign of any entrance among the ferns and piles of leaves below the tree.

"Maybe it's just a trail marker," Cory said.

"What trail?" Sophie asked.

I realized the Fae would use magic to conceal a tunnel opening, to make it invisible to human eyes. But maybe not in all cases. The gopher tortoise burrow where Cervantes had disappeared was not concealed.

"Send a message to Cervantes," I said.

Sophie and Cory closed their eyes. Their lips moved wordlessly.

We stood in silence for several minutes. There was no answering call in my head, only frustrated thought fragments from Sophie and Cory. A slight breeze rustled the leaves at the top of the oak. A crow cawed from a nearby tree.

We continued to plow through the thick woods, rays of late-morning light streaking through the canopy above. I was afraid we wouldn't get back to the inn before Teatime. As if that would be the worst calamity.

Our concentric circles, or erratic curves, were bringing us closer to the center of the large forest. I didn't know if any of this land was part of the Gilley estate, or if it was owned by the state or another landowner. We might be trespassing and needed to fear coming upon a human as much as stumbling upon a faerie.

"Do faeries come out during the day?" Sophie asked. "Or are they nocturnal?"

"I don't know," I said.

Cory gave me a sideways glance. "You didn't exactly do your homework before this expedition."

"I'm not much of a planner. You knew that before you married me."

"How was I supposed to know I'd be following you on a mission to find dangerous, mythological creatures?"

"Life is full of surprises."

As if to punctuate my cliche, Cory yelped suddenly and shot up into the air upside down. Sophie screamed. My heart stopped.

Cory hung from a cord wrapped around his ankle and tied around a bough of a large oak tree. His head dangled about four feet above the ground. He'd been caught not by faerie magic, but with an old-fashioned snare.

"Are you okay?" Sophie asked.

"Do I look okay?"

"Your hair is really messed up," I said.

"Get. Me. Down. From. Here."

"Do you think you can climb the tree?" I asked Sophie.

"Yeah."

"Here." I handed her a pocketknife. See, I wasn't totally unprepared. And, I should add, we also had my handgun in Cory's backpack, though I don't know if bullets harm faeries.

I needed to boost Sophie to reach the lowest limb. After that, she had no problem climbing to the limb where the snare was tied, shimmying out to it, and leaning over to saw at the cord.

"I'm going to break my neck," Cory said.

"Use your arms to brace yourself. I'll try to catch you."

"Darla, I'm much bigger than you. You can't catch me."

"I'll soften the impact."

"Don't stand there, you're going to be—"

The cord severed. Cory dropped and landed on me, knocking my wind out.

"Hurt," I gasped.

"Are you guys all right?" Sophie called down to us.

We untangled ourselves. There were no broken bones, but probably some bruises.

"So far, it's faeries one, humans zero," Cory said.

"We're lucky they didn't attack us with magic," Sophie said.

"Don't speak too soon. Man, that was not good for my back and ankle."

"Can you walk?" I asked.

"I'll manage."

We continued onward, our circles getting smaller according to the GPS on my phone, though it was impossible to tell visually in the dense woods. Soon, though, I noticed a change in terrain. Pine trees dominated, and there was less undergrowth. The ground was carpeted with pine needles. It was easier to move around.

Despite not having the magic gene, I sensed an otherworldly presence here. The hairs on my head prickled.

"The pearl!" Cory whispered.

In his outstretched hand, the tennis-ball-sized pearl glowed with a pulsating light from within.

I searched for signs of a tunnel opening.

"Send out messages for—"

I jumped as something rubbed against my leg.

It was Cervantes. I shushed Sophie and Cory before they could make any sounds of delight. The Fae surely had sentries nearby.

Cory put the pearl in his satchel and picked up our black cat.

"Cervantes asked what took us so long," he whispered.

"Tell him if he escaped from the tunnels now, he should have done so a long time ago."

"He said they've only allowed him out of his cage recently."

"Ask him where the tunnel entrance is that he escaped from."

Cory said, "At the base of this tree here, he says. But I don't see any opening."

He kicked the leaves away from the roots of an oak tree. There was no sign of an opening.

"Is there a hidden trapdoor?" I asked.

"No. Cervantes says you can only enter and exit using magic."

"Then how did he escape?"

Cervantes let out a cocky chest-beating *meow*.

"That's his version of bragging about his magic," Cory said.

"Okay, let's get out of here fast." I beckoned to the others to follow me on a path bisecting our circles to the place where we had entered the forest and our car waited.

As soon as we set out, the orbs appeared.

I've seen orbs before at the inn; the glowing white or yellow spheres would shoot by in my peripheral vision as manifestations of yet-to-be-identified ghosts.

These orbs here in the woods were different. Larger than those in the inn, purple, and seemingly intelligent, one buzzed right over our heads before disappearing into the trees. Soon, another appeared, hovering above us.

I had no doubt they were faerie surveillance. Magic drones, if you will. By the looks on Cory's and Sophie's faces, they knew it, too. We had no choice but to keep walking and hopefully get away from their territory without being attacked. I believed the fact it was daytime prevented the Fae from coming above ground to chase us.

I have been known to be wrong, though.

After we left the pine forest, I found a faint trail made by animals, so it made the travel much easier through the denser oak and palmetto woods. Up ahead, I was surprised to see a masonry wall at the edge of someone's property. Further back behind the wall, the second story of a large house came into view.

I recognized the Gilley house. Boy, the Fae territory was much closer to the house than I had realized.

As we drew near the road, the trees thinned out somewhat. The orbs, thankfully, had disappeared. Mom's SUV sat on the dirt shoulder waiting for us, our salvation.

Mom jumped out of the car.

"Thank goodness you're back," she said. "You were gone so long I was about to panic. Oh, look, it's Cervantes!"

He mrmphed in greeting.

Cory got into the back seat, still holding Cervantes as if he feared the cat would bolt from his arms. Sophie climbed into the seat beside him. I was about to get into the front seat when I heard a rattling noise approaching and the whirring of tires.

A golf cart appeared from around a curve in the road. It stuck to the shoulder and came right at us before stopping inches from Mom's vehicle. It was a red two-seater with a rearward-facing flip seat in the back.

The driver was Dorothy Gilley.

"Darla, what brings you out here?"

"Um, just going for a hike in the woods."

"There aren't any trails in there."

Yes, I realized my lie was very lame.

"Besides," Dorothy continued, "most of this is our property."

"It is? Sorry. Didn't mean to be trespassing. The truth is, we were searching for our cat who escaped."

Dorothy peered into the SUV. "I see you found him."

"Yes. I'm so relieved."

"Why would he be here, so far from your inn?"

"We were out for a drive. Cervantes jumped out the window and ran into the woods. He must have seen a critter. It took forever to track him down in there."

My new lie seemed to satisfy her.

"Any news on the investigation into, you know?" she asked.

"The police won't tell me anything. I still think Hugo's partner did it."

She seemed unsatisfied. "Oh, I don't know."

"Then who do you suspect?"

She shrugged and glanced behind her toward her home. "Oh, I can't say for sure. Jealousy can come from other directions."

"Who do you mean?" I asked, feigning incomprehension.

"Nobody. It doesn't matter."

"Well, we must be going," I said. "Sorry for going onto your property."

"They're only woods. I'm glad you found your cat."

I jumped into the front seat and breathed a sigh of relief. The golf cart turned around on the shoulder and whirred off toward Dorothy's home.

"That was weird," Cory said.

"Yeah. How did she know we were here?"

I thought of the orbs, of course, but how would they alert her? Maybe there are cameras.

"No," Cory said. "I was talking about the pearl. It stopped glowing after we left the pine grove, but it started again when the lady showed up."

"Really?" Sophie asked. "The jar of Grammer's potion got super-hot while she was here."

"Does that mean Dorothy is a faerie?" I asked in disbelief.

Cory opened his satchel to examine the pearl more closely.

"The glow has a different hue to it than when we were near the tunnels."

"I think our spell is saying the woman has magic," Mom said. "Plain old witchy magic."

"Hugo was a better instructor than I thought," I said. "Maybe even better than he realized himself."

I wondered if she had magic powerful enough to murder her instructor. If so, why wouldn't she encourage my theory that Vance did it?

"Cervantes says when he was on the beach that night, after Sophie and I left, he returned to where we had been. He heard a woman's voice arguing with Hugo. He admits he got scared and ran away, so he doesn't know what happened next."

It figures our magical witch's familiar would be a scaredy-cat, just like the rest of his species.

It appeared Dorothy could be involved in all of this far more than I had imagined, both in Hugo's murder and with the Fae.

How could I learn more? Let's see, I could rely on a certain detective to plod ahead methodically. Or, not having any true detective skills, I could use my paranormal abilities.

And you know that saying, if all you have is a hammer. . .

CHAPTER 18

SNEAK ATTACK

I awoke to a sharp buzzing in my ears. It was like a chainsaw cutting through my head, hurting everything from the top of my skull to my teeth.

I thought I was having a stroke. This is the way your mind works at my age: "What is the most likely bad thing that could happen to me now? Heart attack or stroke."

It wasn't either one, as it turned out, though I wasn't certain at first. The buzzing continued so insistently I thought it was coming from somewhere in the cottage. However, Cory slept unbothered. If he was snoring, I wouldn't be able to tell with all the buzzing. No, the buzzing was coming from my head.

Please stop, I thought. This is painful.

Without a transition, I was standing in the meeting hall of the Memory Guild. I glanced down to make sure I wasn't wearing only a T-shirt and panties like I was in bed. Thankfully, I was dressed as I was before retiring for the night, in a high-collared Victorian-style dress that I wore to add color to the evening Wine Hour.

The painful buzzing continued. The expressions on the faces of my fellow guild members told me they were experiencing the same thing.

Dr. Noordlun wasn't here.

"Where is the professor?" I asked. "What's going on?"

I was met with frustrated stares. Hey, sorry, I'm the new girl.

"This has never happened before," Diana said. "I believe there's something wrong at the Hall of Records."

Summer said, "I think it's under attack. Dr. Noordlun is probably there trying to defend it."

"Is it the Fae?" I asked.

Summer nodded, her face solemn. "I sense they are involved. Probably under the influence of the Father of Lies."

"Diana, send us there," Laurel said.

"It's not that simple. I can't drop us right into a cauldron of trouble. It would be too dangerous. The Fae's magic can harm us even while in our astral forms."

"How could attackers get to the Hall of Records if it's a virtual plane of existence created just for us?" I asked.

"Betrayal," Diego said gravely. Every face turned toward him. "One of our minds betrayed details of the hall's existence."

I figured I would get blamed as the new kid and the only guild member to be interacting with the Fae, as far as I knew.

"None of us knows how to get there," I said.

"I get us there, but I don't have any information that would help an outsider," Diana said. "I only use my memory of the place to guide the magic that enables our astral travel."

"Then it must be Dr. Noordlun," Diego said.

I gasped, as did a few others.

"No, I do not mean he betrayed us intentionally. The intruders hijacked his mind. Dr. Noordlun knows more than any of us about the Hall of Records. He was behind its conception and located the Tugara to bring there. Only he could show Diana how to get there so that she could then send the rest of us. But we have been there only as our astral selves. Dr. Noordlun has been there physically."

"I thought the plane of existence was only astral," I said.

Diana shook her head. "The Tugara are physical creatures. They need actual brains to hold all the memories we have given them and must live in a physical place. We visit the Hall of Records as our spirit selves because it is so much easier."

"I don't want to tell you what to do," I said. "But I think it's time you drop us into the 'cauldron of trouble.' We're all uneasy because we don't have our leader with us and don't know what we're getting into. Dr. Noordlun needs us, though."

"I agree," James said.

"Me, too," said Gloria,

The rest of our guild's tiny membership voiced their consensus.

"So be it." Diana closed her eyes and chanted something unintelligible for a few moments. "Into the cauldron, we shall go."

She clapped her hands.

And we were instantly in the Hall of Records. A cauldron of trouble was putting it mildly.

The Tugara were no longer in orderly rows but were clustered together at the end of the hall like herd animals stalked by wolves. The wolves were the faeries in their natural forms, buzzing above them like mosquitoes, before darting in to stab the giant beasts with small spears.

Dr. Noordlun stood in front of the Tugara, trying and failing to protect them. Bolts of electricity shot from his fingers, driving the faeries back, but only temporarily. Though he wasn't a witch, Sven Noordlun had the paranormal ability to amass and manipulate energy from the ley lines like Cory could.

One faerie dropped to the floor after being hit by the mini lightning bolts. Otherwise, the energy only held the swarm at bay. Observing Dr. Noordlun, I saw the power of his bolts was fading as the energy within him was used up.

Including the faerie twitching on the floor, the attackers numbered eight. While the rest of us stood around, unsure of what to do, Diego rushed toward the swarm and leaped into the air. His arms encircled a faery.

Then he passed right through the faerie's body like a ghost and dropped to the floor.

"We're here as our spiritual selves," Diana said. "The faeries and Dr. Noordlun are here in their corporeal bodies."

"How did they get here like that?" I asked.

"I don't know."

"What are we supposed to do to stop the faeries?" James asked.

I knew of only one way to travel in my physical body to other planes of existence. Via the In Between. But how could I get a gateway to bring me here?

I would have to wing it.

"Diana, please send me home."

"You're throwing in the towel?" Archibald asked.

"I'm going to come back here in my own body."

"How in heaven's name will you do that?"

"I'm not sure yet. I'll figure it out as I go along. Diana?"

She made her hand gestures, and I was instantly lying on the bed next to a snoring Cory. The displacement of energy woke him up, and he blinked at me in confusion.

"Did you go somewhere?" he asked.

"In a manner of speaking. Get dressed fast and grab the pearl. We have an errand to do."

"What are you talking about?"

"We have to fight faeries."

"Oh. Silly me for not having guessed."

He jumped out of bed and threw on jeans and a T-shirt while I did the same. As if fighting faeries was a normal errand that didn't require questioning.

The first stumbling block of my by-the-seat-of-my-pants plan was how to summon a gateway. They had been notably more cooperative with me of late, but I couldn't summon them at will or direct them where to take me without help from magic, such as Missy's Red Dragon talisman.

I hoped a gateway was nearby and would be sympathetic to my request.

Turns out, I was lucky.

As soon as I said, "I need a gateway," a shimmering oval appeared in the bedroom doorway. It was almost too easy. I wondered why.

"Do you have the pearl?" I asked Cory.

He nodded, looking at the gateway with unease. It took a long while to get accustomed to traveling this way. Even I wasn't used to it yet.

Gateway, I hope you can understand me, I said to it telepathically. *We need to go to the Memory Guild's Hall of Records. I don't know how to get there, but here's a mental image of it.*

I pictured the hall as it was the first time I had seen it: pristine, orderly, and lacking a swarm of faeries.

Can you take us there without us having to change trains at the In between?

Traveling to a different moment in time on earth required going from the earth to the In Between, then traveling back to earth to the different time period. Since we were remaining in the present, I hoped the gateway could take us directly to the Hall of Records.

The gateway faded somewhat. I didn't trust walking through it in its weakened state.

"I think it's calculating how to get to our destination," I said to Cory.

The gateway disappeared. My spirits fell.

"What did I do wrong?"

The gateway was back, its shimmering air nearly opaque.

I turned to Cory. "Ready?"

He nodded. And we walked, hand-in-hand to the bedroom doorway, the usual nausea and headache hitting me. I led the way into the portal.

We landed in the corner of the magical hall, with a view of the battle before us. Dr. Noordlun was still crouched in front of the Tugara, shooting electrical bolts at the swarming faeries. His power was clearly fading, and the faeries were pushing in.

One got close enough to thrust its spear into a Tugara. The giant, slug-shaped beast made a whimpering sound, and a jumble of random memories I didn't recognize briefly filled my mind. Memories that were lost, like blood flowing from the creature that had held them.

My fellow Memory Guild members jumped up and down powerlessly, trying to distract the faeries. It wasn't working.

Cory and I had to do something fast, or the battle would be lost.

We rushed to Dr. Noordlun's side. It felt so different being in the hall physically. The air was dry, the temperature cold, and my sensations were a hundred times more vivid. The light pouring in through skylights seemed like normal sunshine. I ventured a look up and saw a sky that was purple instead of the blue of the earth's.

I knew we weren't on another planet. Nor were we in the In Between. The hall was on a plane of existence all its own, though I didn't know how it had been created and with what kind of magic.

I returned my thoughts to the crisis at hand.

"What can you do with your magic?" I asked Cory.

"I'm trying to build a protection spell around us and these. . . creatures. I'm using the power of the pearl to add strength."

Another of the beasts whimpered as a spear struck it. I raced over and pulled the weapon from the giant creature as lost memories arced across my vision.

The faerie who had thrown the spear swooped in to snatch it back. He grabbed the shaft, but I clung fiercely to it. Being that the faerie was only about twenty-four inches tall, this was a rare moment I was actually taller than another adult.

The faerie was stronger than I thought. His feral face with the long nose and pointy ears grimaced, his wings beating furiously, as he kicked me and tried to pry the spear from my hand.

I punched him with my other hand, clocking him in the jaw. To my surprise, the faerie went limp and fell to the floor. Enraged, I picked him up and threw the stunned body at the nearest faerie, knocking him out of the air. I ran to this one and kicked him with all my might, sending him crashing into the marble wall before dropping to the floor.

The faeries, realizing Cory and I were corporeal, flew away from our reach. Just because we were physically stronger than they were didn't mean we weren't vulnerable to their magic.

As soon as they hovered further away, Cory let out a whoop.

"I've closed off a protective bubble around us and the creatures."

"They're called Tugara," I said.

A faerie spear bounced off the outside of the bubble, proving the bubble's efficacy.

"How long will it hold?" Dr. Noordlun asked Cory.

"No clue. I'm kind of new at this."

"How did the faeries get here?" I asked the professor.

"I don't know. Perhaps the same way you did."

How did Dr. Noordlun get here? I wondered, afraid to ask. I didn't think he had ever traveled through a gateway before.

"We need to kill them or drive them away quickly," Dr. Noordlun said. "Can the pearl help us?"

The pearl was aligned to Fae magic to some degree. Yet, its power was primeval, from long before the Fae even existed. I hadn't handled it in a long time. I wondered if anything would be different now.

"Let me have the pearl," I said to Cory.

"Now? I think I need to keep holding it to keep my spell activated."

"You might be right." I stood next to him. "Keep the pearl in your hand, but turn it so I can touch it, too."

He turned his hand so that the pearl was resting on his palm. I placed my hand atop the gem, which was wildly hot to the touch.

Nothing happened, though I didn't expect anything in particular.

The faeries flew around the bubble, poking it with their spears to look for weak spots. They jabbered at each other. The oldest one landed just outside of the bubble and knelt upon the floor.

"He's conjuring magic," Dr. Noordlun said. I'd never seen him so exhausted and frightened before. "We need to keep them out of here. This is just a raiding party, and they could call for reinforcements."

Who was singing? A haunting female voice made it difficult to hear what Dr. Noordlun was saying. I looked around the hall. It wasn't anyone in here.

No, the song was coming into my head from the pearl. It flowed up my arm, through my heart, and into my head.

My vision became hyper-focused, yet at the same time, I felt less present in the hall. It was as if I were above it all. Beyond space and time. What was coming over me?

Barely perceptible whimpering came from the wounded Tugara. Empathy and love filled my heart. I wanted to heal these creatures, my children. Though I sensed they lived for millennia, I knew they could die from injuries or disease.

Dragging the pearl and Cory with me, I approached the two wounded Tugara. I placed my free hand upon each wound, feeling it close beneath my palm, knowing the pain was subsiding.

When I removed my hand, none of the wounds had a scar or mark at all.

I was stunned. Was the pearl alone powerful enough to enable me to do this? Somehow, I felt as if something inside of me had changed.

The skin I touched was old and leathery, as much like a book cover as the hide of an elephant. The markings, which at a distance made the creatures' sides look like rows of books, were natural patterns on the skin like reptile coloration.

When the healing was complete, I stepped back to regard the twelve creatures. The song that ran through me from the pearl flowed into them, as well. I felt like one with them. As if they were my children, although my human body was the smallest fraction of the age of theirs.

On the Tugara nearest to me, it looked as if a fresh wound was opening in its hide. The opening revealed a giant eye that looked at me with great intelligence. And gratitude.

Jabbering from the faeries broke my mental connection to the Tugara and brought me back to reality—somewhat. I still felt dreamy, and the song still played in my head. But I remembered I had unfinished business.

The Fae raiding party. How could I help get rid of them?

For some reason, any thought of harming or killing the faeries was impossible to consider. In fact, I had a brief flash of guilt for my very human acts of hitting and kicking them.

The solution came to me: an ally would assist.

A large patch of shimmering air appeared at the far end of the hall. It moved toward the protection bubble, growing gradually in size until it was nearly as high as the three-story ceiling.

A gateway had answered my summons.

No, it was not an escape hatch for Dr. Noordlun, Cory, and me. We remained safe inside the bubble, while the gateway swooped in on the faeries. They were so preoccupied with us, they didn't sense the gateway or turn to see it until it was too late.

The gateway sucked up the faeries like a giant vacuum cleaner. It simply moved close to them, and its gravitational pull plucked them from the hall, singly and in pairs, until all eight were gone. I assumed they were deposited in the In Between, but who knows?

"Did I just see what I think I saw?" Cory asked, astounded.

"Yep. The gateways and I are becoming buddies. Go figure."

"You don't know how grateful I am, Darla," Dr. Noordlun said. "I speak for the entire guild. Unfortunately, now that enemies have breached the Hall of Records in corporeal form, I don't know how to make it safe again. I never imagined this could happen."

"I don't understand how this place exists in corporeal form."

"Magic. Many years ago, when my father founded the Memory Guild, he enlisted a wizard, one of the most powerful of his time, to create this place. It is based on the physics behind the In Between, which, of course, has divine origins as a stopover for recently departed souls, but has been enhanced over the millennia by the imaginations of humans.

"The Hall of Records is a much humbler endeavor. It, too, is a separate plane of existence, but it is adjacent to the one we inhabit. It's not dissimilar to the chamber where the guild meets in astral form, but it needs a physical component to house the Tugara."

"And where did they come from?" I asked.

"The In Between. Where else?"

"How did you heal them like that?" Diana asked.

"I don't know exactly. Because of the pearl?"

"There's more to it than that," Summer said, looking at me like she knew something I didn't.

"How did the Fae find the hall?" I asked.

"We need to learn the answer to your question." Dr. Noordlun studied me with a grave expression. "I assume the Father of Lies found it, perhaps by reading my mind. I will consult with the Magic Guild for help in protecting the archives. We need to expect more attacks upon the Hall of Records. And upon ourselves."

CHAPTER 19

GOING ROGUE

The logical part of my brain kept telling me this was a colossally stupid idea. I told the logical part of my brain to shut up.

It was about 10:00 p.m. and I was making my way through the same part of the forest we had emerged from last time. The moon was nearly full, and the sky was clear, which was fortunate. I needed the light to keep from tripping on tree roots and breaking my bones, since it was too risky to use a flashlight.

As if simply coming here at all wasn't too risky.

I was determined to read as many of Dorothy's memories as I could get my hands on. Specifically, from her golf cart. If I could find the cart, its steering wheel would be accessible, unlike the one in her locked car. If the cart wasn't locked away somewhere, that is.

I hoped it wouldn't be. The people I knew who had golf carts were rather lax about security. If I was lucky, the Gilleys' cart would be outside somewhere, charging. If it was in their garage, maybe I could get inside.

The important thing was, I wouldn't need to get inside the house itself to handle her stuff. That would be suicidal.

Speaking of suicidal, did I mention I wasn't armed? If I was caught, and the police were called, I did not want to have a weapon on me.

You probably think I'm a nut, and you're right. However, this mission was meant to be quick and surgical. If I couldn't get to the golf cart, or find something else outside that might hold memories, such as lawn chairs or gardening tools, I would leave immediately.

I didn't tell Cory or Sophie that I was coming here, because they wouldn't have allowed me. Or, if they had wanted to go with me, I couldn't put them in needless danger while I only wanted to read memories.

Cory went to bed early, and I slipped away soon afterwards. I had my phone if I needed help, and just in case, I left a note in the bathroom telling Cory where I went. Like most middle-aged men, he reliably wakes up more than once in the night to go to the bathroom. I was pretty sure I'd be home long before his bladder called.

Now, if I could only make it to the Gilleys' yard without getting lost. I wouldn't climb over the wall but go around it to the front yard, which was open. I figured this was much safer than strolling up their long driveway.

See, I was being totally careful and smart. Ha.

The distance between the road and the home seemed a lot longer tonight than it did earlier today. Going through the dark woods alone—with roots trying to trip you, branches smacking you, and spider webs clinging to your face—does that to you.

Hearing unidentifiable creatures skittering through the underbrush does, too. So does hearing strange animal calls that sounded like crying. I hoped beyond hope that floating purple orbs wouldn't appear this far from the pine grove.

Yeah, I admit, this was a dumb idea. All of me, not just the logical part, now agreed.

Finally, a glimpse of masonry in moonlight. I angled to my left and reached the wall. It was too tall for me to climb over. They probably built it not for security, but to prevent the encroachment of the forest into their backyard.

I wondered if faeries ever encroached. Would they raid the garbage can like raccoons?

Keeping close to the wall, I followed it around the perimeter of the homesite. The Gilleys had a big house and a proportionately huge yard. Finally, the wall took a forty-five-degree angle to the left and ended at the back of the detached garage. The golf cart was hopefully nearby.

I had thought little about outside security systems, because of how open the front approach to the house was. Now, though, I worried about triggering an infrared beam. And what if the golf cart was locked in the garage behind a security system?

Poor planner who acted on impulse. That would be my epitaph.

I circled the garage, keeping an eye on the main house, the back of which faced me. The lights were off, except in one bedroom upstairs.

The garage door was closed, but an SUV and the BMW from my scooter fiasco were parked outside. The BMW had a new windshield. I peeked into the garage through a side window. Enough moonlight seeped in to reveal that a sports car was parked inside, but the rest of the three-car garage was filled with junk.

In Florida, basements were rare, thanks to the high water table. It meant many households couldn't fit their cars in their garages because of all the stuff crammed in there. It seemed rich people, like the Gilleys, were no exception.

No sign of a golf cart in the garage. I crept around the other side until I reached an alcove between the garage and the perimeter wall. The roof extended from the rear of the garage above a concrete slab.

There sat the golf cart, plugged into a charging cable. With no moonlight here under the roof, the darkness felt safer for me. I approached the cart, and touching no surfaces, moved my hands about, feeling for psychic energy.

Golf carts were popular in Florida suburbia. Families rode around the neighborhood with the kids and dog in the back. I was never quite sure what the purpose of the carts was, aside from entertaining the kids. As far as I knew, the Gilleys didn't have any, at least none who still lived at home.

The other non-golf purpose of the carts was to transport you around a large property for utilitarian purposes. The Gilleys had a large tract of land. Why did they need to travel throughout it?

Were there paths through the forest we hadn't come across?

My survey of the cart told me the most powerful energy was on the steering wheel, as expected, but also on the handrail on the passenger side, as well as those on the back seat.

Standing next to the driver's seat, I focused on the steering wheel, since it was Dorothy who had held it most recently. Anxiety practically radiated from the wheel, with anger slightly less intense. Time to jump right—

—on our property. Why are they here? (View of an SUV parked on the shoulder ahead with people getting in, as the cart rattles toward them.) Are they spying on us? Oh no, that Darla woman is one of them. She must know too much about me. Why didn't my spell work properly on her motor scooter? I thought it was ingenious. No one would have suspected anything other than an engine malfunction. And somehow, she

puts the darn thing through my windshield! As I stop the cart by the SUV, Darla looks stricken.

"Darla, what brings you out here?" I ask.

Yeah, right, you were going on a hike. Please. Now, she's claiming they were looking for a cat. There's one in the back seat. Maybe that wasn't a lie.

(Turn around and drive away.) But it's too much of a coincidence she's out here. I know she suspects me of killing Hugo. Why does she even care about him? I'm sure he was a lousy magic tutor for their daughter. He was lousy for me. I should have been the ideal pupil for him since I already knew magic the Fae and Dick had taught me. I simply wanted to learn more, and Dick cut me off from that.

I didn't plan on falling for Hugo. Dick drove me into his arms. Treating me like a possession he had no use for anymore. Disappearing for days for his "strategic planning sessions." It was his own fault I ran around behind his back.

It was an insult atop an insult when Hugo broke things off. The pompous fool. Once he, too, began treating me like a toy he was tired of, I snapped. Didn't plan to do what I did. He just pushed me too far. He deserved to be killed by his own silly staff. I showed him who the true witch was. A water witch pumped full of energy from the ocean, just like he had taught me. He learned the hard way who had the true power and how easy it was for me to kill him with it.

I hope Dick gets charged with the murder. Couldn't happen to a better guy.

(Pulling up behind the garage.) I don't like it that Darla was on our property. I know she suspects me. Probably doesn't have a clue what Dick is up to, though. Maybe I should tell her. How would Dick like that? I could blow the lid off this whole thing, and he'd get blamed because it was his wife who did it.

I need to plug the cart in and—

(Flash of light)

—Her memory cut off just like that.

What had happened? When I read memories, they usually end when the person's mind wanders elsewhere or when they release the object they were touching. Dorothy was still sitting in the cart with her hands on the wheel when the memory ended.

I hovered my hand just above the seat. She had been wearing shorts, and her bare skin could have left memories on the vinyl.

Nope. Only a sudden, strong contraction of her thigh muscles, probably from getting out of the cart. If I climbed into the seat, maybe I'd pick up more memories from other sources.

I reached for the opposite side of the backrest to pull myself in when my hand touched something sticky. I jerked my hand away. A dark substance was on my finger, viscous and almost dried. There wasn't enough light to see what color it was. I sniffed my fingers and caught the coppery scent.

Of spilled blood.

Oh, boy. I pulled a tissue from my pocket to wipe my fingers as best I could and had to stuff the nasty tissue back in my pocket because I couldn't leave it here.

There was no escaping the fact that something bad may have happened to Dorothy. That was why her memory cut off so abruptly. Should I find out if she needed help? It wasn't any of my business, and the woman had tried to kill me with my own motor scooter.

If a woman was in mortal danger from a man, how could I abandon her?

My eye caught the tennis shoe on the concrete slab, just outside of the rear door to the garage. It was the same brand and color Dorothy was wearing when she confronted us on the shoulder of the road.

The door was locked. I returned to the window I had investigated before and took a more thorough look at the garage's interior. The moonlight didn't dispel enough of the darkness inside for me to see everything.

Yet, it was hard to miss the blue tarp on the ground near the back door. It was rolled around an object. And the object looked an awful lot like a human body.

It was Dorothy, the sinking feeling in my gut told me.

It was time to make my departure. Yessiree, I needed to get a move on.

Almost running, I went around the garage until I was behind the masonry wall that I had followed before. I tried to be quiet, but I was moving too quickly in my panicked state, rushing through the underbrush, tripping on tree roots.

The purple orbs appeared out of nowhere, swooping down and aggressively getting in my face. There were three of them, and they weren't observing from afar as they had when we were hiking out of the woods this afternoon.

They weren't watching me. They were intercepting me.

I pushed on, more desperate to escape these woods and get to my car.

The night noises I had heard tonight on my trek to the Gilley house suddenly stopped. The forest was eerily silent, except for the beating of my heart and the noise from my steps.

My head darted around to see what had scared the night creatures. All I saw in the moonlight were looming trees and tangled vines.

That's when I heard the fluttering of wings. Giant insect-like wings.

Then, several feet hit the ground all around me. The black silhouettes and glowing eyes of a dozen faeries encircled me, trapping me against the wall.

A bee stung me in my neck, and I involuntarily yelped.

Another sting in my left shoulder. They burned terribly. I touched my neck and pulled out a dart hanging from my skin.

My eyes found the moon and stayed locked upon it as I dropped like a tree backwards, hitting the wall and sliding to the ground. My face plunged into the forest floor, and total darkness swallowed me.

CHAPTER 20

A FAERIE BAD SITUATION

"Tell me what you know about us," the man said again and again.

I think it was a man. It could have been a faerie in human form.

When my eyes finally came into focus, I recognized Dick Gilley. I lay on a couch in a family room or den. The room had a super-sized television mounted to the wall with a blank screen. The decor had no personality. At least I wasn't in an underground cavern, though.

Dick looked down at me. He really was a good-looking guy, even at this unflattering angle. Even though I appeared to be his captive.

Focus, Darla, I told myself.

"What do I know about you?" My voice was torpid and scratchy.

"Yes," he said sternly.

"Not much. You guys are obviously rich. You're a hedge-fund manager. Dorothy is. . ." I stopped before I said the fatal word.

"Dorothy is a student of magic. I don't believe she has a job now."

Gilley frowned. My answer wasn't sufficient.

"Where is the key?" he asked menacingly.

"What key?"

"I know you have it. Where is it?"

It was unsettling that he suspected me of having it. Logically, I don't know how he'd make the leap. Either he was accusing everyone, including the mail carrier, of having the key, or he pieced together that I might have it based on my conversations with Dorothy. I hoped he hadn't sensed my psychic reading of the key.

And in case you're wondering, I didn't have it on me tonight. It was safe at home. My phone, however, was now missing from my jeans pocket.

"I barely know you and your wife. Why would I have your key?"

Try as I may, I couldn't convince this guy that I didn't know what key he was talking about.

"Dorothy gave it to the cartoonish magician. He's a friend of yours, I know. He gave it to you."

"Sorry. I don't know about any key. What's it for? Is it a house key?"

"It unlocks a precious container that doesn't belong to me. It was a duplicate key, but still extremely valuable to the owner of the container."

"Wish I could help you, but—"

He slammed his fist on the side table. I jumped.

"How much do you know about the Fae?" he asked. "And don't act ignorant of what I'm talking about. You've interacted with us before."

Us?

"You're a faerie?" I asked.

"I am."

"Was—I mean—is Dorothy one, too?"

He smiled bitterly. "You discovered she's dead. I'm not surprised, since you're so resourceful. No, she was not Fae. She was human. That is why we couldn't have children. I can take a human form and stay this way day and night, but my DNA is slightly different from yours. Our two species cannot procreate together."

That didn't bother me one bit. The guy was stunning, for sure, but knowing he was a faerie seriously reduced his sexiness in my eyes.

"Then why do the Fae kidnap human children if they can't expand your species?"

"Prior to adolescence, humans can be magically altered to make them grow into faeries."

"Oh." That was a scary thought.

"Back to the key. The container it unlocks is extremely important to the Fae," Gilley said. "The lock cannot be changed because of its magical nature. Therefore, we can't allow the key or its copy to be lost or stolen. I searched you, and I know you don't have the key with you."

It freaked me out, but didn't surprise me, to hear I was searched while unconscious.

"You must tell me where the key is. Don't bother refusing. I'll get the information from you, anyway."

My heart rattled beneath my ribcage. I've never been a good liar. Even if I were, I wouldn't hold up under torture or magical means of getting the information. In fact, I forced myself not to think of where the key was—not to even risk a brief mental image of it—in case Gilley knew telepathy or could read minds magically.

A door opened and closed in the house. Multiple pairs of feet walked across tiled floors until they entered this room.

Texas Tom stepped in and smiled when he recognized me. Two other men entered. They were dark and handsome in an otherworldly way that suggested they were faeries in human form. Tom, though, looked like a dork. A dangerous dork.

"I finished the assignment," Tom said to Gilley.

"I know. Make sure everything is clean."

"Yes, sir."

I guessed the assignment they were referring to was Dorothy. It was disconcerting to see Tom, who had been the Alpha Male imprisoning my husband and attempting to rule the Magic Guild, now taking orders from someone else. It shouldn't surprise me, because he was clearly an opportunist. And a worm.

"I believe this woman has the Queene's key," Gilley said. "I want her to tell us where it is."

"I can make her beg to give it to us," Tom said with a sadistic grin.

"I'm sure you could." Gilley turned to one of the faeries. "Balen, I prefer to use Fae magic for this."

The only thing I could do to save my butt was to attempt to contact another telepath for help. Namely, Mom. Last time I was in deep doo-doo (I have a habit of getting into it), I reached her telepathically and asked her to call the police.

My situation now was trickier. Though I was being held against my will, I was a trespasser here, and they haven't harmed me. Yet. I wanted to report the probable murder of Dorothy, but I'd rather do it when I was far away from the murderer.

Mom! I called in my mind. Shouted is a better way to describe it. *Mom, I need help. Tell Cory I'm at the Gilley house.*

I repeated this several times but received no answer. Did my message get through?

"Let's leave Balen to his task," Gilley said, exiting the room with Tom and the other soldier following.

The faerie named Balen approached, sizing me up. He had a slighter build than Gilley but was just as handsome: dark hair and eyes, light olive complexion. He wore a black designer T-shirt and slacks. It was hardly the outfit you'd expect a faerie would wear.

"Where is the key?" he asked in a gentle voice, with a slight accent I couldn't identify.

He was merely asking me like Gilley had. How was this magic?

"I don't know of any key," I answered.

Searing pain split my head. Oh, *this* was the magic.

I sensed something probing my mind. It was a creepy, invasive feeling. I had no magical defenses, but my mind was my paranormal tool, so I was good at opening and closing it. At this moment, I closed it as tightly as I could.

The intrusive probe snaked along my synapses, searching for a way into my thoughts. I resisted it.

Soon, it stopped. Balen frowned.

What time is it? Surely, Cory had awakened to go to the bathroom and had seen my note. I hoped he had consumed a great deal of water before going to bed.

Then, I grimly realized: what could he do? Storm the house like this was an action-adventure movie? He wouldn't even know where in the house I was.

Don't despair, Darla. You must be strong and resolute to get through this.

The pain returned, and the probing sensation began again.

"Where is the key?"

He didn't expect a verbal answer. He wanted to break my

concentration and trigger my mind to answer him with a mental image of the key's hiding place.

Instead, I tried to fake him out. I pictured Hugo's house and the jewelry box on his dresser, concentrating on this image as much as I could. I mentally fused upon it an image of the key from my memory. You could call it a mental Photoshop job.

Ever since my ability of psychometry has bloomed, I have become a student of memories. I search for them, study them, rewind them, looking for clues. This is the first time I've tried to manipulate my own.

The pain in my head went away. Balen studied my face for a moment before leaving the room and closing the door.

Did my altered memory work?

The drugs or magic from the darts that struck me had worn off enough to allow me to sit up and take unsteady steps across the floor. The door to the room was locked.

I looked at the window. Since I was on the first floor, it was worth seeing if it was an escape route.

I undid the latch on the window, but when I tried to lift the sash, it wouldn't budge. A faint static-like crackle when I touched it told me magic was involved. A purple orb floated by outside, stopping at the window to look in at me.

As I was wracking my brain to devise a plan for escape, Balen came through the door. He was not pleased.

"You've been playing games with me," he said. "Now, you must receive the full treatment."

I didn't like the sound of that.

He pointed at me and made a gesture like a mime pulling a rope. Indeed, it felt as if there was an invisible rope tied around my neck. Balen yanked me painfully, and I followed as he walked through a hallway and into a giant kitchen.

The kitchen was beautiful, one that I would normally be

jealous of if I weren't being yanked by a magic rope to my possible doom. Texas Tom sat on a stool at the expansive quartz-top island. He casually drank coffee and watched me with a smirk on his face.

"I look forward to working with your husband again," he said.

"Keep dreaming," I said. "You need to return my car first."

He laughed. "It's at the bottom of a lake."

I really, really hated that guy.

Balen pulled me out of a door onto an expansive patio surfaced with pavers, then through a large backyard. I felt the dissonance of being in the banal setting of a McMansion while under the thrall of Fae magic.

The banality soon ended. Balen reached the masonry wall, the other side of which I had traversed. He motioned with his hand, and a section of wall opened outwards. There had been no sign an opening existed here earlier tonight.

We stepped out onto a dirt pathway leading straight from the wall into the thick woods. The path was wide and smooth enough for a golf cart. And it hadn't existed when I traveled here before. I was certain of that. It must have been camouflaged with magic.

There was a tension in the forest. The insects and night creatures were silent. Even the trees seemed to be frozen with apprehension. I picked up a faint chattering from the dense network of roots beneath me. There was no chance for me to attempt to decipher it as I was marched deeper into the woods.

The elevation rose slightly, the underbrush thinned out, and the oak and palmetto trees gave way to the pines of the grove my family had passed through earlier. The psychic energy was powerful here. Fae magic.

Balen strode ahead of me, easily visible in the moonlight. He wasn't tall in his human form, but, of course, taller than me. Until he wasn't anymore.

With no discernible transition, he was suddenly in his natural faerie form. Now, only about two feet tall, he kept his humanoid shape, but had gossamer dragonfly-like wings and a head slightly larger in proportion than when he was in human form.

He stopped near a large pine and uttered a sing-song verse in an unrecognizable language.

Light poured from an opening in the ground. Balen pulled me toward it. The opening was only slightly larger than he was.

"Wait—I can't fit in there."

He turned back to me and smiled. The smile looked evil on his doll-sized face. Stepping into the opening and down a steep slope, he yanked the invisible rope viciously.

I fell forward into a bright light that blinded me, landing hard on a rock surface.

Now, I was in a cavern that was cold, as if it was deep underground. A single torch mounted to the wall blazed. Yellow light came from the tunnel that led to the cavern. The tunnel was the same height as the one leading outside. How had I gotten in here?

The answer to that question was like any other in the Fae world: magic.

The cavern appeared to be naturally formed within the porous limestone that lies beneath much of Florida: craggy rock filled with holes, pockets, and larger caverns like this one. The rounded ceiling was about eight feet tall at its highest point, sloping down to a few feet above the stone floor. The space was about thirty feet long and twenty wide.

It was spacious by faerie standards, but claustrophobic to me, trapped within it beneath the earth. I suspected the entrance to the tunnel was blocked with magic, but I was too afraid to crawl through it, anyway. Who knows how many hundreds of yards I would have to crawl on my belly, while possibly getting stuck?

The sound of tiny feet on rock came from the tunnel opening. Balen, and another faerie I didn't recognize, came inside in their natural state, but instantly transformed to human form. Balen's expression was grim. The other faerie was the only one I'd seen who was ugly, with a bent, pointy nose and a hideous scar running up the entire left side of his face.

"This is Magor," Balen said. "He will make you tell us where the key is."

Magor grinned. Several of his brown, crooked teeth were missing. You'd think he would have adopted a less gruesome appearance, since it was magical anyway.

It quickly and painfully dawned on me that a torturer did not need to be attractive.

CHAPTER 21

WITCHING

When Cory stumbled into the bathroom not long after midnight, he needed his reading glasses to decipher the handwritten note Darla had propped up behind the sink's faucet.

Oh no, he thought. She returned to the woods alone to trespass on the Gilleys' property and read their golf cart. What if the Fae catch her? What if the police do?

Both frightened and angry, he grabbed his phone from the bedside table and called her. She didn't pick up. He tried twice more before leaving a voicemail for her to call him. He hastily threw on clothes.

What had caused this change in Darla after he was taken from her? This was insanely risky behavior. Impulsive and unwise. The Darla he used to know would never risk being arrested or harmed over something that didn't immediately affect her or her family.

Why did she feel it was so necessary for her to find out who murdered Hugo? Let the police do it. She had told him of her frustration at Detective Samson's slow pace, but still, who cares?

Hugo wasn't a family member. The police weren't suspecting Sophie any longer.

And why was she so obsessed with the Fae? It wasn't up to her alone to battle them.

Why insert herself in all of this unnecessarily?

Glancing at her note again, he realized her transformation must have something to do with her psychometry. She had mentioned once, offhand, her frustration with how society treated her as a midlife woman—like she was unimportant and invisible.

Darla had told him her paranormal abilities made her feel powerful. That she had a say in the world and could make a difference.

Cory realized helping solve a murder case by using her psychometry was immensely rewarding to Darla, even if she had no personal stake in doing so, unlike earlier cases she had told him about.

He understood she believed that without her paranormal abilities, some of these cases might not have been solved at all. She must feel a responsibility, then, to take matters into her own hands.

But why take such great risks? There had to be a safer way to read the golf cart than sneaking onto the property at night, passing through a forest infested by faeries. She slipped out while he was sleeping because she knew he wouldn't approve of this. The reality that it was 1:30 a.m., she hadn't returned, and wasn't answering her phone meant things weren't going well for her.

What an understatement.

He didn't have the training to take on the Fae with his magic. But he did have the ability to juice up his power to incredible levels. Despite his urgency to search for Darla, he forced himself to not race to the Gilley house unprepared.

PAIN RECEPTORS I NEVER KNEW I HAD THROBBED IN AGONY throughout my entire body, outside and in. On my head, in my brain, in my soul.

Where was Heaven's mercy?

I had fallen to the stone floor, but neither faerie had touched me physically.

Magor stood above me, proud and straight, his arms gesticulating like an orchestra conductor as he inflicted a symphony of torture upon me.

Possibly the worst part was the unexpected nature of his torments. One moment, my feet burned as if on fire; the next moment, an invisible fist punched my stomach. Immediately afterwards, my ears would feel like they were being cut. This went on, startling and horrifying me, while Balen chanted in a monotone:

"Where is the key? Where is the key?"

Finally, I must have told him. I don't remember uttering the words, but I pictured the rear of the drawer in my bedside table, where I had placed the key inside an envelope. Yeah, it wasn't a safe enough spot, but I had stuck it there in a hurry after our reconnaissance mission to find Cervantes.

Balen smiled and told Magor to stop.

Shame flooded me. I tried to convince myself that it didn't matter if the Fae retrieved the key; I didn't need it for anything.

Deep in my heart, though, I knew the key was too important to lose to the Fae. Humankind would have a better chance against the Fae if we had the key. Somehow, I knew the jar it unlocked held secrets that would help us.

I failed.

My last thought before falling unconscious was a cry for help to my mother or any other telepath who could hear me.

The darkness that enveloped me was the only non-cruel thing Magor gave me.

CORY STUCK DARLA'S HANDGUN IN THE BACK OF HIS PANTS, then threw gear into a satchel. Flashlights, rope, a carving knife, first aid kit. . . What else? Too bad they didn't have any explosives lying around in the cottage. Don't most people?

Rummaging through kitchen drawers, he saw the sack that held the giant pearl. He should bring it along. Exactly what it could do for him, he didn't know. Still, its association with the Fae assured him it might come in handy. He placed it in the satchel.

As he took one last look in the bedroom, the satchel grew suddenly hot when he neared the bedside table. He opened the drawer and saw the envelope in the back. The mysterious key was inside.

It could be common sense, or intuition, but he knew not to bring the key along. In fact, he felt a strong urge to hide it better. He stepped outside into the courtyard, and something drew his eyes to the fountain gurgling away in the corner.

This time, it was intuition that told him the water might block certain magic. He tucked the key beneath a smooth rock at the bottom of the pool beneath the fountain.

His phone rang. It was Darla's mother, Sadie, gushing hysterically about Darla being in danger. She repeated over and over that she didn't know where Darla was or what to do. Should she call the police?

"No, don't call them yet. Hold tight, Sadie. I know where Darla is, and I'm heading there now." He didn't mention Sophie was going with him, because it probably wouldn't go over well with her grandmother.

Now, they needed to make a trip to the ley lines.

CORY WOKE SOPHIE IN HER BEDROOM IN THE INN. SHE WAS grumpy and groggy, but once he explained the situation, she leaped from her bed and threw on clothing while he went downstairs to start the car.

The nearly full moon gleamed upon the water of the bay when he parked the car, and they walked to the small park where Old Courage, the ancient Southern live oak tree, held court. The grassy area just south of the tree was the location where two underground ley lines intersected, a major one and a minor one. These conduits of electromagnetic energy could be mined by a witch with the right abilities. It was the main reason Cory had been enslaved by Texas Tom for so long.

While Sophie watched, Cory knelt upon the grass above the precise point where the two lines met. The current of energy rushed into him, making his entire body sing from his head to his toes. His euphoria was greater than any drug high; the power flowing into him would kill a man if it were in the form of electricity.

When he stepped away, Sophie's eyes widened as she looked at his face. He didn't know what she saw, but he knew he had been transformed in some way, at least while the energy was still in him.

He had an idea.

"Let me have your hands," he said.

"Why?" Sophie asked.

"To share some of the energy with you. It will make your magic much stronger, and you might need it to help Darla."

He took her hands and willed power to flow into her. He almost laughed when he saw strands of her hair rise into the air. When he felt it was time, he let go and stepped backwards.

"Wow! What just happened to me?" Sophie asked.

"Before you cast a spell, when you gather your elemental energies to mix them with your own inner energies, this new power will come naturally with it. Cast your spells as you would normally do, and they will be magnitudes stronger."

"I'm not sure if I know any spells that can help Mom."

"You'll know when the opportunity presents itself."

He drove toward the countryside and the Gilley estate.

CHAPTER 22

YOU SAY THAT TO ALL THE GIRLS

When I regained consciousness, I was alone in the cavern, sprawled on my back on the stone floor. My pain was blessedly gone, aside from the discomfort of lying on the unforgiving surface. There were no bruises, burns, or any wounds on my body despite the abuse I had suffered from Magor's magic.

The trauma, though, was fresh and severe.

A scuffling sound in the tunnel drew my attention, and a faerie walked into the cavern. He remained in his natural form, the only elderly member of their species I'd seen so far. He had a long white beard and closely shorn white hair. His elongated ears were pointier than those of the other faeries. Wrapped in a woolen cloak, he seemed just as healthy and vibrant as the others. Perhaps faeries aged in outward appearance, but not in their physical health.

"You are Darla?" he asked.

"Yes." My voice was hoarse. Had I screamed during the torture?

"I am Wilference, the priest of our local clan. I came here to give you company and comfort during your travail."

"Thank you. Please tell me there will be no more torture."

"No, not before the end."

"The end?"

"Has no one told you?" He seemed genuinely angry. "What kind of leader behaves this way?"

"Told me what?" I'm not sure I wanted to hear.

"My poor creature. You have been sentenced to death before dawn."

I was shocked, but the significance of what he said wasn't sinking in yet. Remind me, whose idea was it for me to come out here alone tonight?

"Who sentenced me to death?"

"The chieftain of our clan, of course. He has the power to do so unilaterally. Though, I thought he would have announced it to you."

"Would that be Dick Gilley?" I asked.

"That is the human name he uses. We call him Dorn."

Reality was setting in, and my thoughts were going dark.

"Um, how exactly am I to be executed?"

"A ceremonial dagger in your heart. It is quick and painless, I assure you."

"No one who has actually experienced it can verify that."

Wilference smiled uncomfortably as I pulled myself up into a sitting position.

"Can I get blankets and pillows to make you more comfortable?"

"What's the point?"

I glanced at my watch. All the magic used against me had fried it.

"How long until dawn?" I asked.

He ignored my question and stared at me strangely, as if I were a long-lost relative. This went on for a while and was beginning to creep me out.

"You know, dear creature, you look remarkably like. . . No, it can't be. Though, it has been prophesied."

"What are you talking about?"

He laughed and added, "I'm only a silly old fool."

But he continued staring at me.

"Come on," I said. "You're making me self-conscious."

"Do you know Danu? Also known as Anu. Those names were what your people called her. We have a different name for her. You look remarkably like the way she has been depicted in our art for millennia."

"Who?"

"You haven't heard of her? I keep forgetting how brief human lives are."

"Mine is going to be even briefer."

"She is the earth-mother goddess. We worshipped her long before humans came along. She was a major goddess of your Celtic people, from Ireland to Eastern Europe, at least until they adopted Christianity. But you humans keep changing your minds about which gods you worship, don't you?"

"I look like a goddess? I bet you say that to all the girls."

"You look just like her in hundreds of paintings and carvings. She is the mother of life, the goddess of nature. For the Fae, she is one of our most important goddesses."

I realized he was trying to distract me, to keep my thoughts away from my impending appointment with the dagger.

Why was he still staring at me?

"It has been prophesied that she will return to earth one day. As a mortal, but of the goddess. Similar to how one of your human gods had a son who was born on earth."

He was making no sense to me.

"I will return to you shortly," Wilference said, bowing his head to me. "I wish to bring the priest of one of the clans who have come here with their armies."

He slipped away into the tunnel. What the heck was he talking about? I looked like a mother-nature goddess? Did that mean I looked fat? I certainly wasn't a symbol of fertility. It was getting a little late for that.

Oh, wait. It was getting late for anything. I was a dead goddess walking.

While thoughts swirled in my head, I remembered the strange thing I had heard while communing with the trees in the state park recently. The trees, through their root systems, seemed to speak to me.

Mother, they had said.

I didn't understand what they meant. Could this "goddess" nonsense have something to do with it? But the trees didn't know I looked like the Fae's artwork of a goddess.

Wilference returned with another faerie who was dressed and groomed like him and had an even older outward appearance.

"Do you see what I mean?" Wilference asked the other priest.

"The resemblance is striking. Did you know the prophecy says the daughter of the goddess would be born among a non-magical species?"

"You are right. I had forgotten."

"I never imagined she would be born to humans," the other priest said.

They both stared at me for an overly long time.

"We should speak to Dorn," Wilference said. "Her death sentence should be commuted."

"Absolutely."

"We will return, Darla."

The two little priests scurried into the tunnel, and I was left alone again with my thoughts. What Wilference said about the death sentence was encouraging, but what would happen to me if I were spared? Would I be freed? Or would they expect me to do goddess stuff? Whatever that might be.

I wished this was all just a crazy bad dream after a too-spicy dinner. Please, let me wake up in my bed and not be in an underground cavern with faeries everywhere. Please, make my only problem be the foul smells in my inn.

A long time went by, though I had no means to tell how much, while I sat in the cavern beneath the flickering torch. Then, footsteps echoed from the tunnel.

Balen and the other faerie from the Gilley house entered in their true forms. They didn't say a word. The other faerie forced me to my feet and bound my wrists behind me with magic. Balen cast his rope spell, yanked me to my feet, then pulled me toward the tunnel I couldn't fit through.

Darkness overtook me as magic transported us to the surface. The next thing I knew, I was being led down the path from the pine grove through the hardwood forest.

Balen and the other faerie said nothing to me. They definitely weren't treating me like a goddess. More like a cow to the slaughter.

We passed through the hidden door into the Gilleys' backyard. Several faeries in human form were gathered in the yard and the patio, chatting in small groups as if it were a garden party without the food and champagne. Something was different now.

Wooden steps led up the back of the wall to a small platform at the top. Texas Tom stood on the platform watching me.

This wasn't good.

Dick Gilley, AKA Dorn, strode up to me, accompanied by two important-looking faeries and followed by the two elderly priests. All were in human form, dressed in Medieval-style clothing. None looked happy.

The faeries stopped in front of me. Gilley pulled out a thick slip of paper and held it before him.

"I, Dorn of the Magnolia Clan, and principal of the war council, decree the sentence of death to Darla Chesswick, human and enemy of the Fae, for crimes against our people, including theft, and plotting to stop our righteous war to take back our lands. By the consent of the gods, I call for the sentence to be carried out."

My heart rattled in my chest, and sweat poured down my back. I'm just an innkeeper, for Pete's sake. How did I end up here like this?

"What about Danu?" Wilference asked Gilley.

"You're mistaken. This human is not the child of Danu. In any event, in this time of war, the god we must please is Haarg, the God of War. Not Mother Nature."

"Don't mess with Mother Nature," I said, but no one listened to me.

Balen pulled me toward the wall. I sank my heels into the grass, and he pulled me with impossible strength.

I resisted climbing up the first step of the stairs. He yanked the invisible rope, and I fell forward, painfully knocking my chest and knees on the wood.

"The daughter of the goddess must exhibit grace," Wilference whispered behind me.

Yeah, sure, exhibit grace so you all can watch me die without feeling so guilty about it.

Balen tugged on the invisible rope very ungracefully. I got to my feet so I wouldn't be dragged up the stairs by my neck, face thumping upon the wood.

When we reached the platform atop the wall, I felt the collective excitement of the Fae behind me in the yard and throughout the forest on the other side. Thousands of tiny pinpricks of light glowed among the trees.

The eyes of the faerie army watching me.

Then, a unique pair of eyes caught my attention. Cervantes was perched atop the wall, just past the platform, behind Tom and Balen. The cat must have heard my telepathic calls for help and answered them.

He stared at me urgently. What help would a cat be for me, even if he was a witch's familiar?

His yellow-green eyes bore into mine. What was he trying to tell me?

Texas Tom pulled a long dagger from a scabbard on his belt. It had a strange, wavy blade and a jewel-encrusted hilt. He held it aloft to show it to the audience.

You are the goddess' daughter, a male voice with a slight Spanish accent said in my head. *Use your powers*.

Were those Cervantes' words? They must be. I could finally communicate with him telepathically, like Sophie and Cory could. But what good would it do for me now?

My thoughts turned to my family and away from my self-pity. The thought of leaving them was crippling. The guilt over having caused it through my rashness was devastating.

Use your powers, Cervantes said. *Nature is yours; the forest is yours. The trees can help you.*

What was he talking about?

However, in my heightened consciousness from being at the doorway to death, my senses were extra sensitive. The chattering of the trees poured into my ears. I sensed their concern and alarm.

Their mother was in danger. Pests were all around them, having invaded their soil and disturbed their roots. The pests must be driven away. Just like parasitical insects, they must be repelled.

Texas Tom turned to me, the moonlight glinting off the exotic dagger blade. He smiled sickeningly. The paunchy, balding grifter was having a grand time playing executioner for his masters. It made him feel important, instead of the evil loser that he was.

Command them! Cervantes' words implored.

Tom stepped closer to me, his eyes focused on my throat, the dagger held before him. Balen's magical rope slipped away, but he wrapped an arm around my chest and forehead from behind, holding me firmly.

Repel the invaders! I said telepathically to the trees. *Save your mother and rid your forest of these vermin!*

Tom stumbled as the platform shifted atop the wall. He glanced at the wood structure below him, then back at me. And smiled.

The earth rumbled again, and the wall shook. Tom, Balen, Wilference, and I lurched and almost fell.

Enormous popping, tearing sounds came from the forest beyond us. The noise came from right below the wall as well as deep in the woods. A cloud that had obscured the moon slipped past it, and the bright light illuminated what was happening.

The forest floor churned as roots rose to the surface and broke through like a sea of snakes. All the forest, as far as I could see, was erupting in sprays of soil and dead leaves. The ground shook as if from an earthquake, making the wall tremble.

Texas Tom, his dagger held dramatically before him, opened

his mouth in terror and fell from the platform. Balen staggered behind me and almost brought both of us to the ground. Wilference fell off, landing on the forest side of the wall.

With both arms, I elbowed Balen in the ribs and kicked the heel of my right foot up backwards, hitting him in the knee. That, and the bouncing of the platform, sent him reeling, losing his grip on me. I turned and kicked him in the gut. Arms flailing, he fell off the platform onto the lawn.

Meanwhile, more roots were breaking to the surface as far as I could see into the trees. Huge roots, the size of my legs, broke free along with networks of smaller roots like veins and capillaries.

And then it was as if the floor of the forest was swarming with ants. They weren't ants, though. They were faeries driven from their tunnels and thrust through the soil into the night. Their underground passageways destroyed, they scurried about in panic, tripping on the roots, becoming ensnared by them. Some were even being strangled by the roots.

A large chunk of the masonry wall broke away and fell in a cloud of dust. The Gilleys' backyard was experiencing the same fate as the forest. The exterior light blinked out as the home's electricity failed. Roots from the trees on the other side of the wall broke through the turf, tripping and tangling the faeries who were in human form.

The brick pavers of the patio fell apart among rising piles of soil. The swimming pool basin cracked open in several places, water quickly disappearing. Even the house sagged in places, as the ground moved beneath it. Windows popped out and went flying from the pressure on the walls. Cracks snaked out across the stucco surface.

I rushed down the wooden stairs before the platform fell from the wall, and when it did, it just missed me. There in the backyard, with the ground boiling beneath me, my path was blocked by Texas Tom about twenty feet distant.

"You're not getting away," he said angrily. "I blame you for my failed takeover of the Magic Guild and for my arrest. And I blame Cory, too. This is how I'm going to get revenge—with your blood."

CHAPTER 23

HOPE IS A PLAN

Tom ran toward me. A rope-like root emerged from the ground and grabbed his ankle as if it were a tentacle. Tom cursed and hacked at the root with the dagger.

I sprinted toward the driveway, hoping to make it to the road and back to where I left my car. If only I could get away from Tom, Gilley, and the Fae on this side of the wall.

But Tom had freed himself and was coming at me again.

"Hey, Tommy! Good to see you."

Tom stopped in his tracks.

It was Cory's voice! He and Sophie walked out of the shadows on the side of the house and stood at the edge of the driveway.

"Good," Tom said with a sneer. "You can watch your wife die before I kill you and your daughter."

As soon as the last word escaped his lips, Tom went flying backwards and smashed into a chair that had fallen off the patio.

My heart surged as I realized the magic hadn't come from Cory, but from Sophie's outstretched hand. Both of them seemed to glow, as if brimming with energy. And, knowing Cory, they probably were.

Tom tried to untangle himself from the chair, was then hit with an invisible blow, flipping him backwards. Again, the magic had come from Sophie's hand, while Cory stood beside her, the pearl glowing in his own hand.

"Not bad for a beginner," Tom said. "I'll show you how it's really done."

He crouched behind the fallen chair, pointed his open palms at my family, and shot fireballs at them. Fireballs were bad news. I shouted at Tom, trying to break his concentration, but the balls continued to fly at Sophie and Cory.

They didn't get past the shield of a protection spell that was radiating from the pearl. The fireballs bounced off, landing on the lawn sizzling. Two hit the house, one of them going into an opening where a window had fallen out.

Sophie and Cory advanced toward Tom like soldiers in formation. Tom screamed in frustration and tried a different spell. He sent an intense gust of wind at the two of them. Their hair flew backwards, and their clothing pasted against their bodies. A small palm tree toppled beside them. Still, they continued toward Tom.

I had been circling around behind him, looking for a way to attack. Suddenly, he bolted, sprinting to escape his attackers. He chose the wrong direction. I threw myself at his legs, and he went sprawling, landing on his face among the broken pavers of the patio.

My ribs hurt, but I had successfully executed my first—and hopefully last—football cross-body block. By the looks of Tom, it was highly effective.

Cory raced over and held Tom down with a foot on his back.

He pushed the pearl against the back of Tom's head. The smell of singed hair came to my nose.

"May the healing power of the pearl cleanse you of your evil magic," Cory shouted.

Tom screamed and squirmed. The pearl was truly burning him. I stood on his lower back to help keep him down and took the dagger from its scabbard.

"Cleanse him of the magic derived from the blackness in his heart," Cory intoned. "Render him impotent of all magic that is not pure and good."

Tom went limp, crying. It was an ignominious defeat for a truly bad person. I called 911, figuring it was safe now to bring in normal humans. The Gilleys' backyard was deserted, and I figured the faeries in the woods had retreated far from the house.

Heavy smoke poured from an upstairs bedroom where the deflected fireball had landed. I told the 911 operator about the fire, as well as the captured escaped prisoner and the murdered homeowner.

"Guys, thanks for showing up," I said to Sophie and Cory. "Your work isn't finished yet, though."

I pointed to the SUV parked by the garage. Gilley had just sprinted from the house and hopped into the driver's seat.

As soon as the ignition kicked in, the vehicle died. The starter whined, but nothing happened.

Cory smiled. "That was the easiest part."

Gilley got out of the SUV and slipped into the BMW. The same thing happened to the battery.

"You need to put him out of his misery," I said to my family.

Gilley leaped out of the car and ran toward the woods. He didn't get far. Sophie's spell was like a lasso encircling a calf's legs at a rodeo. He went down hard.

"Make sure he doesn't get up," I said to Cory. "I'll keep this worm from wiggling anywhere."

Cory headed over to Gilley and stomped on his back.

Still on top of Tom, I crouched and placed the dagger blade on the back of his neck, below what was left of his burned hair. I pressed down just enough to draw a little blood.

"I bet you think it's a shame this beautiful dagger wasn't used tonight," I said. "If you so much as move an inch, I'm going to use it to shorten you by about ten inches."

I was relieved to hear the approaching sirens. Smoke now belched from all the windows of the second floor and flames danced from the former windows. Our two prisoners were subdued, but for how long?

I felt enormous relief when I spotted the police cars coming up the drive, followed by fire engines. The fact I had almost died tonight was far from my mind, and I refused to deal with it now.

Our cute black cat strolled up to observe what his humans were up to. For now, I wasn't going to think about myself. I was only going to think about the family I had almost lost and how much I loved them.

OF COURSE, ME BEING ME, I COULDN'T KEEP MYSELF FROM poking around a bit before I went home. After Gilley and Tom were led away in handcuffs, the fire captain shooed away bystanders. Which, with all the faeries having fled, was my family. I told Cory and Sophie that I would meet them at home.

"You will not get in trouble again," Cory said. "You're going home now with us."

"I have to get my car."

"Please, folks, leave the property," the fire captain said.

While he stepped in front of Cory, I slipped away unnoticed to the rear of the garage.

I wanted to do more memory reading.

Samson and crime scene techs were inside the garage with Dorothy's body, so I had to work with what I could access outside. The golf cart was the best target. I had read the steering wheel and the handrail, but not the rest of the cart. Maybe I would find something useful for dealing with the Fae.

I went to the passenger side. Hovering my hand above the seat, dashboard, and handrail, I sensed that there had been a variety of passengers, including Dorothy. A recent memory was on the handrail. I carefully placed my fingers on—

—*top of injury. He's allowed our property to become infested by his "people." They're not his people. I'm his people. He promised me he'd live as a human with me, to have a normal life. He's built a great career. We have a wonderful home with all this property to insulate us from the world. All we lacked were children. We had an idyllic life, and now he's ruining it.*

This trail is bumpy. Need to hang on tight.

Because of his Queene. He says he has been called to serve. I think it's just a male midlife crisis, a chance to play soldier. Run around in the woods and talk big about conquering humans. What does that mean for me? Does it make me the enemy?

He's asking me about the key again. He's really concerned about it. Now's the time to drive the bargain.

"What if I could find the key for you?" I ask.

He slams on the brakes, and my head snaps forward.

"You know where it is?" His face is red with rage. I hope this isn't a mistake.

"I might know," I say. "But only if you give me what I want. Either tell your Queene you can't play soldier anymore, so you and I can rebuild our lives together. Or I want a divorce under the terms I dictate."

He's furious. He jerks his arm, and I flinch involuntarily.

"Are you crazy? I can't tell the Queene anything. She's the absolute ruler, empowered by the gods. She can have my throat cut at whim. And are you telling me you took the key?"

"No," I lied. "There's someone I suspect."

"I think you took it in your petty, spiteful way. You don't realize how dangerous this is. The key unlocks an amphora that was a gift from the gods. It holds the only thing that allows our people to survive in these dark times. It literally gives us hope, and no one can live without hope. The Queene herself has the only other copy of the key. In case of regicide, there must be a copy. Just recently, I was asked to lend the key to an alchemist who is said to be the only person who can make another duplicate that will actually open the box."

"Let me see what I can do."

"Stop lying to me. Give me the key. Or I'll . . . You'll be sorry."

I'm frightened. That look on his face is deadly.

"Let me off here," I say. "You're dangerous."

If I only knew what Hugo did with the—

—memory ends as she climbs from the golf cart, leaving an earlier fragment behind of her standing on a sand dune, watching Hugo die.

I walked around to the driver's side. Dorothy's memory of confronting us on her property was the most recent and dominant one. Yet Dick's memories of the conversation I just experienced must be on the steering wheel as well.

This is where psychometry is just as much a learned skill as a paranormal ability. It's all about controlling your psychic impressions, taking a jumble of memories left by different people at different times, and sorting them out to make sense of them.

So, as I hover my hand just above the wheel, I ignore Dorothy's memories from yesterday and try to look beneath them.

Oh, it's a jumble, all right. More memories from Dorothy, tons from Dick, and even some from Balen. Being emotionally aroused makes your psychic energy more powerful, and thus, the memories you leave are stronger.

Right here, at the top of the wheel, are angry memories of—

—*I know she took the key. She's such a silly fool to think taking the key will hurt me. Yeah, it could mean my execution, but she's hurting not only me but all the Fae. All the humans in the world, too. Without being able to open the jar, no one can survive.*

The jar contains hope itself.

The jar is Pandora's Box, and the Queene has it. I'm one of the few who know this. It's—

—Blowing my mind. *Pandora's Box?* That's only a myth, a silly ancient folktale.

Dick Gilley surely believed it, though.

Should I believe it, too?

If so, should I try to find it? Maybe if it was taken from the Fae, they would end their campaign against humans. If I found the jar, I had a key to open it, after all.

However, that didn't work out so well for Pandora, did it?

The improvised, cobbled-together spell my witch family had created was supposed to lead us to the jar, but it's not here. If it's actually true the Queene has it. Does she live nearby in the tunnels, or did the spell simply lead us to the greatest concentration of Fae in the area?

I wished I could search the Gilley home for more clues. That would not happen, considering the second floor was still ablaze, and firefighters were dousing it with their hoses. I took one last survey of the golf cart.

After several minutes, I hadn't found anything worthwhile, nothing but mundane thoughts of those who traveled on the hidden paths through the enormous property. Until, at last, I came upon an interesting fragment. It was on the right handrail of the rearward-facing back seats.

Balen had been sitting here. Someone else on the cart mentioned the Faerie Queene. Into Balen's mind came the image of a mansion. "The Winter Palace" was how his mind classified it.

What was odd to me was that the mansion looked like your typical human mansion. What was even odder, I was pretty sure I recognized the setting, based on some exploring Cory and I did on vacation years ago.

The Faerie Queene's Winter Palace was located on the ocean, and with its faux French estate design, looked an awful lot like similar homes in Palm Beach, Florida. My guess was it was just one of many winter palaces owned by human billionaires. I wondered if she belonged to a country club, too.

"Darla, come with us now."

It was Cory. I thought he had already gone home.

"We're walking you to your car," he said. "I'm not letting you out of my sight."

I RETURNED HOME TO FIND A DISASTER SCENE. OUR COTTAGE bedroom was trashed; both bedside tables had been broken apart into pieces.

"I thought the Fae would be more sophisticated than this," I said to Cory, who stood forlornly beside our upended bed.

I explained that my mind had been read while I was in their captivity, and I inadvertently had pictured the key's hiding spot.

"I guess I was naïve to believe I could keep the key from them."

"They didn't find the key," Cory said proudly. "I had a hunch telling me to move it, and I hid it under a rock in the fountain."

"Thank you!" I said, as I grabbed him in a bear hug, then covered his face in kisses. He remained in my arms for a long time while I savored being alive and with my family again.

I would never tell them how close to death I had come.

"Do we really need to keep the key?" Cory asked. "If you don't know what it's for, maybe we should just let the Fae have it. It's too dangerous for us."

"I learned what it's for."

I explained to him it unlocked the lid of Pandora's Box, which the Fae considered critical to their survival. If the guilds of San Marcos could acquire it, they could rid us of the Fae threat.

"You've got to be kidding," he said. "You expect me to believe an ancient Greek myth is actually real?"

"I believe it is. And you gave me a good idea. I think I *will* return the key to the Fae. Just not this one."

The next day, I took it to James.

"Ah, good to see this beauty again," he said when I handed it to him. "Have you learned anything about it?"

"Not really," I said, hedging. It wasn't the time to babble about Pandora's Box. That called for a bigger discussion with the guild, which I needed to do right away.

"Do you want me to speak with it again?"

"No. Actually, I'm here to ask if you could replicate it. The Fae want the key back, and I don't want to put myself and my family in any more danger. I don't want to return it, either, because I believe the guilds of San Marcos will need it."

He raised an eyebrow questioningly.

"I know. I promise to explain at our next meeting. In the

meantime, do you think you can create a replica that will fool the Fae enough, so they'll leave me alone?"

He studied it again, more closely. "Cosmetically, yes. I obviously can't get ahold of whatever rare metal this is, but I can use a metal of comparable weight, coat it with gold, then distress it to make it look old. Will it fool the Fae? I don't know. They would sense it lacks remnants of their magic on it. And I doubt it would work to open the box without the rare metal and the magic."

"It doesn't need to work. It only needs to fool them for a while. Arch Mage Bob probably has the expertise to put some magic on it that would fool them. So, please, begin your work."

James took several measurements and photos of the key before returning it to me. When I got home, I returned it to the hiding place in the fountain.

Now, I had to hope I could get the fake to the Fae before they came after me again. Even Gilley being behind bars wouldn't stop them.

CHAPTER 24

TREATS

"You're *what?*" I asked Samson.

"We're not going to be able to keep Dick Gilley in jail. He'll bond out," Samson said in the small conference room next to the detective bureau at the police station.

"But why?"

"We don't have enough evidence to tie him to his wife's murder. Forensics matched her wound to the unusual dagger Tom Sykes had. Tom's prints are all over the weapon. But we can't prove Gilley hired Tom to kill her, unless Tom flips on him."

"Let me read some of Gilley's possessions. I bet I can find incriminating memories."

"I shouldn't have to keep reminding you that your psychometry can't be used in a trial."

I sighed. Yeah, he keeps on reminding me, and I keep wanting to smack judges on the upside of their heads for not accepting paranormal evidence.

"Well, you can get Gilley for the attempted murder of me."

"Accessory to attempted murder. Based on your testimony. That's what we have, and it probably won't be enough for a judge to deny him bail."

I stewed in frustration.

Samson continued. "Not to rub salt in the wound, but we don't have any physical evidence or testimony that Dorothy Gilley killed Hugo Starbright. It would have taken great strength to kill him with his staff. That's why I thought Vance Puggle was the perfect suspect, especially since the cell towers placed him in the area. As for Dorothy Gilley, she had a motive, but again, all we have are the memories you read. And your cat's claim that he heard a woman arguing with the victim." He chuckled darkly. "Obviously, she can't confess to the crime now."

"That's your problem, then. The unwritten agreement between you and me is even if my findings can't be used in court, they're supposed to point you in the right direction. Then, you go find evidence that can be used."

"If such evidence exists. Murder cases are rarely cut and dry."

"You're saying sometimes murderers get away with it."

"Sometimes. Rarely. Remember, we have a strong case against Tom Sykes for murdering Hugo's partner: prints and other physical evidence from the scene. As well as a neighbor who will testify she saw Sykes at the townhome around the time of death. And we can probably nail him for Dorothy Gilley's murder, too."

"I want to take down Dick Gilley, too," I said.

"We'll work on it. First, by getting Tom to flip on him as a murder for hire. If Tom doesn't break out of jail again with his magic."

"Funny how magic can get you out of jail, but not into jail."

"Because of the narrow minds of the unbelievers. Presumption of innocence. All that fun stuff in our criminal justice system."

"Anyway, I wouldn't worry too much about Tom's magic. I believe Cory neutralized most of it with the help of the pearl."

"Let's hope so." Samson leaned back in his chair. "Tell me, how big of a threat do you believe the Fae to be?"

"I don't know. It doesn't help if Dick Gilley goes free. What I don't understand is when the Fae say they want to take their lands back and be the dominant race again, do they mean a literal armed conflict? Or are they going to remain a secret to most humans and just influence us with their magic? Also, I don't know if this is only happening here in Florida, or everywhere."

Samson shrugged. "You realize there's nothing the police can do about it at the moment?"

I nodded. The only folks I knew who could combat it for now were the supernatural guilds of San Marcos. If they could actually work together, which was a big question mark.

"OH, MY," MISSY SAID OVER THE PHONE. "SUCH A BRUTAL murder."

"What kind of magic spell could do it?"

"I wouldn't know from personal experience, of course, but you would have to metaphysically bind the two materials."

"Materials?"

"Yes. The wood of the staff and the flesh of the victim. This way, the magic recreates in the real world what you've symbolically created. It's not as gross as it sounds. You would need a sample of wood from the staff—it would only have to be a splinter. And then, a sample from the victim, say, a hair. "

"Would you have to be present at the crime scene when you cast the spell for it to work?" I asked.

"The most powerful witch could do it remotely, but it's a lot easier if you're nearby and have the victim in view. You would combine the materials, either in a potion or burn them together within a magic circle. Then, you would—"

"Thanks, Missy. That's all I care to know. I don't need to prove she performed the spell. I need to find an alternate, non-magical way the perp did it."

"'Perp'? That sounds like cop talk."

"I guess I've been hanging around cops too much."

I thanked Missy and said goodbye. Everyone should have at least one highly experienced witch in the family. It comes in very handy.

Now, it was the hard part. I could ask Samson to send a forensics team to the Gilley house and see if they could find wood fragments that matched Hugo's staff or any of his hairs. All that would do was indicate she attempted the magic spell. It would be worthless in determining that she was the murderer.

I needed to prove she was at the scene and was capable of impaling a man with a wooden staff. And I couldn't use my psychic abilities to do it.

Why did I care so much about proving she did it? After all, she was deceased now and would face divine justice. I guess I simply wanted to solve the case I had been puzzling over for so long. For my sake and Hugo's.

Aside from Dorothy's own memories, my best evidence was Cervantes' testimony. It was worthless to the police, but invaluable to me.

I found the cat sprawled on the cobblestones of the courtyard, soaking in the sun.

Good morning, Darla, his words said in my mind. *Got any treats?*

Silly me, I believed a witch's familiar would have profound thoughts.

"Why is it we can communicate telepathically now, when we couldn't before, even though I'm a telepath?" I asked aloud.

I can only communicate with witches. Now that you're awakening to the goddess in you, it's a different story. You have another form of magic, you know.

"This awakening frightens me," I confessed.

It shouldn't. Let it happen naturally. Chill out.

"I need you to tell me more about the night when you disappeared on the beach."

Oh, that. Can I have some treats?

"If you tell me what I need to know. Exactly where on the beach was Hugo when you last saw him?"

He was standing on the tallest of the coquina rock formations.

"If I take you to the beach, can you point it out?"

For treats up front as a deposit. Then more treats when we get home.

"Deal."

I grabbed his favorite treats (crunchy on the outside and soft on the inside), borrowed Sophie's car, and drove Cervantes to the small sandy parking lot at the public beach where Hugo met his end. I carried Cervantes up over the dune crossover, the few sunbathers on the sand giving me strange looks.

You can set me down, Cervantes said.

"I don't want you running off again."

No danger of that. Believe me. The rocks are over there, to your left.

Shelves of coquina limestone stretched for dozens of yards, punctuated by large, flat, boulder-like formations. I walked toward the tallest, which was closest to the sand dunes.

He was standing on top, right there.

"Was this where he was when you heard the woman arguing with him?"

Yes.

I put Cervantes down and climbed carefully atop the rock. It provided a splendid view of the beach to the north and south, as well as of the ocean itself and the gentle, lazy breakers. I wasn't sure what I should be looking for.

The shelf of rock below me had lichen and barnacles on it in places. There were also holes of various sizes from erosion and the activity of microorganisms over the centuries. In the rocks closer to the water, these holes would remain filled with water when the tide receded. The rock below me looked like it was rarely touched by water this far up the beach. Only in months with the highest tides would it get wet.

One hole in particular caught my eye. It was perfectly round and went deep, with a small diameter that looked perfect for holding a fishing pole.

Or a wizard's staff.

I climbed down to the beach and examined the hole closely. Could those be particles of scraped wood on the edges of the hole? It looked like there might even be a piece from the end of the staff in the dark bottom of the hole.

What if Hugo had placed his staff in this hole, maybe to keep it handy, while he climbed up the rock? The staff would stand perfectly upright.

I glanced up at the boulder where I had stood. If Hugo had fallen from up there and landed with his soft belly right on the tip of his staff, a guy as heavy as he could be impaled.

Dorothy's magic could have thrown him down here. Or, in a non-magical, acceptable-to-legal-minds scenario, she could have pushed him. If Samson's consulting witch was right, and magic was used here, the amount of energy required to topple Hugo from the rock was much less than that needed to launch his staff like a spear with enough force to impale him.

Very clever, Cervantes said.

If Samson could get those wood fragments in the hole tested, and they matched the staff, that would be brilliant.

Now, how could I prove Dorothy was here? Her phone records didn't show she was here. She was smart enough to leave her phone at home.

I picked up Cervantes, who protested with a whine, and carried him back to the car. The sandy lot held the impressions of hundreds of tires. I doubted the police had taken impressions of them at the time. It would be too late now with all the cars that have parked here since then. If they had, we could try to match the impressions with the tires of Dorothy's BMW. I had to give the police the benefit of the doubt and believe they had thoroughly investigated the scene.

Could Dorothy have parked somewhere else? To the north and south were oceanfront homes and no place to park. The nearest public lot was about a mile north of here. I drove there.

This parking lot was much larger than the other one. As a busier park, it had public bathrooms.

An idea filled me with excitement. I jogged over to the bathrooms. Sure enough, there were surveillance cameras mounted above the doors.

Dorothy could have parked here and easily walked the mile to the beach where Hugo was. If she was here, hopefully there would be camera footage that picked up her BMW, and maybe even her.

"Thank you, Cervantes. I'll bring you home for your treats now."

NEXT, IT WAS *MY* TURN FOR A TREAT.

"How are you proposing she did it?" Samson asked me as I sat across from his desk.

"With gravity."

I explained my theory of the murder and where Dorothy might have parked, keeping my voice low so the other detectives wouldn't hear. Especially Billy Reyna, who was not known for his discretion.

"Okay," Samson said. "The case is still open, so I'll subpoena the videos of the beach parking lot from the Department of Recreation. Since they're part of the city, they'll respond right away."

"Then there's the wizard's staff. As I recall, the bottom was damaged."

Samson glanced at the case folder opened on his desk. "Yeah."

"Any theory for why it was damaged?"

"No, not at the time, aside from wear and tear. The staff was found with the victim lying on the beach. No one would have thought it had been held upright by the hole in the rock. You have to understand, your theory is not a likely one. The way you describe it, though, I can believe it."

"How kind of you," I said, sarcasm creeping into my voice. "Even if you remove magic from the history of what happened, this theory explains how she could have done it without magic."

"Absolutely."

"Can you send a tech to the beach to collect those wood fibers and check if there's a piece that broke from the staff still in the hole?"

"Will do. I have to say I'm impressed." He smiled. "Nice sleuthing, and no psychic stuff involved."

"Well, there was a talking cat, but we won't count him."

"Let's not."

Samson called me the next day to report the crime scene tech did, in fact, find a broken section of wood at the bottom of the hole. Forensic tests determined that it and the wood fibers on the rim of the hole had indeed come from the staff.

"I feel confident the staff was held upright in the rock, and once the body landed on it, it broke at the base from the weight," Samson said. "Also, you'll be pleased to know we found footage from that night, shortly before and after the time of death, showing Dorothy's make and model of vehicle parking in and leaving the lot. The driver is visible, too. We need a little more work to confirm it was Dorothy Gilley, but I'm sure we will."

"Then what?"

"I'll write a report, get it approved by the DA, and the case will be closed. Dorothy Gilley will be recorded as the murderer."

"Thank you for your help, Michael."

"Thank *you*."

"Now, get your butt in gear and nail Dick Gilley to the wall."

CHAPTER 25

FOOL A FAERIE?

I was in the utility room helping Bella and Sophie fold sheets when Samson called.

"I thought you'd want to know that Dick Gilley bonded out of jail already. He's hired a high-powered attorney."

"Of course. Gilley's rich. Have you made any progress in investigating him?"

"He's a slippery eel. We haven't found any evidence tying him to the murders so far. Nor have there been any incriminating communications between him and Tom Sykes showing he ordered the killings. We've been working Tom hard, though. I think he'll flip on Gilley. For now, all we have is the abduction of you on his property."

"Okay," I said, dejected. "Thanks for the update."

"I'm going to post an officer outside your inn. Just in case."

Just in case? It was a certainty that Gilley would continue to search for the key. He or his faeries would show up, eventually.

Fortunately, when I called James, he told me he had just finished making the replica key. I drove to his smithy in my rental car, truly missing the convenience of my motor scooter in the parking nightmare of Old Town. When James opened a wooden box in his shed, revealing the replica key lying on a piece of velvet, I was thrilled.

"Brilliant, James! It looks just like the original. How did you make it look so worn?"

"With a file, sandpaper, and black paint that looks like tarnish. I'm not a locksmith, but I'm pretty sure this key would work in the lock. If the lock isn't magical."

"It probably is," I said, giving James a sisterly hug and profuse thanks.

Now came the hardest part—imbuing it with enough magic to convince Gilley the key belonged to the Fae, but not enough for him to identify what kind of magic it was.

No, I take that back. The hardest part was convincing Arch Mage Bob to help.

"What is 'the essence of Fae magic' supposed to mean?" he asked me from his desk in the back room of his surf shop.

I sighed and handed him the real key. "You tell me." I hadn't wanted to risk bringing it here, but I knew Bob would probably be a little dense.

"Whoa, dude," he said, as the dainty key rested on his beefy palm. "This is, like, loaded with magic and stuff. Not just from the Fae, either. I've never felt anything like it. What is this key for?"

"Oh, some special container belonging to the Fae."

"Like, what's so special about it?"

I was reluctant to tell him, because it sounded so crazy, but I suppose it couldn't hurt to try it out on different audiences, as if I were a standup comic testing a new routine.

"I haven't told anyone except my husband. I read a memory

from a faerie, and the memory referred to the box as Pandora's Box. Probably just a nickname or a metaphor, right?"

Bob's eyes widened. "Holy shizzle! So, the legends are true!"

I was expecting ridicule. Not this.

"What legends?"

"Everyone knows the Fae have been on earth longer than humans. Some dudes say the ancient gods were actually faeries. Like, who knows? Anyway, there was this famous wizard in Byzantium who said Pandora's Box really existed and the Fae had it. The whole myth, about Pandora opening the box when she wasn't supposed to and letting out all the bad stuff into the world, was true. Same with her closing the box to keep hope inside. Other dudes say the Fae have stuck around all this time because of the hope in that box."

"That's amazing. By the way, it's not really a box."

"Huh?"

"It's an amphora—a large ceramic jar or urn, the kind the ancient Greeks stored wine, grain, and stuff in. An incorrect translation hundreds of years ago called it a box."

"Whatever. Like I was saying, there's some powerful witches and wizards who would give their left foot to get a hold of that box—I mean, jar. Hope is, like, such a powerful force. Think of what it could do to their magic."

"Who cares? Think of what it could do for the suffering people on this planet."

"Um, yeah. That, too. Do you know where the jar is?"

"No," I said. "But it can't be too far away if the duplicate key is right here. It makes me think the Faerie Queene has it with her, and I believe she's in Palm Beach, at least sometimes. I think if we can find the jar and steal it from the Fae, they would give up on their campaign to take the world back from humans.

Or, maybe we could use it to negotiate a peace treaty with them."

"Good luck with that, dude. The Fae have had that jar for thousands of years. No one's gonna steal it from them."

Never say never, I thought.

"Okay, back to my original request. Can you put some sort of spell on the duplicate key so that a faerie holding it will think it's the real thing?"

"Fool a faerie? Dude, that's a lot to ask. I mean, their knowledge of magic is, like, tons better than humans."

"Just the essence of magic is all I'm asking. Nothing specific. Only enough that they feel like the key has been around a long time and has been in the presence of magic."

Bob frowned. "Let me think. What do we do with our keys? We lose them. I could put on a spell that attaches it to its owner. It's a very common spell."

"The actual key didn't have a spell like that, obviously, because Gilley lost the key."

"He didn't lose it—it was stolen from him, and it wasn't really his. Anyway, I'll make the spell weak, like it's old and faded."

"How do I keep it from attaching to me?"

"Try not to handle it too much. And definitely don't put it in your pocket."

I handed him the replica key and took back the real one. This, I put in my pocket. As soon as I got home, it would go straight back into hiding again.

As Bob examined the key, he suddenly snapped his eyes back to me.

"You know what? I can tweak the spell a bit, so I can track it. It will give us an idea where that Gilley dude is whenever he has the key with him. Who knows, maybe it could help us find Pandora's Box if he tries to use the key on it."

"Good idea. Please let me know if the key goes on a long road trip. Say, to Palm Beach."

After Bob cast the spell, my next task was to get the counterfeit key into Dick Gilley's hands without him finding out it was from me. Then it dawned on me, this horse was already out of the barn. He had me tortured because he suspected I had the key, or at least knew where it was, so what's the point of going to great pains to arrange for him to stumble upon it himself?

I wrapped the key in blank paper, stuck it in a stamped, addressed envelope. Then I dropped it in the mail. At a post office in the next county. I had to keep the guy guessing a little, you see.

CHAPTER 26

NATURE IS A MOTHER

S ummer and I were in the same state park where I had first heard the communications between trees. Where I had first heard them call me mother. Where this strange goddess odyssey had begun.

As we walked along a trail through thick woods, I gave her a condensed version of what happened that night in the forest behind the Gilley place, about what the faerie priests said about me, and how the trees responded to my call for help.

"Elves are distantly related to faeries," said Summer, who was half-elf. "We share some of the same gods and goddesses. I never said anything before, but I sensed a bit of the divine in you. That's not the kind of thing you say to someone lightly. It tends to go to their heads."

"I don't think it would go to my head at all. My brain can't process it."

"I should have known something like this was the case when the trees called you mother. But today, there's something differ-ent, like you're changing."

"You mean menopause?"

Summer laughed. "I mean, you're answering the call of your destiny."

"Why is this happening to me now?"

"Only the goddess has the answer to that. Come, let's see if the trees behave any differently around you today. Forget I'm here. Connect with the forest, and allow me to observe."

Easier said than done. We walked along the trail of hard-packed soil and sand, coated with dead leaves, and textured with the curving tops of roots that had pushed their way to the surface. Roots that could trip a careless hiker or trail runner.

Images of the night at the Gilleys' property wouldn't leave my head. Roots behaving like the tentacles of krakens in a bad horror movie. They didn't scare me in the least. They only impressed me with their silent strength and resolve.

And the fact they came to my rescue.

To humans, trees are silent and unmoving. In reality, they are highly dynamic, constantly battling enemies and struggling to survive. Many of them flourish, rising into the sky above the competition to spread their branches and expose their foliage to the sun. While hidden to human eyes, their roots do the same, exploring beneath the soil in search of water, communicating with other trees.

I was one of their family now. I could feel all this activity going on around me as if I were part of it.

A low murmur filled my head from their communications. Previously, I needed my psychometry to sense what was going on in their root systems, but now it came to me more naturally.

There *has* been a change in me, I realized. How did it happen and why? What caused me to answer my call to destiny now? Have I always had this calling? If so, the guidance counselor in high school never mentioned it.

And why me? I was just a girl in a tiny, old city whose lineage included witches, but who didn't receive the gene.

My head swung toward a giant Southern live oak just off the trail. It was as if she were calling me. I came right up to her, wrapped my arms around her, and rested my cheek against her jagged bark.

I heard the swoosh of water rising up the trunk from her roots to her leaves, like the sound coming from an echocardiogram. The tree knew I was here and welcomed me.

Before you disparage someone as being a tree-hugger, make sure she's not actually a nature goddess.

I returned to the trail, a warm glow in my face as if I had just hugged a loved one.

"The trees know you," Summer said. "They know you as representing Danu, their mother."

"I can't really be a goddess. I mean, my knees ache in the mornings, and I have trouble opening prescription bottles. How can I be a goddess?"

"Like the faerie said, you are Danu's daughter."

"A woman named Sadie Chesswick would beg to differ."

Summer laughed and shook her head. "You are Danu's manifestation in human form. Does that sound better?"

"Yes, but just as wacky."

Just then, the sky that was visible through the treetops turned dark, as if a thunderstorm were brewing. The temperature plummeted. Goosebumps appeared on my arms.

The forest was alarmed. I wouldn't think trees would be afraid of rain. Lightning probably. Tornadoes most definitely. The problem was, there was no wind like you'd expect from an approaching storm.

"Is a storm coming?" I asked.

Summer shook her head. "Something supernatural is causing this. Can't you feel the energy?"

She was right. There was an energy that I could only describe as wrong. Evil. I'm not exactly a connoisseur of supernatural energies, so I couldn't identify it any better than that.

"We should get out of here," Summer said. "*Now.*"

I followed her back along the trail to the parking lot where I had met her today. Before we each got into our cars, Summer turned to me.

"The Memory Guild needs to know about your destiny and the supernatural event we just experienced."

"Okay," I said. "Let me know when we're meeting."

I didn't want to be the one to request it, because I didn't have a direct line to Dr. Noordlun. Having to go through Archibald to set up a meeting was simply too much trouble. I waved goodbye and got into my rental car.

Somehow, I found myself standing in the torch-lit hall where the Memory Guild meets. All the members were there. I guess Summer had a direct line.

"Why is everyone staring at me?" I asked.

"I, for one, am gobsmacked," Archibald said. "I never saw it in you."

"Oh, I did," Summer said.

"So did I," James said.

"I didn't," Gloria complained. "I'm a psychic who's supposed to see everything."

"To be fair," Dr. Noordlun said, "those of us who have lived in a strictly Judeo-Christian world would have little awareness of what is dismissively called paganism."

"Yes," Diego said. "Even though I'm a vampire, I was a strict Catholic when I was human."

"Can someone please tell me how this is going to affect my

life?" I asked. "Can I still be an innkeeper and a member of the Memory Guild? Or do I have to move to Mount Olympus?"

"That would be only for ancient Greek deities, dear," Archibald said.

"Well, do Celtic deities have their own mountain?"

"Actually, Danu, or Anu, has certain places in Ireland or Eastern Europe associated with her, but that's irrelevant." Dr. Noordlun had segued into his lecturing voice. "To answer your question, I simply do not know how this will affect your life. Or our mission here at the Guild. If there is some greater purpose for you, I suppose that will be revealed to you somehow."

"Will I have special, god-like powers?" I asked. That would be cool, wouldn't it?

"My, aren't you full of questions? If you have special powers, I'm certain you will discover them in due time. In the short term, however, I'm concerned about the supernatural event Summer and you experienced in the forest today."

"Does it have something to do with me?"

"I'm afraid it does, Darla. It might have been an old friend noticing you and paying you a visit."

When she saw my confused face, Summer said, "The Father of Lies. In Fae mythology, the god they associate with him is an enemy of the mother-earth goddess."

"If I'm attracting his attention, am I bringing danger to the Guild?"

Dr. Noordlun gazed at me, deep in thought. I don't believe he'd considered this possibility.

"If so, you must learn how, as a goddess, you can fight him."

"Perhaps Darla should stay away from the Guild," Diego said.

Dissenting murmurs spread through the group.

"It would be premature to take that course of action," Dr. Noordlun said.

He looked at me funny, though.

"DID YOU JUST SAY YOU'RE A GODDESS?" CORY ASKED WHILE he, Sophie, and I ate dinner in the cottage. "In a *literal* sense? Not like you're 'the goddess of inn-keeping hospitality'?"

"I'm not making this up. A faerie priest told me, and Summer pretty much confirmed it."

"How did she confirm it?"

"She asked the trees."

"Oh, of course."

"Don't be sarcastic, Cory," Sophie said. "You saw what the tree roots were doing at the Gilley house."

"Yeah." Cory took a bite of baked flounder and sulked.

"You don't have to complain anymore about being the only non-witch in the family, Mom."

"I didn't complain that much."

"Constantly," Sophie said.

"I was mostly jealous of the relationship the two of you have with Cervantes. Now, I can speak with him, too."

"A goddess." Cory shook his head and stared at his plate.

"Is this bothering you?" I asked.

"Yeah. How am I supposed to measure up as a husband to a goddess? I'm just a mere mortal with a little magic. Far from perfect, like a deity. I mean, how is a goddess going to tolerate a spouse who leaves the toilet seat up?"

"You can learn to leave it down."

"I'm fifty-six years old. That ship has sailed."

"Don't worry. It's not like I'll run off with Zeus because of a toilet seat."

"Speaking of age, does this mean you're immortal?" Sophie asked hopefully.

"I don't think so. Look at me—do I look ageless?"

"You just began being a goddess. So maybe the clock was paused beginning now."

"A goddess. Can you believe it?" Cory muttered.

"Listen, both of you, I am not Danu. I am her daughter, in a symbolic sense. I'm her physical manifestation on earth."

"So, you're not God, you're Jesus," Cory said. "Talk about setting a high bar."

"No, no, no." I was getting frustrated. "Pagan gods weren't all powerful like our modern conception of God. They represented elements of the world and the universe. Danu was a human-like symbol of nature and the concept of motherhood. I'm a representative of Mother Nature. I'm like her agent."

They stared at me blankly.

"Look, I'm trying to come to grips with this. I don't know what it all means yet. Maybe it means nothing except that I can communicate with trees. And that plants are popping up everywhere in the inn. Does it bother you, Cory, that I can talk with trees?"

"Not particularly. It sounds rather goofy when you put it that way."

"Good. We'll leave it at that."

I mentioned nothing about the Father of Lies, the Fae, and whether I had a responsibility to battle them. They were not suitable topics for the dinner table.

And, at some point, I would have to break the news to Mom that while she was certainly my biological mother, she was not the only mother in my heritage. I did not expect that conversation to go well.

CHAPTER 27

BILLIONAIRE'S ROW

My phone rang. It was Bob, which was surprising, since the mage never called me and never answered his phone.

"You told me to let you know if the fake key was going on a road trip," he said.

"How far away is it?"

Bob laughed. "I put a spell on it, not a GPS tracking unit. All I can tell you is it's leaving the San Marcos area and is headed south. You wanna try to catch up?"

"I don't know if I—"

"I'm parked outside the inn. Let's go."

Sophie was in the kitchen with me. I told her to hold down the fort, then jogged out the door, where Bob was waiting in a vintage Ford Mustang rather than the open-cab Jeep with the oversized tires he takes to the beach when surfing.

I hopped in, and Bob took off at twice the speed limit of the narrow city streets. It seemed to take forever to reach the interstate highway, but as soon as he merged from the entrance ramp, he floored it.

I felt like an astronaut slammed by multiple Gs during a launch.

"You're going to get a ticket," I said.

"I put on a spell that blocks the State Troopers' radar. If I see any of them hiding on the median ahead, I'll wrap the car in a cloak of invisibility."

"Do you do this often?"

"Ever since I almost got my license suspended. See, magic is a force for good."

"Don't you believe in safety?"

"I believe in getting to the beach with the best surf conditions before all the other surfers get there."

"I see." I clung to the armrest as if my life depended on it. Maybe it did.

About a half hour later, we blew past a familiar-looking blue BMW. Bob grunted.

"Dude, I just got a surge from the spell."

Looking in the passenger side-view mirror at the BMW receding behind us in the middle lane, I noted the German license plate on the front. Dorothy had one on her car.

"Slow down," I said. "I think the BMW you just passed might be him."

Bob glanced in the rearview mirror, then switched two lanes to the right. He allowed the BMW to catch up. The glass was tinted too dark to tell if the man driving was Gilley.

"I need to see the rear of the car," I said.

As the BMW drew ahead of us, I spotted the bumper sticker with an offensive political slogan. The same one Dorothy had.

"That's him. I can't believe he's driving the car of the wife he murdered."

"You gotta admit it's a nice car, though," Bob said.

"Just follow him."

For a long time, we traveled two car lengths behind Gilley. Bob talked at length about the surf shop in Daytona Beach advertised on several billboards, a competitor he believed was inferior. Then, the long silences got awkward as Bob spun through the radio stations. It can be uncomfortable being on a long drive with someone you don't know well.

"So," Bob said, "you're, like, a goddess now?"

"Who told you that? It's supposed to be a secret."

"The Memory Guild knows about it, right?"

"Yeah."

"The other guilds find out about stuff like this, eventually."

"Who told you?" I demanded.

"Your gargoyle."

I sighed in exasperation. Archibald didn't have permission to blab about this.

"I'm happy for you," Bob said. "We'll need all the help we can get fighting back the Fae, and a goddess might be just the ticket. I feel kinda responsible for letting things get this far. I didn't want to deal with Texas Tom when he tried to take over the Magic Guild. His association with the Fae, and his pact to help them, encouraged them to get involved in San Marcos."

"I sure hope Tom doesn't get out of jail again. Thanks to him ditching my car in a lake, my car insurance rates went up."

"I hear he had his magic neutralized."

"Yes. Thanks to the pearl. Ironically, a gift from the Fae."

"You shouldn't accept gifts from them, dude. It means you'll owe them forever."

I hadn't thought about it that way before. But I had no intention of giving the pearl back, which I said to Bob.

"If you're gonna keep it, you should play around with it, see if it has any special magic with you."

"What do you mean?"

"You're a nature goddess. The pearl was a product of nature —of some monster-sized oyster thousands of years ago. Who knows? Maybe you can coax some special magic out of it."

"I'll keep that in mind."

I thought about when I healed the Tugara. At the time, I gave the pearl all the credit, but maybe my being a goddess was the secret ingredient.

Gilley's BMW moved into the right lane, then eased its way onto an exit ramp. We followed him through the streets of West Palm Beach. We crossed a drawbridge over the Intracoastal Waterway, and, just as I had anticipated, entered the island of Palm Beach.

We were south of the city's small downtown of luxury retailers and restaurants. With Mar-a-Lago to our left, we curved around a traffic circle and headed south on A1A, passing one mansion after another.

"Ah, Billionaire's Row," Bob said.

A1A shifted slightly to the east and ran directly along the beach, so no mansions blocked our view of the calm Atlantic. To our right were the carefully manicured lawns and facades of homes that looked like they were plucked from European royal estates. Most of the properties had tunnels beneath the road, allowing easy access to the owners' cabanas on the beach below us.

"I can't believe the Faerie Queene has a place here," I said. "I mean, it's hard to imagine the leader of the Fae living among the banking CEOs and heirs to media empires."

"It's just her winter home, dude."

I shook my head. Here I was, supposedly a goddess, and I

felt inferior to these mega-rich folks. I suppose power comes in many forms. In this age of ours, when magic has been forgotten and scorned, money has taken its place.

The Faerie Queene obviously had both kinds of power. Now, she was poised to rule over her neighbors, who believed they were gods and goddesses themselves through wealth and influence alone.

The BMW ahead of us slowed, then turned into the driveway of a gigantic mansion, stopping at a metal gate. This estate was hidden behind a stone wall, unlike the other estates that had clear sight lines from the windows to the ocean—and for passing drivers to be able to admire them.

Dark towers topped with spires of steel that twisted like entwined snakes were the only feature of the mansion you could see from this angle. Definitely not a Palm Beachy look.

"Do you feel that?" Bob asked as we continued driving past the estate. "Tons of magic radiating from there."

Though I wasn't a witch, I felt the power in the air. My goddess role, having kicked in, must be why I could feel it, beyond my normal paranormal sensibilities.

"Let's find a place where we can park and come back to watch how long Gilley is here," I said.

We were in a strictly residential neighborhood. However, we soon came upon a small public beach where we parked. We had a long walk north along the beach until we arrived across A1A from the Faerie Queene's palace.

"How long do we have to sit here?" Bob asked.

"No idea. Something tells me he's not here to spend the night. My hunch is he's returning what he believes is the key. There could be strategy meetings planned. But I'm guessing he'll head back to San Marcos before long."

So, Bob and I sat on the beach, strange-looking beachgoers

who lacked towels and beach chairs, and faced the road instead of the ocean. Below the road was a sandy embankment covered in sea oats, abruptly severed by a sea wall. At the bottom was a heavy steel door to the tunnel beneath the road. The door was undoubtedly built to withstand the extra-high tides of a hurricane or nor'easter.

The Faerie Queene did not have a cabana or any structure near the tunnel. I guess faeries weren't big fans of hanging out on the beach.

I checked the door to the tunnel. It was locked, of course. And it radiated magic, probably some sort of warding spell.

"Dude," Bob said, "I got a sign from my spell that the key has been separated from Gilley."

"Okay, he handed it in. Errand accomplished."

About an hour later, the estate gates swung open. I stood up to see if Gilley's car had left. No, it was a black van that drove away.

Not long afterward, the gates opened for a tow truck that had arrived. When they opened again, I finally saw Gilley's car.

But it wasn't driving out. It was being towed by the wrecker.

"You really think his car died?" Bob asked doubtfully.

"No. I think Gilley died. The Faerie Queene recognized the key as a fake. Gilley and his car were disposed of."

"Kinda brutal for a faerie as high up as he was, you know?"

"It shows how important the key is to the Queene. Even the duplicate key. She probably thought he was deliberately counterfeiting it."

The realization that I was indirectly responsible for his death washed over me. Even though I had wanted to bring down this man, it wasn't a good feeling. He murdered his wife and was going to have me executed. Guilt, nevertheless, made my insides ache.

"We don't know for sure that he's dead," Bob said, consolingly.

"He's dead."

The ride back to San Marcos was long and free of talk. Over and over, I told myself that my job was done. Hugo's murder had been solved, Vance's murderer was in jail, and Dorothy's husband found a ghastly justice beyond the law.

My job wasn't done, though. No way could I convince myself it was. I had a key to Pandora's Box. Getting ahold of the box might be the only way we could stop the gathering Fae army.

Hours later, after the night had fully settled in, and we were approaching the exit to San Marcos, a thought came to me.

Was I behaving just like Pandora—too obsessed with the darned box to leave it alone?

"I AM *NOT* A GOSSIPING BLABBER-MOUTH, AND I RESENT THE insult," Archibald said in the inn's front room. Since he was carved to look like a demon, whenever he was angry like this, it was truly frightening. With his English accent and his voice up an octave, he sounded almost like he was singing.

"You told Bob I'm a goddess."

"Arch Mage Bob is a leading figure in the supernatural community, and I'm a senior member of our guild. I had every right to inform him of such an important development."

"It's nobody's business but mine."

"To the contrary, young missy. It is all of our business. Your new status could have severe repercussions throughout the supernatural community."

Only a stone entity who was nearly a thousand years old could call me a young missy without irony.

"Why is that?"

Before I got an answer, I got a summons. One that I had no say in. The instant my question had left my mouth, I found myself standing in the virtual meeting hall of the Memory Guild, complete with torches lit and members assembled on the imaginary stone floor.

"The repercussions have already occurred," Dr. Noordlun said to me sternly. Don't underestimate the effect of a large, white-bearded, Moses-like figure speaking to you sternly.

"The emergence of your goddess identity would naturally attract the attention of other divine entities," the professor said. "Such as the Father of Lies. Especially since you are engaging in conflict with the Fae, who treat him as a god instead of the devil he truly is."

"But I—"

"The attack on the Hall of Records was not random."

"Are you saying it's my fault?" I asked, stricken with guilt.

"Only that you have attracted the attention of the Father of Lies. He has always been our antagonist, but we are only mere pilot fish, swimming with a giant shark, unnoticed by the monster, cleaning up the mess he creates with every meal. Now, the shark has noticed us."

"And wants to eat us," Archibald chimed in.

"You can shut your trap, rock-head," I said in a low voice.

"We are grateful for all the information you have provided to us about the Fae," Dr. Noordlun said. "However, I ask you to please step aside and let the guilds of San Marcos handle this."

It was now or never: I had to tell them about Pandora's Box, as nutty as it would sound coming from my lips.

And boy, did it sound nutty. I hedged on the details of exactly how I gained possession of the key, but I told them it was given to Hugo by Dorothy, who stole it from her husband, a leader of the Fae, who was now most likely fish food.

I went into great detail when I described the memory I read on the golf cart about Pandora's Box. More description made it sound more believable. That my counterfeit key most likely spelled Gilley's doom couldn't be left out of the story.

I repeated what I had read in the memory: the hope remaining inside the box was critical for the Fae. And for us humans, too.

The case for stealing the box from the Faerie Queene, I thought, was cut and dry.

"You must surrender the key," Dr. Noordlun said, "and refrain from involving yourself in this matter. I applaud you for your accomplishments, but we shall take it from here."

"Who is 'we'?"

"The Executive Council of the Guilds of San Marcos. This moment is too monumental for any individual to freelance and create havoc. San Marcos will be in good hands."

I happened to catch Diego's eye. The vampire did not seem as confident as the good professor sounded.

CHAPTER 28

MUST BE THE WEATHER

"I heard you were supposed to surrender the key," Bob said, rubbing a towel across his considerable beer gut as we stood beside his jeep on the beach.

The few dozen other surfers in view all lacked big bellies. They were lean and trim, being several years younger than Bob. Despite his stomach and its effects on his balance atop the board, Bob was among the best surfers in San Marcos and surrounding beaches. I always wondered if magic had a role in that.

"If someone gets hold of the box and needs my key, they're welcome to use it. But I'm not simply going to give it up and have it sit in a drawer somewhere to punish me like a kid. What, I can't have it back until I get my grades up?"

"Like, why did Hugo give it to you, anyway?"

"He gave it to me accidentally." That was all I would say for now.

"I don't know if the kind of spell you want me to cast would work. The spell is supposed to alert me if the box is opened by the other key?"

"Right," I said. "The key is impregnated with Fae magic and is made with a metal that's not found on earth. The counterfeit key could open the lock—mechanically, that is. But the Faerie Queene knew it was fake. I'm guessing it's because the key fit the lock but wouldn't work. There must be a magical or some other connection between the box and the actual keys."

"So, like, you think your key will know if the other one opens the box?"

"Exactly."

"Uh, why would you care?"

"Because it's Pandora's freaking Box! When it opens, serious crap happens. If the Faerie Queene opens it, we need to know. It could mean the war is beginning."

Bob looked at me dubiously.

"I don't know," I said, frustrated. "I have a key to the most famous box in history and I can't use it! We need to find a way to advantage the humans while the faeries are plotting to destroy us."

"Okay, I'll give it a try." Bob shrugged. "The thing is, I'm not sure if it will work. There must be an attachment between the key and the box or between the two keys. You know what I'm saying?"

"You could be a little clearer."

"Like, your key was used before to open the box. That would connect it psychically to the box. Or the two keys were made together at the same time and shared the same magic."

"Okay. Fair enough. We'll never know unless we try."

"Yeah, try is all I can promise you. Let's go back to my shop. I have some potions in my office that I need."

I realized it wasn't an easy spell to create. It was like

installing a car alarm from a distance. Bob brought several small vials with him back to the beach, to the rocky area near where Hugo was found. Bob claimed this was an excellent area because there were few beachgoers, and the minerals in the rocks enhanced the energy he drew from the ocean.

He sat atop a flat rock and fiddled with the key, his potions, seashells, and an osprey feather. He even burned a small pile of dried seaweed. The whole thing took over an hour.

"Okay, dude. I did my best. I'm hoping there's enough of a connection now between this key and the box, as well as with the other key. If the box is opened, the key will let you know. If the spell works, I mean."

"How will it let me know?"

"Beats me. The key will tell you one way or another. But if you ask me, I don't think anyone's gonna open the box. Pandora opened it once, thousands and thousands of years ago, and all the gnarly stuff escaped into the world. If all that's left in there is hope, why open it and risk losing it?"

"Because the Fae need hope if they're going to take back the world? I don't know. Plus, there could be other ills that didn't escape the first time."

"I sure hope there aren't."

I KEPT THE KEY WITH ME AT ALL TIMES, NOW THAT I DIDN'T need to worry about Gilley coming after me. Of course, other faeries could come after me. I hoped suspicion that I had the key was restricted to Gilley and his inner circle, and that his circle wouldn't take any risks with their leader dead.

The key sat in a zippered cloth pouch, the kind you wore under your clothes to hide valuables from pickpockets. The pouch rested against my skin, just above my left hip. Frequently, I unconsciously patted my side to make sure it was still there.

No one from the Memory Guild had mentioned the key again, and I hoped they would forget about it. They had a lot more to worry about than me and the key.

Reports of faeries being spotted doing reconnaissance around San Marcos came in from the supernatural community. It was up to us to be vigilant, because regular humans were no help. They couldn't see faeries when they were in their natural form. When faeries were in human form, normal humans who spotted them would have no inkling the creatures were magical.

At the same time, Dr. Noordlun and the Memory Guild were increasingly paranoid about the Hall of Records getting attacked again. I felt horrible that my presence might have drawn the attention of the Father of Lies. I struggled to learn if my goddess status could cease being a liability and, instead, provide a way to fight the Father of Lies.

So, that's the crazy stuff I had to deal with, on top of the everyday crazy things that arose when running a bed-and-breakfast. You know, things like Darren's odors and tree seedlings growing in showers.

Today was one of those days. The kind when everything seems to go wrong, and everyone is in a bad mood. I used to think days like this happened when the weather was rotten, but today was sunny and beautiful. The bad stuff didn't seem to care that it was a perfect beach day.

First, a rotten-egg stench in the dining room had ruined breakfast and angered guests. It had only just ended when I had another problem. An argument broke out between Cory and an electrician he had hired to bring a bunch of wiring up to code.

When you have a 300-year-old inn, you're constantly going to have problems with things no longer meeting the building codes.

Too bad. The wiring had been installed when the house was first electrified in 1897.

"I'm telling you, I have to rip out the paneling in this room to get to the line that runs through here," the elderly electrician insisted.

"Forget it! This paneling is too valuable to be messed with. It's historic, can't you see? I know there are ways to get to the wires without tearing out the freaking walls."

It was very unlike Cory to be so argumentative.

"Well then, you can find yourself another electrician to do it."

The man stormed out of the inn with Cory looking like he wanted to clobber him.

"Everything okay?" I asked Cory.

"Oh, come on! I don't need another person on my case."

Cory stormed out of the room, with even more drama than the electrician's storming.

Okay, then. Something was truly off today.

It wasn't until Teatime that I learned why. I was pouring hot water into a cup for an ancient woman from St. Petersburg when the pouch under my blouse buzzed. It was a buzz ten times more intense than when your phone vibrates. In fact, it startled me so much I spilled hot water all over the old woman's plate of scones and finger sandwiches.

"Blast it all to Hades!" she said. "I'm not putting up with your delirium tremens while I'm trying to enjoy an egg-salad finger sandwich!"

She pushed back her chair and stood. Then, you guessed it, stormed out of the dining room.

Meanwhile, the preacher and his wife from 203 were complaining about the lemon tarts. I couldn't take it anymore. I set down the kettle next to the ruined finger sandwiches and left the room.

"Bob, the key was buzzing like crazy," I told him over the phone.

"Whoa, it worked!"

"Is there any way to know if the opened jar released anything into the world?"

"The key to the box won't be able to tell you that. I'll try to whip up a spell to find out. I have a few that detect when powerful magic has been cast by someone, but I don't know if they'll work. The evils of the world aren't actually magic. They're just evil."

"Whatever it is, everyone is in a foul mood today."

Bob grunted. "Bad sign, dude, bad sign."

THE NEXT EVENING, I SAT IN THE FRONT ROOM READING A book in the small sitting area. It was the original parlor of the house, but the door to the outside was no longer used. I'd moved the small desk that had been in here, which served as the inn's front desk, to the wide hallway just outside of this room, facing the foyer.

There were two comfy chairs and a loveseat facing the fireplace where Archibald lived, with an antique oriental carpet in the center. It was a cozy room, but people rarely came in here. Which was why I chose it.

I didn't want to deal with anyone tonight. Every social interaction I'd had today ended in bickering, including with my own family. It appeared more and more likely that whatever the Faerie Queene had released from the jar had something to do with it.

Before you accuse me of blaming my family arguments on some ephemeral concept that came out of a mythical urn, you should know how cranky every person I interacted with today was. In normal times, you'd pass it off as, "must be the weather," or, "there's something in the water."

These were not normal times. The cantankerous moods among us were not from the weather or the water. They came from evil. I was certain of it.

Archibald, who had been missing from the fireplace mantel, reappeared in animated form. He confirmed my theory.

"Oh, for heaven's sake, I had hoped this room would be empty," he said, not happy to see me.

"It was, and that is why I'm here."

"What a bloody awful evening this has been!"

"Why?" I asked.

"The Executive Council of the Guilds met tonight. It did not go well."

I felt rather left out, though I reminded myself that I was only a junior member of my guild, and the council is comprised of guild leaders and their adjutants.

"Was everybody in a bad mood?"

"You are putting it mildly, Darla. We met to come to a consensus, and instead, everyone spent the time finding points to argue about, most of which were trivial. I would like to point out that many of the guild leaders are human, and that made things worse. Humans are so illogical and, frankly, stupid. I wouldn't mind not speaking to one ever again."

"I should remind you I'm human."

"You are the only creature here to whom I can complain. And one could claim that you are no longer merely human, with this goddess silliness about you."

"Silliness? It sounds like you're trying to pick a fight with me,

Archibald. I have it on good authority that the Faerie Queene opened Pandora's Box and released another evil into the world. I believe that's what is causing all the disagreements lately. It's been nonstop—with everyone."

"Arch Mage Bob told the council about the spell he put on your key and what it reported. The key, I should add, you were supposed to surrender to Dr. Noordlun."

"Oops. Guess I forgot."

"You can keep the bloody key as far as I'm concerned. Currently, we face the problem of an impending Fae invasion. The guilds of the city are unable to come together to face the Fae. The Memory Guild and The Magic Guild have completely different priorities. Of course, The Clan of the Eternal Night wants nothing to do with either of us, which is exactly the snobbishness you'd expect from a bunch of vampires. And the Shifter's Guild? Spare me. They're behaving like a pack of dogs distracted by squirrels. Then, you have the trolls, pixies, sprites, elves, zombies, and others—all in disagreement."

"There's a zombie guild?"

"There was. Until tonight, when they all quit and wandered off looking for brains to eat. Bunch of morons, if you ask me."

"Divisiveness and distrust," I said. "I believe those are the evils that were released into the world."

"Some of us in the council came to the same conclusion. Though nowadays, there have been quite a lot of those particular ills already, wouldn't you say?"

"Yeah. Only the amount seems to have quadrupled now. What is the council going to do?"

"They couldn't agree on doing anything," Archibald said. "One member pointed out that spreading distrust and divisiveness was clearly a strategic move by the Faerie Queene, making organized resistance against her impossible. Despite the obviousness of this point, we couldn't overcome it and unite. It was pathetic."

"Surely, the common threat of the Fae is greater than any disagreement among us."

"You would think so."

"Then it's up to ordinary humans to save us all?" I asked.

Archibald shook his stony head. "The Fae can retake all their lands and dominate all the inhabitants, and the humans will never notice. There don't have to be armed battles or physical confrontations. The Fae will simply infiltrate the existing power structures the humans already have that keep most of their population under control. Humans make a lot of noise about being free, but they aren't as free as they like to believe."

I thought about the Faerie Queene's mansion among those of the human billionaires who run the world. She was already fitting in quite nicely.

"Well, that was quite a dose of despair," I said.

"One of the ills Pandora had already set free upon us all."

Still, according to the myths, hope remained inside the jar. Perhaps a little dose of it could turn things around.

It made me yearn once again to get my grubby little hands on the jar.

CHAPTER 29

THE VAMPIRE THIEVES

Archibald transitioned to stony slumber. Now, I assured myself, I would enjoy my book without interruption. I sat in the front room, beneath the Tiffany lamp, and read an old-school mystery novel without a trace of the supernatural in its plot. It reminded me of my previous life, before I was forced to accept the existence of all sorts of creatures that used to only appear in novels and movies.

In the book I was reading, I was absolutely certain the bad guy would be human, and the means of murder would obey the accepted laws of physics and credulity. For you, this would be normal. For me, in my crazy world, it was like reading an outlandish fantasy novel.

To prove my point, I'd only read half a chapter when someone walked into the room.

A vampire.

"Diego," I said, "what brings you here tonight?"

What brings you into my home without knocking, was what

I was thinking. That myth about vampires needing permission to enter your home was just that—a myth.

"I have a proposition for you," he said.

Another legend about vampires—that they were excessively territorial—happened to be true.

Roderick suddenly appeared in the front room.

"Can I help you?" he asked ultra-aggressively, of Diego.

In body age, Diego was in his late-twenties, early thirties. He was elegant and handsome, lean and muscled, his skin a medium shade of brown.

Roderick, on the other hand, had a body age in his sixties with an awkward build and thinning, unkempt white hair. His dark, moldy suit had gone out of style in the eighteen-nineties. His complexion was a deathly shade of white, for which he could be forgiven, being a vampire and all.

If Roderick wanted to fight Diego for territorial reasons, it would be the biggest mistake of his very long existence.

"Please accept my apologies for not asking permission from the vampire of the house to enter," Diego said. "I had an urgent need to speak with Ms. Chesswick."

Roderick looked relieved. "In the future, please do not forget."

Diego nodded, then returned his attention to me.

"Do you still have the key to the jar the Fae possess?"

I nodded.

"The Clan of the Eternal Night wishes to borrow it. As vampires, we have been only mildly affected by the distrust and divisiveness that has crippled the other guilds. We are resolved to act to prevent the Fae from conquering us all. We plan to send our band of vampire thieves to steal the jar and release more hope into the world. Hopefully, this will overcome the negativity everyone feels for others."

"Isn't that risky?" I asked. "You don't want to splurge the hope."

"No, we plan to release not all of it, only enough to counter the recent evils the Faerie Queene has sent into the world."

"How would you even know how much is enough?"

Diego shrugged. "No one could know for sure. We would have to trust our instincts."

"Would vampires' instincts know what is best for mortals?"

"We experience the same emotions you do. Our immortality gives us more wisdom and perspective than you."

I pursed my lips with doubt. "Your plan sounds pretty far-fetched, don't you agree?"

"Of course it is," Diego said with an ironic smile. "We're in an extreme situation, however. If the distrust and divisiveness aren't counteracted, it will mean more than our defeat by the Fae. It could lead to violence between guilds, between humans and supernatural creatures. And, of course, among the different factions of humans, who have a history of such violence."

"Who are the vampires to make such decisions?" Roderick asked stuffily.

Diego stared at him with narrowed eyes. "We are the only ones with the resolve to do anything, unlike the naysayers."

Roderick harrumphed and adjusted his cravat.

"What do you say, Darla?" Diego asked. "May we have the key?"

"No."

"What? Why not?"

"I don't want to give it up. Sorry, but I don't trust anyone else with the key. I've formed a bond with it—at least as much as a human could. You would have to bring me with you so that I could open the jar."

"The band of thieves would never agree to bring a human with them."

My telepathy was tickled by thoughts coming from Diego. Another untrue myth about vampires is that their thoughts can't be read.

"Don't you dare try to mesmerize me to give you the key," I said. "Roderick will stop you from getting it."

"I will?"

"Perhaps we can work out an arrangement so that you can keep the key," Diego said. "I will return with more information."

Just like that, he was no longer in the room, leaving so quickly my eyes didn't register it. The sound of the front door swishing shut came from the front of the foyer.

"I think his plan is preposterous," Roderick said. "And it's not as if the vampire thieves are some sort of mystical ninjas. They are completely fallible, as you recall."

I did recall. One of their thieves was hired to steal a magic coin from me and was foiled by Archibald and Roderick, if you can believe that.

"Frankly, I have doubts that the Fae have Pandora's Box," Roderick said. "Or that it even exists. It's only a dusty old myth. I believe the divisiveness that besets us is caused by cable news and social media."

"Oh, do you? Do you even consume those?"

"Not exactly." Roderick cleared his throat and re-adjusted his cravat.

"I have seen the jar in the memories of more than one individual. Arch Mage Bob told me that many in the Magic Community are adamant about the existence of Pandora's Box. The legends say it fell into the hands of the Fae as long ago as when gods roamed the earth."

"Pshaw, I say. And you are truly bonkers if you go with those thieves to break into the Faerie Queene's palace. Imagine what could happen to you."

I allowed myself to imagine just that, and a certain dagger with a wavy blade came to mind.

"I'd rather not imagine."

I WAS SITTING IN THE BACK OF A VAN WITH A BUNCH OF vampires. Not an optimal situation for the faint of heart. You might think I'm brave because of all the reckless endeavors I stumble into, and it couldn't be further from the truth. My courage is only that of an impulsive person who doesn't game out all the things that could go wrong before I plunge into danger.

I like to say I'm spontaneous. It sounds a lot more fun than impulsive. Tonight, it wasn't.

I'm also very determined to do what needs to be done. Some people with this quality use it to achieve worldly success. For me, determination really came into play when I reached midlife and my paranormal powers bloomed.

At my age, it's easier to realize what needs to be done isn't the same as what you need to do to be happy or successful. Often, doing the right thing brings no reward other than some deep satisfaction and a feeling of righteousness.

So, that brings me back to the van with six vampires, not counting Diego, who wasn't a member of the thieves. They were of different body ages and mixed genders, and all were in excellent physical condition. And darned hot looking. They also had the air of cold ruthlessness. Which kind of reduced the effect of their hotness on me.

The band of vampire thieves had existed in San Marcos

before there were enough vampires residing in town to create a guild. Some of the thieves were over a thousand years old and could boast of lifting valuable objects from famous humans throughout history. Many of the thieves were also accomplished spies. After the Cold War was over, some of them moved to San Marcos in semi-retirement.

Now, they had to enter what was probably the most heavily guarded home—physically and magically—in Palm Beach. When burglarizing humans, the vampires relied on their mesmerizing abilities, as well as the heightened strength, speed, and senses that vampirism gave them.

But what about the Fae's magic that surely guarded the palace? Could the vampires get past that?

To help with that, Arch Mage Bob came along. He rode shotgun while Diego drove. I was in the back with the blood-suckers and a trove of weapons, including darts and crossbows.

This was not a normal activity for a middle-aged innkeeper, was it?

"The house we have rented is half a block from the mansion," Diego said to Bob and me. "Is that close enough for your location spells to work?"

"I think so," Bob replied. "Remember, dude, we'll only be able to give you an approximate location in the building. We don't have a freaking floor plan of the place."

"The approximate location will be of some assistance," said an older, hawk-nosed vampire with a heavy European accent named Olaf. He was the leader of the thieves.

When we arrived in Palm Beach, we went west on a short side street perpendicular to A1A where the palace was. The home the vampires had rented was worth multi-millions but was considerably smaller than the Faerie Queene's digs and didn't have an ocean view.

The van had the signage of a catering company, so hopefully, the neighbors wouldn't be suspicious. Even though we were showing up at 10:30 p.m. You see, we couldn't travel until after sunset, thanks to my undead travel companions.

"We are going to scout the area now," Olaf said. "You do your magic and report the results."

"Whatever, dude," Bob said. He clearly didn't enjoy taking orders from anyone. He also seemed apprehensive about his spell working.

While the vampires piled out of the back of the van, Bob and I wandered onto the carefully manicured front lawn of the rented house. Bob sat cross-legged next to a burbling fountain and faced east. The ocean was only a few houses away. I sat nearby while he went into a meditative state, most likely drawing energy from the ocean and from within himself.

"The key," he said, holding out his hand.

I removed it from the pouch inside my blouse and placed it in his hand—this key that almost got me killed and appeared to be the cause of Gilley's demise. Bob's beefy hand closed around it.

He mumbled rhythmic lines of what sounded to be Latin, and suddenly a glowing light appeared above him.

"Find the lock to which you belong," he whispered.

The glowing light drifted away toward the east. It wasn't a concentrated ball of light like the faerie orbs; this one was fainter and more ethereal.

"The psychic energy that ties the key to its lock was brought to life by my spell," he said. "The ball of energy is drawn naturally to the lock and will find it. While the spell is active, I can see what the ball sees."

"Will the Fae see it, too?"

"I don't think so. As the mage who brought it to life, only I can see it."

"I saw it," I said.

He looked at me with surprise. "Whoa, that's whacked out. It's probably because you're attached to the key yourself, having held it for so long. Gotta hope no one else has a connection to it."

"Gilley did. But he's no longer with us. And I guess the Faerie Queene may have held it at some point."

Bob waved his hand in dismissal and returned his concentration to the spell, his face growing slack as he entered a semi-hypnotic state.

"The mansion has three floors," he said. "The ball just went through a window on the second floor on the north side. Huge suite of rooms running across the entire width of the house. Must be the Queene's personal space. It's going into a small room that looks like a chapel. An altar. Whoa, it's stained with blood! Candles. Creepy paintings on the wall. I see a chest made of gold. Nope, the ball's not going to it. It's going toward a jar in the corner. There's a lid on the jar with a keyhole. Light is seeping from the keyhole. Something magical. Oh no, someone came into the room! The ball of energy went away. I lost contact with it."

Bob came out of his semi-trance and his eyes met mine.

"I hope whoever came into the room didn't see the ball of energy," he said.

"If it was the Faerie Queene, she could have seen it. If she has ever used this duplicate key."

Suddenly, Olaf was standing between us. I practically jumped out of my shoes. I'll never get used to how fast vampires move.

"Do you have any intel for us?" he asked.

"The box is actually a tall jar, and it's in a small room that looks like a chapel on the second floor, north side of the mansion," Bob said. "Probably the Queene's private chambers. The jar is brownish from age, with faded blue and red artwork of planets and stars on it. There's—"

Olaf was gone.

"Vampires really bug me, you know?" Bob said.

"I know."

"Are we supposed to just sit here and wait? What if the vampires are going into an ambush?"

"Even if there isn't an ambush, how are six vampires going to get into the Queene's chambers without being staked? There could be hundreds of faeries guarding her. Plus, faeries are nocturnal, just like the vampires. Whose idea was this raid, anyway?"

"The Duke of the Clan of the Eternal Night. He's totally stoked about his thieves."

Three Fae surveillance orbs flew by overhead.

"Let's go wait in the van," I said.

Before we made two steps, the poop—as the expression goes —hit the fan.

Shouts and screams came from the distance, along with breaking glass. The neighborhood was filled with a chorus of barking dogs. Lights began popping on in the homes around us.

A small swarm of faeries flew overhead toward the palace.

This was Palm Beach, where mayhem was not welcome. Especially not involving swarms of armed faeries.

A siren wailed, from far away but getting closer.

"Dang," Bob said, "I think the raid failed."

I raced down the street toward the mansion. Yeah, I know, pretty stupid and reckless, but the chance of getting my hands on Pandora's Box was slipping away.

Boy, I truly was obsessed with it. That wasn't healthy, but my psychological wellbeing was the least of my worries at the moment.

As I neared the palace, one of the vampire thieves shot past me faster than an arrow. Then another one passed by carrying a crossbow, limping and not moving as quickly.

The grounds of the palace were flooded with light. The front door was wide open, and I moved toward it instinctively. Two dead faeries lay in the bushes nearby.

The sound of clashing swords came from a nearby hall, but I couldn't see what was going on. And why were they fighting with swords? Of course, if they'd been shooting firearms, there would be a hundred police cars arriving right now.

Halfway down the wide hall before me was a grand staircase leading to the second floor. I ran toward it and jogged up the stairs. Crossbow bolts protruded from the stairs and railings, along with darts and small faerie spears.

A buzzing of insect wings came from behind me, and I ducked. Several faeries flew past without bothering me and headed toward the battle noises.

A vampire thief leaped from the second-floor landing, landed lightly in the main hallway, and disappeared through the front door.

I reached the landing and sprinted down a hallway toward the north end of the building.

Toward the Queene's chambers. If the jar was still there, and I could get to it, I was going to open it. I didn't care how reckless I was acting. We couldn't let the raid fail.

At the very least, I had to release some hope into the world if we were going to stop our infighting and defend ourselves against the Fae.

I couldn't live without opening Pandora's Box.

My last thought disturbed me, but I kept running. The

palace seemed deserted. They must have evacuated the Queene for protection.

I passed a large, heavy door that hung open. And now I was in a maze of rooms, all sumptuously appointed with lots of mirrors and gold leaf, but hipper, more contemporary furniture than you'd expect in a palace.

It almost tripped me as I ran down a smaller hallway.

The large ceramic jar lay on its side, half in and half out of a doorway. It was ancient-looking, with painted symbols of stars and planets. Greek lettering wrapped around its base. I instantly knew in my heart it was Pandora's Box. I just knew.

And its heavy wooden lid, with an intricate locking mechanism, lay open.

I dropped to my knees. The jar was too heavy for me to lift, so I bent over and looked into the jar's opening.

It was empty. I sensed nothing inside of it. No magic, no evils, no hope. Nothing.

This had been done deliberately. I touched the two curved handles attached to where the jar's diameter was widest.

A woman's recent thoughts pulled me in. They were the Queene's. The language of her musings was indecipherable to me, but I'd encountered it enough by now to recognize it as Fae. Anger and disappointment motivated her, as I watched her visual memory, having seen Bob's magic ball of light and knowing someone was looking for the jar. Next, her memory of opening it, then of tipping it over.

Where had the hope gone? Had anything else escaped the jar with it?

I sat back on my heels, totally bereft. Defeated. What will we do now?

Heat flared on my side. It came from the key hidden under

my top. Suddenly, I had the strongest urge to try the key in the lock, even though it seemed it was now too late.

I removed the key from the pouch. It was so hot it almost burned my fingers.

The circular mahogany lid lay open at the top of the jar like the mouth of a beached fish. Intricate patterns of gold, silver, and mother-of-pearl covered its top. At the edge was a heavy metal lock with a keyhole.

I slipped the key into it and turned it, watching the bolt slide out. Turning it back and forth, as the bolt went in and out, my fingertips brushed the lock's face around the keyhole.

Someone else's memory came to me. It wasn't the Faerie Queene's. It was from someone who lived thousands of years ago, the individual who had installed the lock on the jar. And the male creature—of what species it was unclear—thought about his task, performed after Pandora had opened the jar. He knew the lock would make people want to open the jar more than Pandora had, and their intrigue would keep them focused on the jar.

And not on the small box he had made with a matching lock that accepted the same skeleton key. This knowledge comforted him, for the box had valuable contents.

What was in this other box? His freaking memory did not tell me!

My arms were seized, and I was yanked to my feet.

"What are you doing here?" Olaf asked, furious.

My mouth opened, but no words came out.

"We must leave here now," he said, tossing me over his shoulder.

The world was a blur as we raced to a large window and crashed through, landing with a jolt in a side yard, then somehow ending up in the back of the catering van.

Everyone was here. Half of the vampires were wounded, but their wounds healed before my eyes.

Diego maneuvered the van out of the neighborhood seconds before the police cars arrived.

The key, back in its pouch against my side, slowly cooled. Was I the only one who knew it opened not just Pandora's Box, but an additional container?

I guess I'll have to keep the danged thing in case I ever need it.

CHAPTER 30

DAUGHTER OF DANU

The end of the mattress near my feet sank from the weight of someone sitting on it, and my eyes snapped open. A woman sat there in the darkness, staring at me. Cervantes, who had lost his sleeping spot to the woman, curled in her lap purring.

"Sophie?"

As soon as my words escaped my lips, I knew it wasn't her. This woman was larger than Sophie, had red hair bright enough to stand out in the moonlight filtering through the blinds. She wore a grey cloak of heavy linen.

"We have a lot of work to do," she said in an Irish accent.

Cory continued sleeping.

"Um, are you here to apply for the housekeeping job?"

She laughed heartily. Cory still didn't awaken.

"No, I'm here to help ye get your act together."

"Please don't tell me you're a life coach."

"I'm a Druid. Me name's Birog. I worshipped the goddess

Danu back in the day. Way back in the day. She sent me here to give ye a little nudge, maybe a kick in yer bottom."

"Why? I'd like to go back to sleep, please. I'm exhausted. I tried to take Pandora's Box from the Fae, only to find it had been emptied."

"I could have told ye that was a waste of time."

"I'm only an innkeeper. All this has been way beyond my pay grade. Please let me go back to sleep, okay?"

"Now listen here, will ye?" She leaned closer to me. I noticed she had symbols, like the triskelion, painted on her cheeks, and the ends of her red hair were braided and tied with small ribbons. "Ye haven't been fulfilling yer duties as the daughter of Danu. Ye got mighty responsibilities."

"I don't know what they are," I said in a whiny voice.

"That's why I'm here—to tell ye. First and foremost, ye got the power to stop these faeries from running amok. The Fae worship ye, too, ye realize that?"

"One of them said something to that effect. How am I supposed to stop them? Just wave my hands? I don't know what I can do as the agent of the goddess, other than get trees to disrupt the Fae's tunnels. The problem with trees, though, is they tend to stay in the same place. I can't make them into an army to march against the Fae."

"I'm not gonna give ye instructions. Ye'll learn your powers in time. First, ye got to be aggressive with the Fae. That's how ye'll discover the powers ye got."

"But really, how much can I do on my own? The supernatural guilds are too busy fighting among each other to fight the Fae. The Faerie Queene made it worse by releasing more distrust and divisiveness into the world. I was hoping to use hope to counteract this, but there's no hope left in Pandora's Box."

"All the hope ye need is already out in the world. It's hidden deep in the hearts, minds, and souls of everyone alive. It's up to folks to look deep inside themselves to find the hope they need, then bring it out. That's what religion is for. And music, poetry, art, and magic. Ye're in a guild that preserves memory, are ye not?"

"Yeah. The Memory Guild."

"We all have hope in us, even if we've forgotten. We're all born with the memory of divine hope. Come on, Daughter of Danu, make it come alive!"

"You said magic brings hope? What kind of magic?"

"Oh, there're many kinds of magic that can kindle hope. Ye got plenty of it yourself, ye know?"

"No, I don't know. I only have a couple of paranormal abilities. I'm not a witch like the rest of my family."

"Ye don't need to be a witch to use magic. Just look at the Fae—they have their own magic."

"I'm a human. We need witchcraft to create magic."

"Ye're not a normal human. Ye're the daughter of Danu. The goddess is in you. Ye got the magic of the divine."

I admit, I'd been jealous of my mother, daughter, and husband who inherited witchy genes, while I didn't. I mean, I never grew up wanting to be a witch, but I felt like I was missing out, especially when Sophie and Cory turned out to have magic after no one knew they did.

Therefore, this whole goddess thing intrigued me. As crazy as it seemed, it also gave me hope. Yes, hope. Half a century on this earth and now I was turning out to be someone special.

I smiled.

Birog the Druid smiled back at me. "Ye will figure it out."

Then she disappeared. The end of the mattress rose to its proper height, and Cervantes sniffed the spot to reassure himself the woman really had been there.

Was Birog yet another ghost in my inn, or was she some other type of entity?

I sat in stunned silence.

Cory snored.

BELIEVE IT OR NOT, I FELL ASLEEP AGAIN, EVEN AFTER HAVING an ancient Druid sitting on my bed. Maybe it was the way Cervantes relaxed and curled up with his eyes closed. Or the way Cory slept on, oblivious to the fact we had a visitor in our bedroom.

I slept, and then I dreamed of Danu: silken auburn hair, shining green eyes, and a face that was young and yet so world-weary. She stood naked in a pool of water beside a forest stream. Her hair was long, hanging beneath her breasts, and flowers were woven into it.

She was the embodiment of fertility, yet she seemed so ancient beneath her youthful features. She smiled at me.

You must bring healing to the world, she said, her words telepathically appearing in my head. *Use the pearl to heal and to enhance your strength.*

Why me? I asked.

I am too old and have been forgotten by humans. A goddess who has been forgotten cannot act upon the earth.

Again, I ask, why me? I'm not really your daughter.

You are, for I have chosen you. You have the power to bring memories to life again. Just like nature's cycle of life, death, and rebirth. Bringing forgotten memories back to life is a form of hope. I fear this world is dying for lack of hope.

Everyone keeps talking about hope.

I chose you to be my representative on earth, so you can resurrect the memories of me. This will allow me to return and save the world from the poisons and the hatreds that are killing it.

How do I resurrect your memory?

Use the human ways of sharing stories. And you must battle the Father of Lies. Falsities are the opposite of memories. They create a world that never existed while wiping out the world that does.

And how do I do that?

She merely smiled, and the dream turned into the one I have all the time about being in school and remembering I'm enrolled in classes I've never attended or done work for. After walking through the school corridors fretting, I tried to go into a classroom but realized I was naked. Then, I dreamed about eating pizza.

Okay, enough of this nonsense, my subconscious said.

I awoke feeling more exhausted than when I had gone to bed.

I SUFFERED FROM THE WEIGHT OF TOO MANY MAJOR responsibilities on my shoulders, with no idea of how to deal with them. Running a 300-year-old inn on a shoestring budget was easy compared to the challenges I had before me.

Like Mom would say, don't get overwhelmed by all the tasks before you. Focus on one at a time and cross it off your list.

When it came to the threat the Fae posed to humankind, that was not for me alone to solve. What I could combat, though, was the threat to the Memory Guild and me. The most dangerous one, of course, was to the Hall of Records, the very memories of the Memory Guild.

I discussed this with Cory in the morning over muffins and coffee as I prepared eggs and sausages for the guests.

"I've already been working on it," Cory said with a self-satisfied grin as he spread Florida orange-blossom honey on a piece of toast.

"You have?"

"Yeah. You've been so distracted by Pandora's Box, and I've been obsessing over what would happen if they attacked the Hall of Records again. It needs a protection spell, a lasting one that doesn't require constant attention from the witch who cast it."

"Right. How can we do that?"

"Sophie."

"Sophie?" I was a supportive mom, but I knew my daughter was still new to spell casting.

"She has the potential to be a great magician, Darla. Let's face it: I'm not cut out to be much of a witch. Yeah, I have the magic gene. Texas Tom recognized it and exploited me for it. But I think I have PTSD from my year as his captive and slave. Practicing magic triggers the trauma."

I placed my hand on his.

"Sophie, though, is special," he said. "I can sense it. Can't you?"

"I do. But she has so much to learn. You know as well as I that becoming a great witch takes years of practice, study, and research. It's like being a leading neurosurgeon."

"Which is why Arch Mage Bob has been giving her lessons."

"He has? He never mentioned it to me."

"I asked him not to mention it for a while. Until you were less . . . distracted."

It stung to be reminded of how my obsessions have led to me ignoring my family and putting them into harm's way. I had to do better. Well, as soon as I got my obsessions out of the way.

Cory continued, "Sophie and Bob have been specifically working on developing a powerful protection and warding spell that can be maintained with minimal intervention. Sort of set it and forget it. The one thing I can contribute is my ability to harvest energy from ley lines. The extra power this can provide could very well make the spell work."

"How is the spell coming along?"

"Yesterday, Sophie told me it was almost there."

"Let's hope the Fae don't attack again in the meantime."

CHAPTER 31

DARREN

I hate to break it to you, but being the material manifestation of a goddess isn't all it's cracked up to be.

You would think I would be above such mundane concerns as the clogged sink drain in 304. You would be wrong. No, I didn't have any goddess-like power to unclog it. The liquid stuff I bought at the hardware store was a waste of money. I had to use one of those snake tools before the drain finally worked again. Half a morning wasted.

Shouldn't a goddess have a handyman working for her to do these things? Yeah, but our profit margin was far from heavenly at the Esperanza Inn. So, the handyman job went to my husband, who recently returned to my life, only to be assigned today to a project even worse than the drain. Getting the rats out of the dumpster.

He was convinced a magic spell would do the trick. But his warding spells only lasted about a day. Any garbage bag that contained food would eventually fall prey to the rats, who would tear the bag open, spilling its contents throughout the dumpster.

That created a horrible smell, which attracted more rats and citations from the city.

Today, Cory was waist-deep in the dumpster, trying to strengthen his warding spell while using conventional ways to get rid of the rats.

Never fall for the myth that running a small inn is cozy and quaint.

After I unclogged the drain, you could say my day went down the toilet. I took the elevator from the third floor, which I normally avoid. However, I was carrying too many tools to use the stairs safely. Before the elevator even reached the second floor, the blasted contraption came to a shuddering halt with a clattering of metal and a jangling of the chain that hung below it.

This cage I was trapped in was a historic relic that should be in a museum, not carrying precious humans up and down dangerous heights. The thing is, the elevator passes every safety inspection. Plus, we can't afford to replace it with a more modern model.

It carried not only humans. The noise, and the offensive odor, alerted me that I shared the elevator today with a ghostly passenger.

"Darren, is that you?"

A masculine moan came from near the door, as if he was as desperate to get out of here as I was.

"Did you stop the elevator, Darren?"

He partly materialized and shook his shaggy-haired head in the negative. Great. I had hoped it was he who stopped it and that I could convince him to change his mind. Instead, it must be mechanical, which meant I—I mean, we—could be stuck in here for hours.

One reassuringly modern feature of the elevator was a "help" button. It connected with a call center for the maintenance service.

A disembodied female voice answered, and I told her my predicament.

"I'll send someone out. You hang in there."

Ha ha. Funny. I was hanging by a delicate steel cable and wasn't in the mood for jokes.

"She tells us to hang in there," I said aloud, trying to make conversation with Darren.

He faded away, no doubt resenting the joke. Okay, so I would be stuck in here alone.

My eyes darted around the metal cage as hints of claustrophobia crept into my brain. I tried to keep my thoughts on something else.

Being in a metal cage allowed me to see the steel elevator shaft surrounding me on all sides. The front of the cage had only an accordion door, which you opened by hand when the elevator car arrived at each floor and aligned with the external doors. Being stuck between floors meant I could see the bottom of the closed third-floor doors above me and the top of the second-floor doors below me.

I was surprised by how much distance there was from floor to floor. Between the support beams for each floor, there was more than enough room for the electrical wiring and ductwork for the HVAC system. These elements did not exist when the inn, originally a large private home, was built.

Why there was so much space between floors stumped me. I had an idea.

"Be honest with me, Darren. Did you stop the elevator? And did you do it to signal to me that your remains are between the third floor and the second-floor ceiling?"

His apparition appeared again, still semi-transparent. He stared at me with an expression that said, "Duh?"

"Give me some help here," I said. "I can't tear out floorboards or ceilings to look for you. If this is where you're resting, can you give me some specifics?"

Ghosts were attracted to me because of the paranormal in me. I wondered if my quasi-goddess status would have any effect on them. So far, it didn't seem to. Apparently, disembodied spirits were not impressed by a nature goddess. Maybe if he were a tree, I'd have better luck communicating with him.

The elevator jolted. I gasped, expecting it to plunge two and a half stories down to the ground and leave me on the floor of the cage like a broken egg.

Instead, it rose and returned to the third floor. The exterior doors slid open. I pulled the lever on the handle and rolled the folding cage door aside, leaping out into the hallway as if my life depended on it. Because it sort of did.

Darren had disappeared. Good riddance to him, I thought, as I dragged my plumbing equipment toward the stairwell.

When I rounded the corner, Darren stood blocking my path. He was manifesting solidly. You'd think a real, live human was standing in front of me in his baggy brown corduroy slacks, white turtleneck, and tan cardigan sweater. He seemed younger than his normal apparition, with his bushy mustache free of any gray hairs.

"What do you want, Darren?"

He turned and walked toward the north side of the building, looking back once as if I should follow him. I placed my gear on the floor and headed after him.

When he reached the door to 303, he looked back at me again, then passed through the door. I should have known; this was the room where I first had an odor problem. The room that was already haunted by another ghost.

Using my pass key, I entered the room, which was currently vacant. It was dark, since the wooden blinds were closed, and the heavy curtains pulled across them.

I was in here only yesterday, when the curtains and blinds had been opened. I opened them now, flooding the room with the morning light. No ghosts were going to mess with me.

Darren stood by the bathroom door. He wanted me to go into the bathroom, and I wasn't surprised.

I turned on the bathroom light and looked around. The room was from the Art déco era, with a pedestal sink, subway tile walls, and black-and-white checkered tile on the floor. The bathtub blended in with the style, but appeared to be of a much newer vintage, long and rectangular with wide rims, a good tub for soaking.

I had long ago searched this bathroom for memories. My psychometry had never picked up anything related to Darren.

At the moment, his ghost stood beside the tub, staring at it with a puzzled expression on his spectral face.

I believed Darren had been trying to convey to me that his body was in between the third and second floors. If I had to guess, I'd say he was in the space below the tub, which had prob-ably been replaced during Darren's tenure as owner of the inn.

Exactly how he got under there was the question.

I felt a strange sensation, as if a switch had been flicked, and I shifted out of the scene, viewing it as if from behind a glass screen. The lighting suddenly changed. It was nighttime now, and the bedroom behind me was illuminated by lamplight. The bathroom lighting was enhanced by a portable work light clamped to the shower curtain rod above.

It shined into a bathtub-sized open hole in the floor. The old tub had been removed and taken away. I couldn't turn my head and avert my gaze, but out of the corner of my eye I saw the new bathtub just outside the bathroom door, still in its cardboard crate.

Darren's ghost was replaying his memory to me. I had a feeling about what was going to happen next in this ghostly movie and didn't want to watch it. But I couldn't close my eyes or turn away.

A very much alive Darren knelt on the bathroom floor, reaching into the hole to fiddle with the drainpipe rising from the darkness. The floor beams appeared to be extremely old, obviously the original ones from 1736, huge and strong looking. Beneath them, I saw only darkness that felt as if it cloaked a large space.

Something moved behind me, but my eyes wouldn't leave the spectral movie screen.

An apparition passed by me into the bathroom. It was Helga, the Victorian-era bride who had been murdered, pushed from the window of this room by her jealous husband. I'd seen her ghost in the room many times.

You could say Helga's ghost and I got along well, especially since she helped me battle Samson's former partner, who had been possessed by a demon at the time. I wouldn't call her a friendly ghost, like that of the Elvis impersonator in Room 202. She was still distraught over her untimely death and behaved as you would expect a ghost to behave—hauntingly. Nevertheless, this room was popular with ghost aficionados, and I'd never received a complaint about her.

She did not, however, like Darren. That was obvious as she swept into the bathroom howling like a banshee, her face twisted in tormented fury.

And Darren did not like her. This was obvious in his look of horror as his face, drained of blood, jerked up from his work to look at her. It was also obvious in the way he rose upright on his knees and clutched his chest.

His pale complexion turned blue as his expression mimicked the torment in Helga's. He wobbled, then keeled over, dropping into the opening where the tub would go. First, he landed on a beam, but as his body fully collapsed, it rolled to the side and dropped between the beams, disappearing into the dark space below.

My first instinct was to rush forward to help him, but I couldn't move. Then, I remembered this scene happened over three years ago.

The sense of being shifted came over me again. And all at once, I was back in the present, looking at the finished bathroom with the tub installed.

Darren was down there, below it somewhere. I shuddered to think of all the guests who took relaxing baths in this tub, with no idea moldering bones were below them.

I was truly surprised that no one had thoroughly searched below the floor when Darren was discovered missing. But I supposed it depended on how his disappearance had been handled. Perhaps the contractor put the new tub in, caulked it up, and left before the body caused an odor.

It was possible that by the time it was obvious Darren was missing, no one knew for a fact he had died, or that he had died in the inn. Therefore, the police wouldn't become involved. If the inn closed down shortly afterwards, without his next-of-kin demanding an investigation, then Darren's story simply ended, the book of his life closed and forgotten.

No wonder he haunted the place. Poor Darren.

Poor me, too. I had to switch the reservations of the couple due to arrive this evening to another room (I hoped they weren't ghost aficionados). And then get a contractor in here to remove the tub.

My mind whirled. Who do you call to remove skeletal remains? How do I explain how I knew they were down there? I guess, after the tub was removed, I'd have to crawl down there and pretend to be surprised when I found them.

Poor Darren. Poor me.

CORY CLAIMED TO KNOW ENOUGH ABOUT PLUMBING AND BATH installations to remove the tub and replace it afterwards, so we kept the situation in the family. It was more difficult than we had imagined, since it wasn't a straight demo job. We needed to avoid damage. And damage was exactly what we did to several tiles. Plus, there were some scratches on the tub.

As soon as Cory pulled it away, the smell of musty air rose from below the floor. No foul smells, fortunately. We both shined flashlights into the opening, revealing a space about three feet deep.

"This is so strange, having a gap like this between floors," Cory said.

At the bottom were narrower beams that sloped downward above the second floor.

"You know what? Those look like rafters," Cory said. "I think the third floor was a later addition to the house, and that used to be the roof down there. The third story was probably built right on top of the roof, but this section of the house here had a lower roof, and that's why there's a large gap below the floor."

"I see. But where is Darren?" That was all I cared about.

"I'll have to go down there to look for him."

"No, let me do it," I said. "I'm much smaller than you."

Before he could protest, I had lowered myself through the opening between the floor beams and squatted upon the rafters that sloped downward slightly. Below them was a framework of regular wooden studs that the second-floor ceiling boards were nailed to.

I shined my flashlight toward the outside of the house, and there, against the wall, was a clump of brown clothing. The flashlight beam glinted off the white of bones among the clothing. The body must have slid down the slope, out of the view of anyone in the bathroom above.

"Hello, Darren," I said.

"You found him?" Cory asked from above.

"Yes. Please call the police's non-emergency number and tell them we've found human remains."

The police came the same day, but it took a couple of weeks before the remains were identified as Darren's. The medical examiner postulated the cause of death was a heart attack. It took even longer for us to repair the bathroom and open 303 to guests again.

The noxious odor problem never returned, thankfully. And the elevator was ghost-free from then on, though I still hated riding the thing.

Oddly, Darren's ghost stuck around at the inn. He haunted the room directly below where his remains were found as a cheerful ghost, not mournful and full of angst.

I immediately added his tale to the page of our website that talked about our ghosts. Bookings increased dramatically. If I could only figure out how to prevent the vegetation from sprouting up everywhere, we might have a profitable inn someday. Being the daughter of a nature goddess does have its downsides.

CHAPTER 32

PRESERVING MEMORIES

Sophie, Cory, Dr. Noordlun, and I stepped from the gateway into the Hall of Records.

"It is quite amazing how you have the ability to summon the gateways and make them deliver you where you want to go," Dr. Noordlun said.

"Only with their permission," I said. "I'm not sure why they've been cooperating with me."

"It can't hurt being a goddess," Cory said. "Talk about being a V.I.P."

He wasn't wrong. There had to be a correlation between my semi-divinity and the gateways' alliance with me. Though I suspected there was more to it. I hoped someday to learn more about the strange creatures.

The Hall of Records was cheery with seemingly natural light that came not from a sun but from magic. Still, it was pleasant here among the giant benevolent reptiles that resembled book-shelves filled with all the knowledge and memories of humankind.

"Let's allow the witches to do their thing," I said to Dr. Noordlun. "Do we need to get out of the way?"

"You can stay where you are," Sophie said. Her brow was furrowed with concentration as she prepared for the spell.

My twenty-four-year-old daughter still seemed like a fragile child to me, her milky white skin radiating purity, despite the ample inking of her tattoos. She had survived being captive to vampires after a drug-recovery company sold her to them. She had watched her mother deal with her second husband disappearing, then opening an inn, while opening our world to all manner of supernatural entities.

She had endured the trauma of losing her magic tutor to murder, but was serious enough in pursuing her craft that she was accepted by the city's top-ranking magician for tutelage. She grew into her craft rapidly and confidently.

As I watched her today preparing to cast her most powerful and complex magic yet, I was overcome with pride and love. And, yes, a bit of awe, too.

Because the amount of energy required for this spell was overwhelming, greater than the feeling of being at a power station beneath the high-tension lines. A buzzing began in my ears, my fingers tingled, and the air crackled.

Sophie was gathering her natural inner energies, those that everyone has, but at a weaker level than a witch's. She added to them the energy she had harvested early this morning from the beach, where, as a water witch, she tapped into the elemental energy of the sea.

However, to maximize her power, Cory had also harvested energy. For him, it came from the ley lines beneath the city: the major and minor ones that bisected, creating a vortex of incredible power. He had been visibly glowing afterwards.

And now he stood beside Sophie and grasped her hand.

I was frightened at first, I admit. Sophie's long, straight black hair sparked with static electricity and rose into the air until it stood vertically from her head.

An aura of white, purple, and yellow surrounded her. The light grew so bright it was difficult to see her inside of it.

The pearl grew warm against my side, inside the satchel that hung from my shoulder. It had seemed like a good idea to bring the pearl, though I had no specific purpose for it. The memory of healing the Tugara after the attack by the Fae made me want to bring it, just in case.

Sophie lifted her arms, and the room brightened even more. She kept them outstretched while she chanted an invocation in Latin. Her rituals for spell casting were different from my cousin Missy's, who used candles and worked within a magic circle. Sophie's approach was more dramatic and commanding.

"Protect this sacred place from incursion by evildoers and those with mal-intent," Sophie intoned in an almost operatic voice. "Protect it from vandals and thieves. Protect it from armies of humans, faeries, and any other race and species. Protect it from attacks of all types of magic. Protect it from everything living or dead, from demons, spirits, or gods. Protect it from all weapons, mechanical or elemental. Protect it from aging or mutability, from all destructive forces of the universe, no matter how benign.

"And, most of all, protect it from lies and misdirection, from forgetfulness and denial. Keep these memories strong and true for all time."

The ground vibrated, and from beyond the windows of the hall came a rippling of light. A sphere of protection solidified around this tiny, artificial island in time and space. The sphere should be strong enough to withstand all forces, physical or otherwise.

The vibrations and rippling ended abruptly.

"It's done," Sophie said, lowering her arms and exhaling with relief.

"I can sense it," Cory said. "The protection bubble is really solid."

I hugged Sophie.

"I'm so proud of you and how far you've come," I whispered into her ear.

"Will this spell need to be maintained?" Dr. Noordlun asked.

"Yes," Sophie said. "Nothing created by humans is eternal. I will check on it once a year and do any repairs or strengthening it might need. We should find another witch who can maintain it also, in case something happens to me. And some to take over after we pass."

"The Memory Guild will take that on as their solemn duty. I am grateful—"

The room grew dark, as if a large entity had blocked the sun. But there was no true sun here. The magically created air temperature dropped. The four of us looked at each other, barely visible in the darkness, with alarm.

"It's the Father of Lies," Dr. Noordlun said. "Will the protection spell keep him out?"

"Is he a demon or devil?" Sophie asked. "Still, it should hold."

"I don't know what he is, or if he's Satan himself. Maybe he's just a concept—the corruption of truth."

"Spells can't keep ideas out," Cory said. "If they come into here through our own minds."

As we looked at each other again, something probed my mind. Paranoia filled me.

"Stay strong," Dr. Noordlun said. "Remember, we are righteous, and he is false and wrong."

A kaleidoscope of images went through my head, frightening

scenes of violence and destruction. Of all people, though, the Father of Lies picked the wrong ones to fill with his conspiracies and perversions of truth.

Unfortunately, the world was full of minds willingly open to his lies.

We stood in silence for a long time until the air grew comfortable again and the light returned. Everyone visibly relaxed somewhat, though we knew the threat from the Father of Lies was ever-present.

The pearl remained warm against my side. In fact, its warmth increased to the point of being uncomfortably hot. Before I could move it away from me, it began to throb.

It had never throbbed before. Was it trying to tell me something?

The book-like scent of the Tugara grew stronger. It gave me a dreamy feeling. All my senses were heightened. I heard the rushing sound of blood flowing through my blood vessels, as well as the heartbeats of everyone in the room.

Including those coming from the Tugara. I was drawn to walk over and stand among them.

Placing a hand upon the leathery skin of the closest one, in my sensitive state, I felt the pulsing of its own circulatory system. Its heartbeat was much slower than one could imagine, barely more than a beat every thirty seconds. It was hard to believe this giant, largely stationary object was a living creature, but now I felt empathy for it.

I sensed, deep within them, not only the memories of humankind, but the creatures' own memories, which were entirely foreign to me.

Dr. Noordlun had said the Tugara were immortal. But they were living creatures, which meant they were fragile in their own way. I had seen their injuries from the faerie spears. And I had healed them.

My dreamlike state became more hallucinatory. Something swelled within me. A motherly feeling.

With my heightened senses came intuition. And with my intuition, I knew these creatures could not reproduce. Taken from the In Between, where they had been created by whatever supernatural force had created that mysterious land, they were never meant to function like earth creatures, sustaining their species for generations. They didn't have to, in a land where they would never age.

Yet, what if the Tugara were killed by the Fae or the Father of Lies? The archive of all the memories of the world would die with them.

I knew what I had to do, and surprisingly, I knew how to do it.

Removing the pearl from the satchel, I walked among the Tugara and caressed each one with my free hand. Something stirred deep within them.

Fertility. The ability to multiply.

It was within my realm, as the mother goddess, the nature goddess, to make species reproduce. It wasn't my job to figure out how these giant slugs would pull off the mating part of the process; all I did was to enable it.

Which meant there would be more Tugara to hold memories as the world's memories grew in volume over time. Most important, it meant redundancy, so if any of the creatures were killed, others could survive with the same memories.

After I did this, I walked away from them and regained my normal consciousness. Sophie and Cory looked at me strangely.

"Mom, you were glowing just now."

"So were you when you cast the protection spell. What about it?"

"Nothing. Just saying. What did you do?"

"Not much. I gave the Tugara the ability to procreate."

"Can we go home now?" Cory asked.

"Sure. Let me hail a cab."

A gateway dutifully materialized on the floor nearby, and the four of us stepped through it.

WHEN WE RETURNED TO THE INN, WE LANDED IN THE FOYER. An air plant had somehow found a perch on the chandelier.

"This nature goddess stuff is really growing old," Cory said. He pulled a stepladder from the hall closet and climbed up to remove the plant.

"You remember the rule?" I asked.

"Yeah, yeah. No killing. I will go to the park and put this in a tree. Is that satisfactory to you, Ms. Divine One?"

"Yes. Thank you."

"Good. Because it only means more work for me."

He was correct. Owning a historic inn, whether you're a witch, or a goddess, or simply a hostess with the most-ess, always means more work.

Believe me, I wish my life was that simple.

WHAT'S NEXT

GET A FREE E-BOOK

Sign up for my newsletter and get *A Ghostly Touch*, a Magic Guild novella, for free, offered exclusively to my newsletter subscribers. Darla reads the memories of a young woman, murdered in the 1890s, whose ghost begins haunting Darla, looking for justice. As a subscriber, you'll be the first to know about my new releases and lots of free book promotions. The newsletter is delivered only a couple of times a month. No spam at all, and you can unsubscribe at any time. Download your free book for all e-readers at wardparker.com

ENJOYED THIS BOOK? PLEASE LEAVE A REVIEW

In the Amazon universe, the number of reviews readers leave can make or break a book. I would be very grateful if you could spend just a few minutes and write a fair and honest review. It can be as short or long as you wish. Thank you so much!

NEXT IN THE MEMORY GUILD:

Book 7: THE FAERIE'S TOUCH
I've really stepped in it this time.

They say if you accept a gift from the Fae, you'll forever be in debt to them. And they always collect on their debts. I wish someone had told me this before a faerie gave me an enchanted pearl.

It comes at an awkward time, because the supernatural guilds of San Marcos are preparing for an invasion by the Fae, who want to restore their primacy over humans. And I'm trying to learn about my new powers and the responsibilities that come with them.

As if I don't have enough on my plate, my first husband has been charged with the murder of his business partner. I agree to help exonerate him with my psychometry, which turns out to be a dangerous decision. There's enough danger already, with the Fae unleashing monsters in our quaint tourist city.

Do you think this will affect the bookings at my inn?

Get enchanted by an alluring world of magic, murder, mystery, and mischief. Order *A Faerie's Touch* on Amazon or at wardparker.com

HAVE YOU READ FREAKY FLORIDA?

Check out this series of humorous paranormal mysteries featuring Darla's cousin, Missy.

Centuries-old vampires who play pickleball. Aging werewolves who surf naked beneath the full moon. Plus dragons, demons, ghouls, and more. They're all in Florida, land of the weird, where even monsters come to retire. That's how Missy Mindle comes in. She's started over in midlife as a home health nurse for elderly monsters and as a witch with growing powers. She uses her magick to solve mysteries, with a little help from a cute reporter. But dangerous secrets from the parents she never knew keep bubbling up.

Dive right into Book 1, *Snowbirds of Prey* at your favorite online retailers or at wardparker.com

ACKNOWLEDGMENTS

I wish to thank my loyal readers, who give me a reason to write more every day. I'm especially grateful to Sharee Steinberg and Amanda Peters for all your editing and proofreading brilliance. And to my wife, Martha, thank you for your moral support, Beta reading, and awesome graphic design!

ABOUT THE AUTHOR

Ward is the author of the Memory Guild midlife paranormal mystery thrillers. The Goddess's Daughter urban fantasy series continues the adventures.

He also writes the Monsters of Jellyfish Beach paranormal mysteries, set in the same world as his Freaky Florida series.

Ward lives in Florida with his wife, several cats, and a demon who wishes to remain anonymous.

Connect with him on Facebook (wardparkerauthor), Book-Bub, Goodreads, Bluesky (wardparker.bsky.social), or Threads (wardparker2223). Check out his books and sign up for his newsletter at wardparker.com.

PARANORMAL BOOKS BY WARD PARKER

Freaky Florida Humorous Paranormal Novels
Snowbirds of Prey
Invasive Species
Fate Is a Witch
Gnome Coming
Going Batty
Dirty Old Manatee
Gazillions of Reptilians
Hangry as Hell (novella)

Books 1-3 Box Set

The Memory Guild Midlife Paranormal Mystery Thrillers

A Magic Touch (also available in audio)
The Psychic Touch (also available in audio)
A Wicked Touch (also available in audio)
A Haunting Touch
The Wizard's Touch
A Witchy Touch
A Faerie's Touch
The Goddess's Touch
The Vampire's Touch
An Angel's Touch
A Ghostly Touch (novella)
Books 1-3 Box Set (also available in audio)

The Goddess's Daughter Urban Fantasies

(Sequel to the Memory Guild Series.)
Of Envy and Empaths
Of Fear and Fae
Of Vampires and Valor

Monsters of Jellyfish Beach Paranormal Mystery Adventures

The Golden Ghouls
Fiends With Benefits
Get Ogre Yourself
My Funny Frankenstein
Werewolf Art Thou?
In Sprite of Herself
Worms of Endearment

www.ingramcontent.com/pod-product-compliance
Lightning Source LLC
Chambersburg PA
CBHW030424180626
46812CB00005B/2158